THE UNICORN QUEST
SECRET IN THE STONE

Also by Kamilla Benko

The Unicorn Quest

THE UNICORN QUEST
SECRET IN THE STONE

KAMILLA BENKO

BLOOMSBURY
CHILDREN'S BOOKS

NEW YORK LONDON OXFORD NEW DELHI SYDNEY

BLOOMSBURY CHILDREN'S BOOKS
Bloomsbury Publishing Inc., part of Bloomsbury Publishing Plc
1385 Broadway, New York, NY 10018

BLOOMSBURY, BLOOMSBURY CHILDREN'S BOOKS, and the Diana logo
are trademarks of Bloomsbury Publishing Plc

First published in the United States of America in February 2019
by Bloomsbury Children's Books

Bloomsbury books may be purchased for business or promotional use. For information
on bulk purchases please contact Macmillan Corporate and Premium Sales Department at
specialmarkets@macmillan.com

Library of Congress Cataloging-in-Publication Data
Names: Benko, Kamilla, author.
Title: Secret in the stone / by Kamilla Benko.
Description: New York: Bloomsbury, 2019.
Summary: Claire and Sophie journey to Stonehaven where Claire can be trained to use her
Gemmer abilities to awaken the unicorns, but Sophie discovers they are in great danger.
Identifiers: LCCN 2018026348 (print) • LCCN 2018033834 (e-book)
ISBN 978-1-68119-247-5 (hardcover) • ISBN 978-1-68119-248-2 (e-book)
Subjects: | CYAC: Sisters—Fiction. | Magic—Fiction. | Adventure and adventurers—Fiction. |
Unicorns—Fiction. | Fantasy.
Classification: LCC PZ7.1.B4537 Sec 2019 (print) | LCC PZ7.1.B4537 (e-book) |
DDC [Fic]—dc23
LC record available at https://lccn.loc.gov/2018026348

Book design by Amanda Bartlett
Typeset by Westchester Publishing Services
Printed and bound in the U.S.A. by Berryville Graphics Inc., Berryville, Virginia
2 4 6 8 10 9 7 5 3 1

All papers used by Bloomsbury Publishing Plc are natural, recyclable products made
from wood grown in well-managed forests. The manufacturing processes conform
to the environmental regulations of the country of origin.

To find out more about our authors and books visit www.bloomsbury.com
and sign up for our newsletters.

For Gabriella Rose and Matthias James,
you're lucky to have me for a sister—
but I'm even luckier to be your sister

"War Chant"

Axes chop
And hammers swing,
Soldiers stomp,
But diamonds gleam.

Mothers weep
And fathers worry,
But only war
Can bring me glory.

Emeralds shine
And rubies mourn,
But there's no mine
For unicorn's horn.

Axes chop
And hammers swing,
My heart stops,
But war cries ring.

Gemmer Army Marching Chant
Lyrics circa 990 Craft Era
Composer unknown

CHAPTER 1

Graveyard.

That was the first word that came to Claire Martinson's mind as she took in the ruined city ahead of her.

The second and third words were: *Absolutely not.* There was no way this could be the city they'd been seeking—the Gemmer school where Claire would learn how to perfect her magic.

Where she was going to figure out how to bring unicorns back to Arden.

This was . . .

"A ghost town," Claire whispered.

"Are you sure it's Stonehaven?" Sophie asked, and Claire was glad to hear some apprehension in her older sister's voice. If Sophie, who at the age of thirteen had already explored a magical land by herself, defeated a mysterious illness, and passed sixth grade, wasn't feeling great about their final destination, then maybe Claire wasn't such a coward after all.

"It looks so . . ."

"Creepy?" Claire offered.

Sophie tightened the ribbon on her ponytail. "Desolate," she finished.

Desolate, indeed. Stone houses stood abandoned, their windows as empty as the sockets of a skull. Weeds grew in the cracks of cobblestone roads, and a fine layer of white dust coated everything. Claire half expected a ghost to jump out at them, and after everything that had happened, she wouldn't have been surprised.

Well, maybe she would have been a little surprised, but in the last couple of weeks, Claire had gotten used to unusual things. Like the fact that other worlds existed, that art could be magic, and that unicorns were real.

"Hold a moment, Princesses!" Claire jumped as Anvil Malchain, their guide and traveling companion, turned the corner to join them.

Another unusual thing Claire now knew: she was a princess.

Only a few weeks ago, Claire and Sophie hadn't been princesses at all—just sisters, who had a mom and a dad, and a summer that they would be spending in their late great-aunt Diana's mansion, organizing all her mysterious artifacts for an estate sale in the fall. But then they had discovered a ladder in a fireplace, and everything had changed.

Because at the end of the ladder it had not been Windemere Manor's roof, but an old stone well that opened into another world: Arden, a land of monsters and magic. A land that had once been ruled by Claire and Sophie's ancestors. A land that now needed saving.

A land that needed unicorns.

Which was where the two new princesses of Arden came into it: they had brought the magical moonstone necklace from their world to Arden. Only they weren't moonstones at all, but moon*tears*—and they were supposed to usher in a new age of unicorns. The only thing was, neither of them knew how to wake the moontears.

And that was why they had been climbing Starscrape Mountain: so they could get to Stonehaven, a settlement of Gemmers who might be able to show them how. The Gemmer Guild, after all, understood the nature of rock and minerals, and was able to harness the magic and power within them.

But Stonehaven was supposed to be a place with answers, not this empty town. A cold wind brushed against Claire's neck, and a low moan rose around them as the wind played through the abandoned buildings.

"Where is everyone?" Claire asked Anvil as he caught up with them. One of the most talented Forgers of Arden, Anvil was famed and feared for his talent with metal and his double-headed ax. But as Claire had gotten to know him, she'd realized he wasn't like an ax at all. Instead, he was more like a wrought iron gate: straight-backed, a bit foreboding, but also protective. He'd been following behind them, covering their tracks so that no one could tell they had passed.

"In Starscrape Citadel, I expect," Anvil said, pointing toward the mountain's peak.

Shielding her eyes, Claire squinted against the sun. The small houses continued to march up the mountainside, spiraling around to the summit's flourish: the gleaming domed roof of a marble castle.

Amid all the other rubble, the castle looked . . . enchanting. *Magical.* Which, she supposed, made sense.

"Now that's more like it," Sophie said, sounding pleased. "A palace! An Experience!" She looked over at Claire. "Maybe they'll help me find my magic, like you."

Claire's chest pinged as it always did when Sophie pointed out this difference between them. It wasn't her fault, but she couldn't help but feel a little guilty. Most everyone in Arden had had the ability to shape the magic found in the natural world around them: members of the Tiller Guild worked with plants, while Forgers crafted metal, Spinners handled thread, and Gemmers carved stone.

Claire had discovered she was a Gemmer, having inherited her family's propensity for rock, when she liberated a legendary unicorn from stone. More specifically, from a monolith called Unicorn Rock.

But for some reason she could only guess at, Sophie didn't seem to have any magic of her own. Which was weird, because Claire had always thought of her sister as the magical one of the two. Sophie was the brave one, the one who had sought out Experiences rather than hiding behind a sketch pad like Claire.

"And here," Anvil said, "I'm afraid, I must leave you."

Claire's stomach swooped, even though she knew firsthand why he—a member of the Forger Guild—couldn't trespass on land claimed by the Gemmer Guild. The guilds were deeply mistrustful of one another, and except for limited trading, interaction between the four guilds was forbidden by law.

"You can't leave us," Sophie protested. "Look at this place!"

Anvil reached under his chain mail shirt and pulled something out.

"Here," he said, pressing a bronze circle into Sophie's hand. Claire immediately recognized it as a Kompass. Not a compass, like back at home in the world of Windemere Manor, which always pointed north, but a Kompass, a rare magic known only to the Malchain family that always pointed toward the one person or thing it was forged to find. In this particular case, it was Aquila, Anvil's cousin and the best treasure hunter in all of Arden.

"Once you've woken the moontears, follow the Kompass to us," he said. "Most likely, we will be near the Sorrowful Plains. And remember what I told you."

Sophie's hand brushed against the small lump under her tunic's neckline. "The unicorn?" she asked, and when Anvil nodded she quickly promised, "We won't tell anyone."

Throughout their weeklong journey, Anvil had made them

repeat that they would not tell anyone how the unicorn had burst from the stone in a blaze of light to heal Sophie from a nearly fatal arrow wound and her illness. But then he had vanished from the Sorrowful Plains, and now Aquila was tracking him, hoping to find the unicorn before someone else did.

Anvil had told them it was the last unicorn.

Unless they could use the moontear necklace to wake more.

Claire's heart squeezed as Sophie carefully put the Kompass in her cloak pocket. Unicorns had once roamed Arden's meadows, until they had been hunted to extinction three hundred years ago, during the great war, the Guild War between the four magics. Without unicorns, Arden's magic was slowly weakening: guild magic could no longer do the wonders of the past, and children were sometimes born without any magic at all.

But worst: ever since the disappearance of the unicorns, dark, shadowy creatures called wraiths had appeared, terrorizing the land. No one knew where the wraiths had come from, but everyone agreed they were a sign that without magic, without unicorns, their world was in great peril.

Magic was weakening. Arden was dying. Claire looked around at the abandoned streets and shivered.

But there was still hope . . . so long as she didn't mess anything up.

"Thank you, Anvil," Sophie said, giving the Forger a quick hug. "We'll see you soon."

Anvil's stern expression softened slightly. "I know you will."

Sophie moved forward through the eerily quiet streets, up

toward the Citadel that loomed above them like a beacon. But Claire hesitated. Her legs felt as sturdy as the moss fringing the abandoned houses. Even though they came here to speak to Gemmers, Claire wasn't entirely sure that she wanted to.

Hundreds of years ago, the Gemmers grew too powerful and conquered the other guilds. As a result, the others rose against them, and the bloody Guild War ensued. As the tension escalated, the people of Arden began to hunt unicorns, believing the rumor that whoever killed a unicorn would live forever. It wasn't true, of course, but it *was* true that any artifact made from a part of a unicorn made guild magic stronger.

The Gemmers—*Claire's* family—caused all that. Their ancestor, Queen Estelle, had led the unicorn hunt.

"Claire!" Sophie called, already far enough up the road that she needed to shout. "Are you coming?"

Anvil looked down at Claire, his dark eyes boring into hers a little too knowingly. "Gemmers are stubborn, but their word is always rock-solid once they have given it."

Claire grimaced. When she'd learned she was a princess, she had promised to help Arden. After all, this magical world had healed her sister from a disease the doctors at the hospital back at home did not even have a name for.

"Just be sure that you and Sophie take care of each other," Anvil continued, "and everything will be all right."

"Thank you." Claire quickly hugged the Forger, not even minding how cold his chain mail was. "Thank you for everything."

"Now then, go on," Anvil said gruffly, but Claire was sure

she caught him smiling before she ran to catch up with her sister.

Keeping her eyes on Sophie's bouncing ponytail, she wound her way up through the city. It was hard to believe that Stonehaven had ever been anything more than this abandoned place, but Anvil had told them that Stonehaven had once been their family's summer palace, the mountain breezes wafting between stone archways were always cool, while the lush blanket of forest on the lower slopes was good for falconry and other . . . sports.

Unicorn hunts.

Claire lifted her feet over another rock pile. There were many such piles littering the mountainside, and they had probably once been the base of a garden wall or bridge. Now, though, they just looked like forgotten tombstones.

The wind picked up, pulling curls from the tangled knot perched on her head. Strands of hair stuck to her sweaty forehead, making her feel itchy all over. The road up to the Citadel was steep—so steep that it eventually became steps carved into the mountain itself. She paused a moment to catch her breath, and took in the view from this high up.

Starscrape Mountain swept out beneath them, a tapestry of towering pines, softly filtered sunlight, and rushing waterfalls that tumbled from its many ridges. At its base, she imagined she could just make out the edge of the Sorrowful Plains, which from this safe height seemed to be nothing more than a pocketful of shadows.

And beyond that, the rest of Arden unfurled. Though she could not see them, Claire knew that tucked somewhere into this land was a Tiller village with a cage of metal vines and a Forger city filled with ringing metal. Somewhere down there were narrowboats carrying merchants of magical objects and even more magical stories, and underground caverns where wyverns sailed through sapphire-studded tunnels.

And among all those wonders sat an old stone well . . . and a way back home.

"HEY!" Sophie's sudden cry echoed down the mountainside.

"Sophie!" Claire looked up the steps, but her sister had already reached the top. So much for following Anvil's advice. Pumping her legs, Claire took the crumbling steps two at a time until she reached the flat summit—and gasped.

The road wound forward a few feet more, then ended abruptly at the base of a cliff face. No, not a cliff—a *wall*, one that rose hundreds of feet into the air.

"Can you believe this? There's no door," Sophie grumbled to Claire. And there wasn't—not even a window. In fact, there were no lines at all in the smooth surface. The wall seemed to have been carved from a single piece of stone and was as seamless as an eggshell.

"HEY!" Sophie shouted again, cupping her hands around her mouth. "LET US IN!"

Trying to see whom, exactly, Sophie was yelling at, Claire followed her sister's gaze up . . . and up . . . and up to a ledge high above them. On top of it, a group of people stared back down at them.

Except . . .

"Those aren't people," Claire said, voice awed. "They're *statues*."

There were about twenty of them, a mix of men and women in helmets or crowns, all in robes that fell in stone folds around their feet. Though they were too high up for Claire to see their expressions, she could clearly see the stone swords and maces they held in their hands.

"Maybe we should just try knocking," Claire suggested, tearing her eyes away from the dizzying wall. She turned slowly to look at her sister. "I don't know what else—Sophie, why do you have your dagger out?"

"Because," Sophie said quietly, "I think that statue just moved."

CHAPTER
2

*W*hat?"

But Claire's question was immediately answered as a stone knight flexed his fingers . . . and leaped off the ledge.

In the several long seconds it took the knight to hit the earth, Claire heard a high-pitched scream. It could have been Sophie, or Claire, or both—but it didn't matter. Either way, the Stone Knight crunched down to the ground behind them, sending pebbles and dust high into the air as his knees bent to absorb the impact.

"Stay away!" Sophie yelled, and Claire felt a pull at her tunic as her sister yanked her back. A second later, Claire felt the solid presence of the wall against her shoulders.

The Stone Knight had trapped them.

Slowly, the knight unfolded from his crouched position,

and rose to his towering height. His feet were as large as trash cans and each leg was as thick as a telephone pole. He strode toward them, shooting tiny tremors through the earth.

Suddenly, Sophie was in front of Claire, holding out the "just in case" dagger Aquila had loaned them. Her feet were spread shoulder width apart, front foot pointing straight out, back foot pointing sideways. It was the position Claire recognized from a few training sessions with Anvil: *En garde*. The attack position.

"What are you doing?" Claire yelled. The dagger was just a toothpick compared to the stomping feet.

"Do something!" Sophie shouted back, not tearing her eyes away from the stone giant. "Come on, Claire. Use your magic!"

"I—I don't know how!" Claire said, struggling to breathe. She thought she might faint.

"*You're a Gemmer!*" Sophie yelled. "*There are rocks everywhere!*"

Flustered, Claire scooped up a handful of pebbles and dirt. Only once before had she done magic on purpose, and then she'd had the help of the Unicorn Harp to strengthen her power. There was no unicorn artifact to help her now. There was no magical hum. The only thing she felt in her bones was *fear*.

"If you're not going to do anything, run!" Sophie yelled as she brandished her dagger. "Get away!"

Sophie's command anchored Claire; she wasn't going to leave her sister alone again. Not today, not ever.

Winding her arm back, Claire aimed, threw—

—the pebbles clattered down harmlessly, woefully short.

The Stone Knight was upon them.

Claire saw Sophie swing the dagger at the stone leg, sparks flying as the blade scraped rock. The knight paused, as though confused about the tiny thing near its feet making such a big fuss. He gave the nuisance a kick, and the dagger spun through the air as Sophie fell on her side.

With a rumble that sounded like slow-moving thunder, the knight pulled his sword from his scabbard.

"Run!" Sophie yelled again as she scrambled away from the stone foot on all fours. The moontear necklace had slipped out from under her tunic and swung about wildly, throwing light into the air.

The Stone Knight raised his sword into the sky.

"No," Claire yelled. "Sophie—!"

And then the Stone Knight paused.

Claire tensed, waiting for the blow . . . but it never came.

Instead, there was another puff of dust as the Stone Knight let his sword tumble to the ground. And then, the knight sank into a low bow—and stayed there.

A deafening silence fell over the odd scene, punctuated only by Claire's quick breaths. Was it a trick? But the knight stayed still.

Sophie looked impressed. "How did you do that?"

"I didn't do anything," Claire said, cautiously looking around. She felt like someone had told her a joke, and she was still waiting for the punch line. But as she took a step forward, a giant *crack* snapped the air.

Whipping around, she saw something was happening to the wall. Thin, tiny lines had appeared across its once smooth face. They raced across the wall's surface, converging and meeting to form the outline of an archway.

A second *crack* filled the air, followed by an explosion of grit and gravel.

"Duck!" Sophie cried. Claire threw her hands over her head as pebbles and dust engulfed them.

Slowly, the air cleared.

A giant stone door stood in the center of the wall, a familiar design of animals and flowers carved into it.

"I guess that's how you get into Stonehaven," Sophie said, blinking rapidly as dust fell into her eyes. Claire didn't say anything; she could only stare. As she watched, the enormous door slowly swung open . . .

. . . and an army flooded out.

"Hide the necklace," Claire whispered, and Sophie shoved the moontears back under her tunic just as soldiers encircled them. Each Gemmer gripped a long spear tipped by a wickedly sharp black rock. Claire had the horrible feeling that if she so much as sneezed, she'd be pinned down as easily as a paper note to a corkboard.

The tallest guard, a man with arms and legs as spindly as a spider but shoulders as wide as a barrel, jabbed his spear in their direction. "Forgers aren't allowed on Starscrape Mountain," he said angrily. "You have violated the treaty!"

Claire exchanged a panicked glance with Sophie. Forgers—the Gemmers thought they were Forgers! The leather clothes that Aquila and Anvil had given them were great for traveling and cleaner than the outfit Claire had arrived in, but they'd forgotten that they looked Forger-made.

"We're not," Claire squeaked out. But the guard didn't seem to hear her, or care what she said, because he spoke loudly over her, "As you are violators of the Guild Treaty, we have the right to punish you under Gemmer law. You can come willingly . . . or not. Your choice."

"We'll come willingly," Claire yelped. "Won't we, Sophie?"

"Er, yes, very willingly!" Sophie said, her spattering of freckles standing out more than usual.

The tall guard looked slightly disappointed, yet he must have given an invisible signal, because all the spear tips suddenly swooped upward like a startled flock of sparrows. Claire took big, gulping breaths of air. She hadn't realized how little she'd breathed while the spears had been leveled at them.

"Wraith Watch," he barked out, "bind their hands."

"Commander Jasper," another guard said in a low voice, "is that really necessary? They're just children."

"In the light of recent events, any Forger is a threat, no matter how puny they may appear," Commander Jasper said flatly.

Unease prickled across Claire's shoulders.

"What events?" Sophie said, asking Claire's own question.

Jasper's expression remained emotionless. "The events regarding the Sorrowful Plains."

Claire sucked in her breath and beside her, she felt Sophie stiffen.

"Yes," Sophie said, her voice carefully measured, "Unicorn Rock is no longer there . . ."

"Not just Unicorn Rock," Jasper said. "Queen Rock, too, is gone."

Claire's heart zigzagged in her chest. She felt as if someone had just taken her freshly painted masterpiece, still gleaming with wet paint, and dragged their fingers across it.

"Gone?" she burst out. "Gone *where?*"

"That's the question, isn't it?" Jasper said, as he signaled to the Wraith Watch to begin tying their hands. "It's not like Unicorn Rock or Queen Rock could have just walked off on their own, now, could they?"

A soft squeak escaped Claire, and Sophie frowned at her. *Keep it together, Clairina,* her expression read. But Sophie didn't understand. Only one person in all of Arden could have woken Queen Estelle: Claire, a royal Gemmer princess who shared the same exact Gemmer blood as Prince Martin. And she would never want to wake the queen. But one group did . . .

Before Claire could stop herself, she heard herself asking, "Is it the Royalists?"

"Diamonds above, no!" Jasper barked out a laugh. "The Royalists and their foolish beliefs! No—this is most likely the work of some Forgers. Only those metal-skulled smiths would have the audacity to obliterate our guild's greatest monuments."

"Don't worry." Sophie's breath tickled Claire's ear as she leaned in close. All the while, the Wraith Watch stepped closer. "Only *you* could have woken her. There's no way Queen Estelle is back."

"But if it's true . . ." Claire trailed off. Maybe Sophie wasn't worried, but Sophie hadn't been the one who'd traveled through the Petrified Forest and heard the echoes of the long-past unicorn hunt. She hadn't been the one to hear the queen's ice-cold voice commanding her armies to kill them all. And now they were willingly entering an entire palace of people whose ancestors had fought for the same queen long ago.

But Claire had no more time to think about it, as Commander Jasper and the Wraith Watch escorted them through the door and into Starscrape Citadel.

"Who are these girls?"

"Did the knight *actually* bow to them?"

"Commander Jasper, what's going on?"

A riot of sound surged around Claire as questions flew from the richly dressed crowd that pressed in around them. Everyone, men and women alike, was bedecked in gemstones. They wore great rings, long necklaces, brooches, and earrings. All together, the Gemmers glittered like a night sky.

"What do the Forgerlings want?"

"Where did they—"

"—DIAMONDS ABOVE!" a voice thundered over the rest. "For all that's strong and stable, return to your evening duties!"

The Gemmers shifted and the crowd parted. Claire could see an old man coming toward them. He hunched over a cane, and the hand that gripped it flashed in the chandelier's light. As he lurched closer, Claire saw why. His fingers were covered in rings. Big ones, small ones, ones set with river stones and others with diamonds that she was pretty sure Mom would have loved.

But as pretty as they were, the sight was unsettling. Claire had been in Arden long enough to know that the most powerful magic could be done with a single thread, the tiniest drop of potion . . . or the smallest pebbled ring.

"Go on, then," the man said, coming to stand in front of them and waving his hands at the Wraith Watch still surrounding Jasper. "Off with you, too. Commander Jasper is plenty of protection from children."

The guards cast their heads down sheepishly and slowly drifted away with the rest of the crowd, while the old man turned to Jasper. "Terra is waiting for us in her study."

The commander shifted his spear. "Grandmaster Carnelian, wouldn't the dungeon be better?"

Carnelian shook his head. "The Stone Knight bowed to them, Jasper. And that changes everything."

CHAPTER
3

Carnelian set off through the Citadel at a fast clip, and with Jasper's spear still pointing at their back, the girls followed. Claire was vaguely aware of beautiful stained-glass windows and vaulted ceilings made to look like stone lace, but it was hard to take in anything when so many Gemmers stared as they rushed by. *Why* had Anvil and Aquila thought this was a good idea? The last time she'd conversed with a grandmaster, Claire had ended up in a cage.

But as Carnelian opened the lone door at the top of a winding staircase, colored light filled Claire's view. She gasped as Sophie murmured, "Spectacular!"

A chandelier threaded with different colored gems hung in the center of a high tower ceiling. Though Claire couldn't see any candles or light bulbs, the stones glowed with their own internal light, throwing splashes of emerald green, ruby red, sapphire blue, and amethyst purple throughout the round, cozy study.

And everywhere, there were unicorns.

In frames as charcoal sketches. On shelves as bookends, propping up tomes with titles like *The Unicorn Chronicles* and *The Hair of a Hare and Horn of a Unicorn*. On the floor, a thickly woven rug depicted a unicorn held captive in a garden.

It was as different from the graveyard village below as it could possibly be.

"These are the intruders the Stone Knight bowed down to?" A woman with a heart-shaped face and a cascade of black curls stood from behind a desk and strode toward them. Her emerald gown swished softly, the actual emeralds sewn onto her sleeves iridescent in the light. But what drew Claire to the woman were her eyes.

Framed by a pair of copper spectacles with the thickest lenses Claire had ever seen, her jet black eyes appeared three times the normal size. From the sides of the frames winged out even more lenses that looked as though they could be swapped in to replace the current ones. With her amplified eyes and shimmery dress, Claire thought the woman resembled a beautiful dragonfly.

She flicked a lens. "I thought you would be . . ." She eyed the girls. "Bigger." She gestured toward Carnelian. "Please have a seat, Grandmaster."

"Thank you, Scholar Terra," Carnelian said as she offered

him an armchair. Terra took a seat behind her desk, while Jasper stayed standing, his spear conspicuously by his side.

No chair was offered to Claire and Sophie, so Claire stood as close as she could to her sister.

"Let's get to the bottom of this," Terra said as she pulled out a slate and chalk from her desk. "What are your names?"

"I am Sophie Andrea, and this is my sister," Sophie said, gesturing to Claire, "Claire Elaina Martinson—er, d'Astora."

That was right, Claire thought, and tried to stand a little taller. They *were* d'Astoras, as their great-grandfather Martin Martinson, formerly Prince Martin d'Astora of Arden, had changed his name when he stole away to another world.

For a moment, all was still as Terra stared hard at the girls.

Then Jasper let out a hoarse yell. Half a heartbeat later, the tip of his spear was pointed right at Sophie's chest. "Lies!"

The man's eyes were so pale that they were the color of ice, though they seemed to burn as they stayed on Sophie. "The audacity of these lowlanders to claim a relationship to the d'Astora family! Grandmaster, I say we take them outside for the wraiths!"

A shriek froze in Claire's throat. *Wraiths*—even hearing their names out loud filled her with a bone-numbing fear, with a feeling of being choked by shadows.

"Grandmaster," Terra said, "if I may be so bold, perhaps that is why the knight bowed. He recognized d'Astora blood."

Carnelian stared at Claire and Sophie for what seemed an eternity, twisting one of his many rings thoughtfully. Finally, he shook his head. "Your request is denied, Commander Jasper. For now. You—Claire, is it? Do you have any evidence to support what you say?"

Claire tried to say the word bravely, but it came out barely more than a whisper. "Yes."

"*But*," Sophie added, "we can only show you if you promise to stop pointing that thing at me and my sister," she nodded at Jasper's spear, "and untie our hands."

Terra gave a start. "You tied their hands? Really, Jasper! They're children!" Standing up, she bustled around the desk and with a unicorn-shaped letter opener cut their ties, while Jasper, grumbling, leaned his weapon against the marble wall.

Grandmaster Carnelian drummed his fingers against the armchair, his rings rattling. "Now, your evidence, please."

Claire held her breath as she watched Sophie tug the silver chain that had been hidden under her neckline. Four luminous moontears dangled from it, shimmering, a quiet beauty unaware of the desperation surrounding them.

Claire's heart beat faster, as it always did when she saw them.

The Great Unicorn Treasure.

The unicorns' final chance.

Arden's last hope.

"By all the diamonds above," Grandmaster Carnelian said softly.

Reluctantly, Claire dragged her eyes away from the necklace to look at the Gemmer grandmaster. His eyes were overbright, like sunlight's reflection on water. He smiled faintly, and the deepest lines on his brow smoothed. It was as if merely seeing the moontears had made him younger.

Carefully, Sophie unlatched the necklace's clasp and laid it on the scholar's desk.

"Are those . . . ," Terra said, her voice oddly choked. She leaned forward and flipped through her lenses. Suddenly, she stopped fiddling with the glasses and let out a soft "oh." She looked up, and Claire was startled to see that the woman's face was streaked with tears. "I never thought I'd live to see the day. *Moontears.* May I?"

Claire and Sophie nodded, and Terra gently placed a slender finger on the necklace.

"Oh," she breathed again, delighted. "They're warm!"

Sophie smiled. "I thought the same thing, but I told myself it was just all the hiking we'd been doing."

Commander Jasper looked like a man at war with himself. Though he placed his hands behind his back, he leaned forward eagerly. He opened his mouth several times, before seeming to finally settle on, "*How?*"

"My great-aunt gave them to me," Sophie said, and Claire nodded, even though technically, Great-Aunt Diana hadn't given them to her. Sophie had found the necklace among all the strange treasures of Windemere Manor. Though now that Claire knew a little more about Arden, perhaps the *moontears* had found *Sophie.*

As Sophie told their story, careful to avoid certain aspects, like that she'd been accused of stealing the Unicorn Harp from Greenwood Village or that Claire had somehow released the unicorn from Unicorn Rock or that they came from another world, Claire silently filled in the actual details. The *full* story, from the very beginning.

Three hundred Arden years ago, Prince Martin d'Astora, younger brother to the evil Queen Estelle of Arden—on whose orders all but one unicorn had been slaughtered—had forged the fireplace-chimney-well as a way to escape out of Arden during the terrible war . . . and into a house in the countryside—in another world. This house had been passed down from generation to generation until Diana. As in, Claire and Sophie's recently deceased great-aunt Diana.

"And so, we journeyed to Stonehaven to ask for your help," Sophie finally finished.

"Can you see a way to open the moontears?" Carnelian asked Terra curiously. Claire held her breath. Finally, they would know! Finally, unicorns would return.

Terra knit her brow and stared pensively at the necklace. "I'm not sure," she murmured, flipping through the lenses again. "I've never come across anything, in all my studies, that says how to wake a moontear. In fact, there is no written record of anyone ever actually finding one, let alone studying it."

Stars, which spent their entire lives emitting light across the universes, would at the end, collapse in on themselves. Claire's great hope had stretched her, tugged her forward, and now, with a simple sentence, it was gone. And without it, Claire felt her great mission fall away, and herself collapsing alongside it.

"But you're Gemmers," Claire said, feeling light-headed and empty. "You're *supposed* to know about rock stuff."

Terra frowned. "*Rock stuff*, as you so elegantly put it, is only one part. Moontears were merely myth, 'fallen from the moon and witnessed by starlight' as Gemmer Historian Eliza the Astute once wrote. These gems are unlike any other—they are unicorn-touched."

The scholar settled back in her chair. "But the d'Astora family rose to the Gemmer throne because they always shared a special bond with unicorns. If anyone can discover the moontears' secrets, it would be a Gemmer princess. So perhaps it is the girls, and not us, who must open them."

"Diamonds above," Jasper said so loudly that Claire jumped. He had come around from the desk and now stood next to them. "They're not princesses! They're clearly imposters. The grandmaster *knows* that they're probably the ones behind the destruction of Unicorn and Queen Rocks!"

"Don't presume to know what's in my mind," Grandmaster Carnelian said, narrowing his eyes, "because you don't. If you *did* know what I thought, you'd realize I want you to be quiet . . . so I can think."

Jasper's mouth snapped shut, and Carnelian looked at Terra. "What are you saying?"

Pursing her lips, Terra tapped the sides of her elaborate spectacles. Looking once more between the moontears and the girls, she finally said, "As shocking as it sounds, it is possible these girls are telling the truth and they really are princesses. They brought the moontears here, after all. And with the wraith attacks growing more frequent, we could use the power of unicorns more than ever."

"This is true." Carnelian nodded in agreement. "But they clearly have no idea how to access the magic of the moontears, either." He glanced at the girls. "I'm not even sure they have basic Gemmer skills."

Claire felt her face get hot, like when you open a toaster oven. "I've only known I'm a Gemmer for two weeks now and Sophie—"

"I'm the same," Sophie cut in. "I've only known that I'm a Gemmer for two weeks, too." Claire didn't look at Sophie, but the room felt even warmer at her sister's lie. So far, anyway, Sophie hadn't demonstrated any magic ability whatsoever.

Silence filled the space around them as the grandmaster and scholar stared intently at each other. Finally, after what seemed like a century, Terra spoke. "We could teach them. If they are truly of the d'Astora bloodline, they might help us find a way to wake the moontears. What do we risk by training them?"

"We risk," Jasper interrupted, "allowing lowland spies onto our mountain!"

"You risk," Sophie said quietly, "a possibility of unicorns."

A possibility of unicorns. The phrase seemed to hang in the air.

Claire held her breath while Carnelian tapped his fingers along the head of his bejeweled cane. Unlike most canes, this one had a stone handle on it in the shape of a ram's head. Its curling horns were chiseled to a point just as sharp as Jasper's spear.

The grandmaster let out a long sigh. "So be it," Carnelian said. "Scholar Terra, you will begin the girls'—the princesses'—training in the morning. But," he added, turning to face them, "if anything happens to disprove your tale . . . we will go with Commander Jasper's original suggestion. Do you understand?"

Take them outside for the wraiths.

Claire nodded. Yes, she definitely understood. Sophie nodded, too.

Terra stood and looked at Claire. Behind her spectacles, her eyes were now magnified five-fold. Claire felt a thrill of fear as the woman ordered: "Follow me."

And so they did, stepping back into the strange and glittering halls of the Gemmers' Citadel, Claire bracing herself for whatever might await them at Stonehaven.

CHAPTER 4

Sunlight streaked in through the diamond-paned windows of Claire and Sophie's tower bedroom. Or prison, as Sophie insisted on calling it.

Still, it really was a nice prison. The arched ceiling above the two small beds was painted a deep blue and inset with real diamonds that swirled together into some of Arden's most famous constellations. Their beds, though small, were comfortable, and the wardrobe was filled with plenty of apprentice uniforms that only had a few patches on them. There was even a window seat that gave Claire a sweeping view that she longed to draw.

But even drawing wouldn't be able to distract her from the tangle of knots in her stomach. After all, it was technically her first day of school . . . *Gemmer* school.

And at the end of the day, Terra said that they would run through their first test. But Claire didn't know what, exactly, the test would be.

"Stop biting your nails!" Sophie ordered. Claire hastily removed her fingers. She hadn't bitten them since she was a kid, but without her pencil to nibble, the old habit had returned. Turning around, she saw Sophie was still sitting cross-legged on the bed, the contents of a Gemmer pack spilled onto the quilt in front of her: a magnifying glass, tweezers, a small hammer, several chisels, and a glass vial of diamond dust—among several other instruments that Claire guessed would help her release magic from stone. That would, maybe, help her release the unicorns from the moontears.

"Do you think Terra forgot us?" Claire asked. When the scholar had deposited them last night, she'd informed them that they would remain in this room until she came to collect them tomorrow at second chime, shortly after dawn.

But the chimes had already sounded three times, and the sun was now fully up.

"Okay, that's it," Sophie said, and rolled off the bed. "We're not going to be some princesses waiting in a tower. We came to Stonehaven to learn. We came to wake the moontears." She swept the Gemmer tools back into the rucksack, and strode to the door. "Coming?"

Jasper's scowl and the glint of spear tips pierced through Claire's memory. "But Terra said—"

"Suit yourself." Sophie turned the knob and the door swung

open easily. Relief flitted through Claire. Last night, she thought she'd heard the click of the lock as Terra shut the door. Maybe they *were* actually guests, and not prisoners after all. But her relief vanished along with Sophie.

Even in another world, Sophie was always Sophie—always off on another Experience. Grabbing her own rucksack of Gemmer tools from a hook on the wall, Claire ran after her.

The Citadel's splendor blossomed around her as she hurried to keep up with her sister. Mosaics of bright stone seemed to gallop across the floors, and colored glass filled many of the windows, splashing color on the walls.

Stonehaven was more than beautiful—it was dazzling. A shot of excitement pulsed through Claire, chasing out her fear. She was going to learn how to make these beautiful things. She was going to learn *magic*.

"Hey!" a voice shouted from behind them.

"Slug soot," Sophie muttered, coming to such an abrupt stop that Claire crashed into her.

Both girls turned around.

A boy also in an apprentice uniform ran toward them. He had the most freckles Claire had ever seen. In fact, with his pointy nose and chin, he seemed to be made up entirely of freckles and angles.

"Are you Sophia and Claire?" the boy asked, panting slightly as he reached them. "Sorry, I mean, Princess Sophia and Princess Claire?"

Claire's neck heated instantly. "Just Claire, actual—"

"Indeed, we are," Sophie cut in, and Claire rolled her eyes at the accent Sophie suddenly had. "And you are?"

"Geode." The boy smiled, his freckles bunching up. "Terra says she's sorry she couldn't get you earlier. The west wing is about to fall off the mountain, and the grandmaster needed her help."

Fall off the mountain.

When they'd first seen the Citadel above the rubble and neglect of Stonehaven, she had wondered if it was somehow held together by magic, and here, she guessed, was her answer. But magic was slipping away from Arden, and if it disappeared entirely . . . would the rest of Stonehaven slip away with it?

Her nerves came clanging back down around her. So much rested on waking the moontears.

"Here," Geode said, seeming not to realize how extraordinary his statement was. "You missed breakfast, so I brought you some crescents." He produced two steaming pastries from his own Gemmer bag, and as Claire bit in, she realized it was stuffed with tangy cheese.

"You can eat on the way," Geode said as he resumed walking. "We're late for S.A.S."

"Late ferr vhat?" Sophie said, her regal act forgotten as she stuffed the rest of the crescent into her mouth.

"S.A.S.," Geode repeated, and picked up the pace, "stands for Slings, Arrows, and Spears. This way, please."

Claire almost choked on her final bit of crescent. Arrows were cool, of course they were, but she would have preferred if her first lesson with magic started off with something a little less . . . deadly.

"Arrows!" Sophie whooped. "What an Experience!"

As they hurried through Stonehaven, Claire noticed that many passageways had been blocked by signs: "Forbidden!" "Danger!" and "Hallway-In."

"Hallway-in?" Claire asked, panting slightly. "What's that?"

"Like a cave-in, but a hall," Geode explained.

"And that? What's that mean?" Sophie asked, pointing to a sign that simply read, "Goats!"

"That's where the goats sleep," Geode said, and at their puzzled expressions, he explained, "With so few Gemmers, it's hard to keep up the village. Years ago, Grandmaster Carnelian decided everyone—animals included—would move into the Citadel to try to preserve it. Everything else, we just had to let go."

Had to let go.

That explained the neglected tombstone houses outside the wall of the Citadel. For a moment, Claire was filled with sadness for the Gemmers. She could only imagine what Stonehaven must have been like when magic flourished and the unicorns still lived. When it was a whole thriving city instead of just one palace above a pile of ruins.

"There's just not enough of us anymore," Geode continued as he turned down another chandelier-lit corridor. "If magic were stronger, or if the lower guilds would lend us a unicorn artifact, maybe things would be different, but for now, the goats are kept in what once would have been the king's chambers. In here!"

They had followed him into a small room lined with weapons. Slingshots dangled from hooks in the wall, while flint spears stuck out of barrels like strange bouquets. Hammerheads chiseled from rock lay across a table, along with a series of walking sticks that each had a large marble orb attached to the top. And in the corner, a cannon carved in the shape of a gargoyle loomed from the shadows.

Unease wriggled through Claire. The Gemmers, for how few they were, were very well armed. She wondered how old some of the stone weapons were. She wondered if any of them had been used in a unicorn hunt. And she wondered how learning to shoot an arrow would help wake the moontears.

"Take these," Geode said, holding out two bows toward them. Sophie snatched the bigger one, while Claire took the smaller. She didn't know a thing about bows, but it was pretty, made of a dark polished wood with soft leather straps wrapped around the grip. It was heavier than the only other bow she'd ever held, the one Mom had made for her from a bent coat hanger and yarn when she was a Merry Man in the fourth graders' production of *Robin Hood*.

"Usually, you only shoot the arrowheads you carve yourself," Geode said as he handed them each a quiver full of arrows. "But since we've missed that part of class, you can borrow these."

"Thank you," Claire said, and she meant it, even though

the arrows in her hand looked as sharp as crocodile teeth. It was nice that he was so helpful. When she'd accidentally joined the Forger academy for class, they hadn't been nearly so welcoming.

"So what's your plan?" Claire whispered to Sophie as they followed Geode to the back door.

Sophie's eyebrows shot up in an umbrella of surprise. "Whatever do you mean?"

Claire rolled her eyes. That wasn't going to work—not on her. "We don't even know if you're a Gemmer. How are you going to get through magic class?"

"Maybe I'm just not a Gemmer *yet*," Sophie said with a shrug. "Maybe I just need training to jog it loose, or something."

Claire frowned. Anvil Malchain had seemed pretty certain that Sophie was not a Gemmer, but Sophie clearly hadn't given up hope. An old worry yawned within Claire, stirring awake at Sophie's words. Did Sophie want to be a Gemmer so badly because she didn't think Claire could handle the pressure of waking the moontears on her own?

And was she right?

But there was no more time to think about it, because they had entered the training courtyard. A handful of children in the same garb as Claire and Sophie stood in an archer's stance, facing a line of targets on the far end of the pebble-filled courtyard.

"Elbow higher, Zuli!" the instructor barked, and Claire

gripped her bow harder. Her first instructor in magic was going to be none other than the glowering Commander Jasper.

"Lapis, stop squinting," Jasper said to the next apprentice. "How can you expect to see a wraith with your eyes practically closed?"

"Commander!" Geode called. "We're here."

Jasper turned, and his already stormy expression darkened further as Claire and Sophie stepped forward.

"What are the *princesses* doing here?" Jasper said, and by the tone of his voice, Claire knew he thought they were just as royal as bird droppings. "They're supposed to be with Terra—"

"Scholar Terra is working on the west wing," Geode quickly explained.

"And she told them to come here first?"

When Claire and Sophie nodded, the furrows of Jasper's brow were so deep that they looked like fault lines. "Join the others, then. AND WHO SAID YOU COULD STOP TO RELAX?"

Claire jumped. She hadn't realized how silent the courtyard had become at their arrival, but at Jasper's bellow, the apprentices tore their eyes away from them and quickly drew back their bowstrings.

Sophie and Claire slipped into line next to a boy and girl who shared the same corkscrew curls, pointed chin, and dimpled cheeks, so Claire knew they must be brother and sister, if not twins. Stealing a glance at the other apprentices, Claire tried to mimic the easy way they gripped the string and pulled back. But her pretty wooden bow was stiff, and didn't seem to want to bend.

It looked so easy in the movies! But Claire could barely get it back one inch. Sophie, meanwhile, had pulled hers taut with ease, and looked as smug as their friend Nettle Green in a trivia contest.

"Pull harder," Sophie urged. "*Come on*, Claire."

Claire gritted her teeth and wondered how the bow could possibly be magic when it seemed to be only clunky and awkward in her hands. The bow budged an inch. She could feel sweat beading on her forehead as she tried to hold her position. Chills broke over her as a cool mountain breeze played between the apprentices. After a few more minutes of stance correcting, Jasper called on Geode to release the first arrow of the morning.

Thwack!

Cheers filled the courtyard as the arrow hit the target, but Claire suddenly felt sick. She glanced at Sophie to see her sister, too, looked ill, and was rubbing a spot under her collarbone, directly above her heart. The same place where an arrow had pierced her only a few weeks ago. The same place where a unicorn's horn had left a pink star-shaped scar.

"Pay attention, Princess!"

Claire tore her eyes away from Sophie only to realize that Jasper was standing beside her. All around, the apprentices snickered.

"I'm s-sorry," Claire stuttered. "What did you say?"

Jasper scowled. "Well then, it seems like you think you know everything already if you're not bothering to pay attention. Go ahead, notch your bow."

Claire's mouth went dry. "But I don't kn—"

"*Now.*"

CHAPTER
5

𝕱ingers trembling, Claire selected an arrow from the quiver and fit it to the string, nearly dropping her bow in the process. This time, with the arrow notched, the bow bent easily. Claire let out a shaky breath.

"We don't have all day," Jasper called. "Fire!"

Taking a deep breath, Claire aimed, then released.

Cold wind suddenly rushed into Claire's face and her hair snapped back as the entire world whooshed past her in a colorful swirl.

"HELP!" Claire yelled as the arrow—still attached to her fingers—dragged her across the courtyard as easily as Dad used to pull her across the ice skating rink.

"Let go!" someone cried.

"I CAN'T!" she screeched as her feet skidded against the cobblestones. She told her fingers to let go, but for some reason they wouldn't—or *couldn't*. She was wildly out of control, her teeth rattling.

Thump!

Her breath slammed out of her lungs as she hit the straw target. She fell back hard on the ground . . . the arrow still attached to her palm. She flapped her hand, trying to shake the arrow off, but it clung to her fingertips, as if glued.

"*Claire!*" There was a crunch of gravel as Sophie ran across the courtyard to her. "Are you all right?"

"Foolish girl!" Jasper said as he stormed over, the rest of the apprentices following in his angry wake. "Just because you think you are a princess *does not mean* you are entitled to a Lode Arrow!"

"A what?" Claire asked, tears prickling her eyes. Even though she was no longer being dragged, the world still seemed to be moving too fast for her to catch up.

"A Lode Arrow," Jasper repeated. "That arrowhead has been carved from lodestone, which, when properly shaped, becomes highly magnetic, clinging to the iron in human blood to allow a *trained* Gemmer to travel far distances quickly."

"You did this on purpose!" Sophie exclaimed, whirling away from Claire to yell at Geode, who stood near the back of the group. But his smile, which had at first seemed so friendly, was now not so much a smile as it was a smirk.

"I don't know what they're talking about, Commander," Geode said. "The princesses insisted on choosing the rarest arrow, saying that they deserved it."

Something hot flashed in Claire's stomach. Geode—he'd set

them up! He'd given her these arrows. Her mind raced to their meeting this morning. Claire would have bet an entire sack of crescent pastries that Terra had no idea they were here at S.A.S. class at all. Anger, bright and scalding, flooded her. *He tricked them!*

"That's not true!" Claire said. "You're lying!"

There was a gasp from the watching apprentices as Claire, forgetting the arrow was still attached to her hand, jabbed an accusatory point at him.

"Put your hand down, girl," Jasper snapped, and she did—instantly. Reaching into his pocket, the commander removed a large black rock and held it up to Claire's hand. There was a slight hum in the air, and then a clink as the arrowhead disconnected from Claire's hand and attached itself to the stone in the same way Claire had seen Mom use a magnet to pick up sewing pins off the floor.

The watching apprentices broke into scattered applause. Claire opened and closed her fingers, breathing with relief as her hand finally obeyed.

"Hey," Sophie said, crossing her arms and glaring at Jasper. "Aren't you going to punish Geode?"

"Geode, as far as I know, has not been lying to Stonehaven," Jasper said. "While you, on the other hand, neglected to mention something to the grandmaster last night. You," he pointed at Sophie, "are clearly *not* a Gemmer. In fact, if I'm not mistaken, you have no magic at all."

Sophie's mouth gaped open.

Jasper ignored her stupefied expression. "The particular Lode Arrows in your quivers are crafted to work only for Gemmers. I would know. I made them myself. If you were a Gemmer, it would have dragged you across the courtyard, too, by now."

"Is he saying she's a lackie?" an apprentice whispered quietly, but someone hushed him.

"S.A.S. is complete for the day. I expect all of you to return your practice weapons to the armory and proceed quietly to Scholar Pumus's workroom. If I hear that one of you so much as puts a toe out of line, I will assign all of you the dawn watch for a month."

The apprentices quickly scattered, scooping up forgotten arrows and returning them to the armory. Claire hefted her Gemmer pack, then looked around for Sophie in the mayhem. She already had her Gemmer pack on and was sidling out the door with the other apprentices.

A spear suddenly appeared in Sophie's path. "And where do you think you're going?" Jasper asked. "You and I have an appointment with Grandmaster Carnelian. Hand over your Gemmer pack, please."

Sophie's shoulders slumped. Shimmying the strap off, she gave her pack to Jasper. "Stand up to them," she whispered to Claire before she followed the commander out the door.

And as Sophie turned left, while the rest of the apprentices went right, Claire couldn't help but feel that it was all her fault. In just the first hour, Claire had managed to break the rules, humiliate herself, and crush Sophie's dream of uncovering her magic.

Her stomach flipped. At the rate she was going, they'd all be lucky if Stonehaven was still standing by dinnertime.

Trailing after the others, she followed them to a door haloed by light. Behind it, she could hear loud voices and a rumbling grind that would have sounded more at home in a construction site than a classroom. A moment later, the door swung open.

"You're all late!" A man of about Claire's height, who was as wide as he was tall, opened the door. His nose was cherry red, and his voice squeaky, as if he had a cold.

"S.A.S. class, er, took off in a different direction than usual," the girl with springy hair said cheerily. "We're very sorry."

"Extremely sorry," her brother added.

"Infinity sor—"

"All right, that's enough from you, Zuli, Lapis," Scholar Pumus said, and held the door open wide. "All of you come in and join the others. All except for . . ." His eyes scanned the group and landed on Claire. "You. Claire, is it?"

Claire nodded as the others trickled in around her to join the other Gemmer students.

"I thought Terra was supposed to bring you here herself at second chime, but no matter," Scholar Pumus said, sweeping her ahead of him into a room that didn't look like any school-room Claire had ever seen. There were no desks, and the kids bustled around different workstations. In one corner, a large waterwheel churned, sending water pounding down onto a pile of rocks. In another corner, some apprentices turned a large tumbler, while others walked around the room, dispersing rags, sandpaper, and polish to the children who sat at long, glimmering tables.

Claire blinked. The tables glimmered because they were heaped with jewels. And not just any jewels—most were as large as her fist. They were bigger than any Claire had ever seen, even in the natural history museum with Dad and Sophie. Just one, she was sure, would have covered the cost for all the paints at her favorite art supply store.

As Claire watched, a boy her age, or maybe even a little younger, reached for a sparkling green stone and began to polish it. A second later, the gem seemed to more than sparkle; it glowed. Holding the stone up, he examined it with a magnifying glass identical to the one Claire knew was in her own Gemmer pack.

Appearing satisfied, he tossed it into a massive clay pot beside him that brimmed with light, and picked up the next gem, this one a brilliant yellow.

"Now," Scholar Pumus said, rubbing his bald head, the only surface shinier than the gems. "How old are you?"

"Eleven and a half," Claire said, trying to speak over the sound of more jewels clattering onto the tables.

The scholar squinted. "With those scrawny arms? But never mind, follow me."

He led her over to a spot next to Lapis, and thankfully, far away from Geode, who was smirking as he watched her pass.

"Listen carefully," Scholar Pumus said as Claire settled onto a stool. "If you don't want the stone to turn to magma, you'll need to follow the three rules of crafting—"

"Scholar Pumus!" Zuli yelped from across the room. Claire saw that her feet seemed to have disappeared into the solid marble floor. She windmilled her arms as she tried to take a step, each of her springy black curls waving wildly.

"Zuli! I *told* you not to play with Impressionism!" Pumus looked around the table and pointed at the boy whose curls stuck out like exclamation points from his head. "Lapis, please help Claire get settled."

"You'll need these," Lapis said, handing her a rag as Claire took a seat. "And the little bit of diamond dust polish that should be in your pack. You just need to dab a little of the polish over the stone, then rub. Then it'll begin to glow."

That was it? Claire could do that. It didn't sound any harder than drying the good silver after one of Mom and Dad's fancy dinner parties. Still, she hesitated, not wanting to take the rag from Lapis.

Lapis stared at her expectantly, then his eyes widened in understanding. "It's safe, I promise! We're not all awful. Geode has pebbles for brains," he confided conspiratorially. "His joke wasn't funny at all. Here, I'll show you." Using the rag he'd offered to Claire, he skimmed the cloth over a pink gem and immediately, his face reflected the rosy glow.

"See? A Gemglow." He tossed it into a waiting pot, then selected a small, white rock and handed it to Claire. "Try a diamond. They're the easiest."

"But how do I—?" Claire broke off her question as Lapis had already ducked his head back down and started attacking his pile.

Cautiously, Claire skimmed her rag over the gem and began to polish. But no matter how many times she ran her cloth across the diamond, it didn't get any more sparkly. Did she not have magic anymore? Is that why she couldn't let go of the arrow? Had she used it all up when she'd released Unicorn Rock?

Magic is in the material. Her friend Nettle Green's voice bubbled up from her memory. *I can only release the potential the seed already has.*

Claire bit her lip. The last time she'd seen Nett, he'd been sick, and their friend Sena Steele was dragging him out of the swamp and to the closest village for help. Claire still didn't know what had happened to them, but Aquila had promised to find out for her while she was questing for the unicorn.

Struggling to remember the times she'd done magic before, Claire rubbed her hands together, trying to get them to feel tingly. When that didn't work, she imagined herself in a long chimney, climbing up through a magical hum that rattled her bones. She even tried to picture, as she had that day on the Sorrowful Plains, that she had *already* called light to the diamond as she had imagined the unicorn already out of the rock. But nothing happened.

"Where are your Gemglows, apprentice?"

Claire looked up to see the scholar's round face staring down at her.

"I'm sorry," Claire said, "I just don't know—I mean, I couldn't . . ."

Scholar Pumus sighed. "After lunch, please join the preambles. They could use some help folding the polishing rags."

Someone snickered. And from behind, she heard Geode whisper, "Some *princess*."

A thread of shame looped over Claire and pulled tight. She kept her head down for the remainder of class.

CHAPTER
6

The rest of the day tumbled by in a rocky sea of classes and worries: What was the first test with Terra going to look like, especially now that they knew Sophie wasn't a Gemmer? What would happen if Claire couldn't wake the moontears after all? Would everyone think she and Sophie were royal imposters, like Jasper and Geode clearly believed?

Claire was beginning to regret ever coming to Stonehaven. They should have gone straight home, climbed back down the chimney, and stayed where they belonged, where it was safe.

But even as Claire thought it, she also knew she couldn't just run away and go home. Because what would happen to Arden then? They'd discovered a magical world. They couldn't just let that world fall apart—and she especially could not. After all, she was the Gemmer princess.

At last, the chimes tinkled, announcing dinnertime, and Claire heaved a huge sigh of relief. Though she'd been nervous attending class, she had secretly thought magic school would have been more like art class: fun and something she was good at. But now, she'd much rather have long division quizzes and spelling tests than relive today. She'd never been more overwhelmed.

Each apprentice helped carry the large pots of Gemglows to the dining hall, and they began to string garlands of glowing gems, bringing both light and cheer to the dark corners of the cavernous space. At least, Claire assumed they were supposed to bring cheer—they only succeeded in illuminating how alone she was. Maybe now that it was dinnertime, she'd see Sophie again.

She hoped Grandmaster Carnelian hadn't been too harsh with her.

Slowly, the dining hall filled up. Choosing a spot as far away from the imperious Commander Jasper and his Wraith Watch as possible, Claire sat at an empty table, nibbling the potatoes in front of her and scanning the Gemmers trickling in through the doors. But as the line thinned out, Sophie still did not appear. The potatoes turned cold in her stomach. She hoped Sophie hadn't gotten into any trouble. Or, more accurately, that trouble hadn't found Sophie. Maybe *she* should go find her.

But before Claire could even formulate a plan, someone was tapping on her shoulder. Terra.

"I'm glad to see you where you're supposed to be," the scholar said. "Commander Jasper filled me in on the day's events."

"I'm sorry!" Claire said quickly. "Geode said—"

"Yes, yes, so I heard from Sophie."

"Where is Sophie?"

"She's where *she's* supposed to be," Terra said. "Now come, it's time."

Before she'd even finished her dinner? "But—"

Claire looked up at Terra and closed her mouth. Terra did not seem like someone who was used to being disobeyed. A wave of exhaustion hit Claire but she stood and trailed after the woman. She knew what this was about.

The first test.

Claire followed Terra into her study, trying to breathe calmly. As they wove their way through the unicorn sculptures, paintings, and figurines, Claire marveled again at how many places Terra had been able to put a unicorn. Perfectly stitched unicorns marched across the deep blue curtains that had been pulled over the windows, and stones carved into unicorn profiles had replaced the dresser knobs.

Claire rubbed her clammy hands on her tunic. She knew she was being silly, but it suddenly seemed like all the hundreds of unicorns in that room were staring at her, waiting for her to prove herself to them. She followed Terra to the desk, now covered with open books—which, of course, were filled with unicorn sketches.

Terra sat down behind the desk. "Now. Did you have a good day?"

"It was . . ." Claire trailed off. *Miserable, awful, disastrous*— all seemed to fit. But she knew that wasn't what Terra wanted to hear. So instead, she settled on, ". . . fine."

"Good, good."

As Claire watched, Terra bent and unlocked the top drawer of her desk. A second later, the moontear necklace appeared in her hands, sparkling in the chandelier's light. Claire leaned forward, drinking in the familiar peace of their rounded edges and gentle gleam. They were luminous and . . . wait, were they bigger?

Narrowing her eyes, Claire leaned closer. She could have sworn they had grown since last night. Maybe they had just needed the fresh air of Starscrape Mountain. Or maybe Claire was just so used to seeing them around Sophie's neck that she wasn't remembering right.

Terra stopped ferreting in her desk and dropped a few polishing rags on top of an open manuscript, which currently was laid out to a page that showed the correct way to braid a unicorn's mane.

"Don't just stand there," she said, glancing up. "Sit. We have a lot—stars and diamonds above, what's wrong?" she exclaimed as she finally looked at Claire for the first time.

Claire took a step back. The current lenses were so thick that they made Terra's eyes look as big as an owl's. Terra rapidly flicked through her lenses, then stopped before she let out a low whistle. "I've never seen someone so *completely* embody misery before. What on earth and underneath it happened today?"

It was almost as if she could see not just Claire's face but inside her head, to her thoughts. But her tone was so warm and so motherly that Claire's eyes immediately swam with tears. She was so focused on keeping them in that the rest of the day spilled out: How Geode had tried to play a prank on her; how she hadn't seen Sophie; how her gems never, not even once, glowed. And how she thought that maybe . . .

"Maybe what?" Terra prompted.

"That maybe I'm out of magic," Claire admitted all in a rush. She held her breath, wondering if she had made a mistake. Terra could call the Wraith Watch, and Claire and Sophie might find themselves at any moment dumped outside the Citadel's wall.

"My dear," Terra said, resting her hand on hers. "Magic never runs out. It's always there, in the material. Magic is really about *seeing*, about finding the possibilities."

Claire frowned. "Possibilities?"

Terra nodded, her large ruby earrings swinging. "Everything has the possibility of changing into something else. Everything contains secret wishes and capabilities. Objects have stories they are longing to tell. Magic is learning how to understand what those are, and then choosing which ones to bring out. Your sister mentioned that you like to sketch, yes?"

Confused at the abrupt turn in conversation, Claire nodded

and felt a familiar itch in her fingertips. It had been so *long* since she'd held a pencil in her hand. Graphite, or letter stone as it was called here, was rare in Arden. So rare that even Anvil and Aquila, the most renowned treasure hunters of all the guilds, had said they'd only seen a handful of them in their lifetime. The graphite mines had shut down years ago.

Still, drawing was one of her favorite things. Slowly, Claire lowered herself into the pink velvet armchair, ready to hear more.

"When you draw," Terra said, tapping the illustration of the braided unicorn on her desk, "what's the very *first* mark you make on a piece of paper?"

Not sure where this was going, Claire shrugged. "A line, I guess."

"And then what do you draw?" Terra prompted.

Claire thought a moment. It was such a simple question, she wondered if it was a trick. "I draw more lines."

"Exactly." Terra nodded. "The line is just a line until you, the crafter, see what that line has the potential to be: the underside of a chin, the swoop of an apple, the curve of a smile."

She reached up to her earlobe and tugged off a ruby earring. It clinked against the table as she placed it on the desk in front of Claire.

"Right now, the ruby has simply been asked to reflect the light *around* it. But rubies once created their own light as they melted in the heart of the earth. By polishing it, you can help the ruby remember how it once shone by itself, and how it can do so again. Now, go on. Try."

Slowly, Claire picked up the ruby, and taking the kerchief Terra handed her, she began to rub it over the stone.

Nothing happened.

"Remember what it feels like to draw," Terra murmured. "You follow the line of letter stone, releasing an image from it. Here, you follow the spark of light, encouraging it to escape."

Claire wanted to point out that polishing was *not* the same as drawing, but Terra would just call that an excuse. So instead, she focused on the tiny sparkle of the ruby. Closing her eyes, she tried to imagine the absolute darkness that this ruby had been born in, the entire heat of the world hugging it close. Squeezing, squeezing, and squeezing, until it would have shaken the molecular structures, making it buckle, vibrate, *hum*, and melt . . . Something flashed against the dark of her eyelids, and Claire snapped them open.

The ruby glowed in the center of her palm.

It was faint, hardly brighter than a strand of fairy lights in daytime, but it was *there*. She had made the ruby glow. *She* had done *magic*.

On purpose.

A flush of joy washed over her, followed immediately by confusion. "Why was it so easy for me before I got here?"

"Ah yes." Terra nodded. "Sophie did mention something about a cave, and a wyvern. At moments of great emotion, sometimes our abilities surprise even ourselves. But learning to control the magic and draw upon it whenever you want takes practice. You don't become a great artist overnight."

Claire nodded, but she was only half listening. She was

again staring at the moontear necklace. "How is polishing going to help with the moontears?"

"You just released light from stone," Terra pointed out. "And according to Timor the Verbose," she tapped the book in front of her again, "a unicorn's closest relative is starlight. As a Gemmer princess, maybe you can call forth the unicorns the same way you called out the ruby's spark of light."

Claire looked at her, dumbfounded. "Really?"

Terra adjusted her spectacles. "It's just an idea, but," she waved her hands at her desk and shelves, all covered with straight-spine covers, "all these books began as just an idea, too. And so did all these paintings, portraits, sculptures, tapestries . . ."

Gazing at the moontears, Claire thought they were the prettiest idea of all. The ruby's glow seemed to reignite somewhere in her chest. Small, but strong.

"Hand me a cloth, Scholar Terra," she said. "I'm ready to try."

CHAPTER
7

An hour later, Claire padded through the marble halls, only the patter of her footsteps keeping her company. She tried to tread softly. Stonehaven seemed like a place to whisper, feeling both as grand as a cathedral and as intimate as a library. Into that echoing quiet, her stomach growled hungrily as she tried to shake off a feeling of doom.

It hadn't worked.

The moontears had pulsed slightly in her hands as she polished them in Terra's office . . . but no light came forth, no magic happened, no unicorns appeared. All the elation Claire had felt moments before seemed to evaporate immediately.

"We'll try again tomorrow, dear," Scholar Terra had said as she picked up the moontears and locked them back into her desk. "These things take time to learn."

But Claire could tell Scholar Terra was disappointed, and as soon as Claire had left the warmth of the study, she felt suddenly cold, and very alone. Now, following Terra's instructions, as she made her way up a set of winding stairs to her and Sophie's shared room, she passed a jade statue of a woman in robes that fell in stone folds, with a bow and arrow across her back. And on top of her long curly hair was a three-pointed crown.

Queen Estelle d'Astora, the last queen of Arden and the hero of Arden's history, who, legend said, had turned herself and the last unicorn to stone to save them both from the fearful blade of the hunter. Who most of Arden believed would one day return, bring unicorns back to Arden, and drive the wraiths away.

But of course, Claire had learned, legends lie. Her heart knocked hard against her chest as she slipped by the statue queen's cold smile. She hoped Anvil had heard about what happened to Queen Rock—who had destroyed it, and why. Had it really been the Forgers, like Jasper had said?

"Hi!"

Claire jumped as Lapis's curly head popped out around a corner, followed immediately by Zuli's sparkling eyes.

"We thought you might need some help getting back from Terra's," Zuli explained. "I know Starscrape like the back of my hand—"

"—and I know it like the back *and the front* of my hand," Lapis interjected.

"—but it's a big place, and easy to get lost in," Zuli finished, completely ignoring her brother.

It was nice of the Gemmer twins, it really was, but after the day she'd had, Claire felt about as trusting as a balled-up porcupine.

"Why are you being so nice to me?" she blurted out. As soon as she said it, she could practically hear Sophie's sigh in her head. But instead of laughing at her, the twins looked at each other in surprise.

"Because," Lapis said, "even princesses need help."

"And you're going to help all of us by waking the moontears," Zuli added. "Once magic is strong again, we won't need to stick around here making sure the Citadel stays put. We'll be able to travel to the mines of Mount Rouge, see the living stone of the Sparkling Sea, and maybe even converse with a wyvern."

Her words seemed to bounce along with her curls. "I could even discover a new mineral or two—all thanks to you!"

Claire blushed, pleased, but also once again overwhelmed by the pressure. So much depended on waking the moontears . . .

"Besides," Lapis added darkly, "we heard Geode bragging at dinner how he got you in trouble. He wasn't supposed to bring you to S.A.S. at all. He was just supposed to let you know Terra would be late. This way!"

Claire looked to see Zuli pulling back a moth-eaten tapestry to reveal a hidden passageway.

"It's a shortcut," she explained. "The Citadel is full of secret halls, if you know where to look."

"And we do!" Lapis said, bounding in. "Mother and Father are in charge of mapping the passageways. No one knows more about the Citadel's tunnels than us."

"Except Mother and Father," Zuli pointed out.

Claire followed the twins, glad they were her guides. Without a map, it would have been impossible to navigate the meandering tunnels. Eventually, the twins pushed on a stone slab, and Claire found herself at the bottom of the spiraling staircase leading to her shared tower room. She barely had time to thank the twins before they were off, racing each other to their family apartments.

Reaching the landing, Claire saw gold light stitching the door to the floor. Good. Sophie was back.

"Claire!" Sophie exclaimed as soon as she walked in. "*Finally.*"

"What happened to you?" Claire asked, taking in her sister. Sophie's hair was pulled back in its ponytail . . . along with enough twigs and leaves to make an entire nest.

Sophie flopped onto her straw pallet and groaned. "*Goats.* It was awful! They eat everything!" She held up the tips of her hair and Claire realized that the ends had clearly been gnawed on. "Grandmaster Carnelian has forbidden me from attending any more Gemmer lessons. He says it's too dangerous for 'someone like me' to be around a bunch of untrained apprentices."

Someone like me. Claire knew what those words meant. Someone without magic.

"But where do the goats come in?"

Sophie sighed. "I'm supposed to be *helpful*. Carnelian took me down to the kitchens, so I spent the day running errands for Cook Koal, weeding, delivering lunch trays, goat watching, that sort of stuff."

Propping her cheek on her hand, Sophie sighed even louder. "I don't get it, Claire. How can you be magic and not me? It doesn't make sense."

Claire flinched. Sophie's careless words buzzed straight into her heart, stinging all the worse because she had asked herself the very same question. But Sophie didn't seem to realize what she had said, because she prattled on. "Honestly, today was the worst."

"I didn't have a good day, either," Claire said, and opened the wardrobe to pull out a nightgown.

Sophie sat up. "Please. You had magic lessons all day. How bad could that be?"

"*Bad*," Claire snapped. "It's not fun when you spend the whole day embarrassing yourself!"

Sophie's eyebrows shot up and her mouth dropped into a round O of surprise.

"I'm sorry," Claire said, her ribs feeling tight. She didn't want Sophie to be mad at her. Not on top of everything else. "I just mean—"

"No, I'm sorry," Sophie said. "I want to hear all of it. Tell me more?"

As the girls prepared for bed, pulling on nightgowns and de-twigging Sophie's hair, Claire told her about her day, even down to the humiliating moment she'd been relegated to folding rags with the preambles. The theory behind magic, however, fascinated Sophie, and Claire tried to answer Sophie's questions as best she could, recalling everything Terra had told her, until her mouth was as dry as a freshly laundered towel. Finally, after checking to make sure the Kompass was still safely hidden at the bottom of their wardrobe, they blew out their candles and clambered into the two trundle beds.

"I miss cell phones," Sophie said into the dark. "Think how much easier it would be to know what Anvil's found out."

Cell phones. Batteries. Internet. How funny all those words sounded in the marble halls of Stonehaven. And how funny that they'd become so strange to her in such a short amount of time. Suddenly, Claire was afraid.

She had been in Arden for weeks now, and already the world of Windemere felt as though it was being erased away. But what if home wasn't what was being erased. What if it was *Claire*?

Everything has the possibility of changing, Terra had said. But Claire wasn't sure she wanted everything to change *that* much.

"Claire," Sophie's voice interrupted the darkness. "I was thinking . . . what if it wasn't the Forgers who destroyed Queen Rock, like Jasper said? Or any of the lowland guilds for that matter."

Turning on her side, Claire stared at the spot of dark where her sister's voice had come from. "What do you mean?"

"I was just thinking, when I delivered lunch to Jasper today, I got a look at his desk. It was covered with papers, but not letters. More like . . . battle plans."

"*Battle* plans?"

"Yeah, you know, maps with little flags and stuff. It made me think that maybe Stonehaven is up to something . . . that maybe the *Gemmers* destroyed Queen Rock?"

"Why would they do that?" Claire asked in surprise. "They love Queen Estelle. She's the only Gemmer everyone likes."

There was a crackling of straw and Claire imagined Sophie turning on her side and squinching her face. "I've seen the kitchens, Claire. There isn't all that much food on a mountain. Despite all the jewels, the Gemmers don't have much else. Maybe they set the Forgers up as an excuse to attack them and take their supplies."

Turning her sister's words over, Claire thought about it. It *could* make sense, but . . .

"Why wouldn't the Gemmers have set up the Tillers, then?" Claire asked. "They're the ones with all the food."

"Oh." Sophie shifted. "That's a good point."

Of course Sophie *would* come up with the most dramatic option. Mom always said that the most dangerous thing was a bored Sophie. When she had too much time, her imagination would run wild, trying to come up with Experiences. Most of the time, they were harmless, but a few times, like when they'd tried to scale the roof of a rotting garden shed, Sophie's Experiences had been dangerous.

Claire snuggled under the goat-hair blanket, trying to cocoon herself away from Sophie's "theories."

"Clairina?" Sophie's voice came once more, and Claire almost groaned. She was *so* sleepy, but her sister continued. "I get that today was hard. But you'll wake the moontears soon. I just know it. There's got to be a reason we found our way here, don't you think? There's a reason we found the chimney. There's a reason we're princesses."

CHAPTER
8

But Claire didn't wake the moontears the next day.

Or the day after that. Or even the day after that.

Every evening, Claire went to Terra's study to try a different Gemmer technique on the necklace—from attempting to deconstruct it on the pottery wheel, to using the erosion of wind and water, to the most obvious use of a chisel. Nothing worked. The moontears remained as secret and silent as they always had been.

Though she could squeeze light out of a jewel, it was never as brilliant as Zuli's and Lapis's or as quick as Geode's, and even the preambles' Gemglows were stronger. She could barely keep up. She wasn't even sure if she was *keeping* up as opposed to *messing* up.

One week after her disastrous first class of S.A.S., Claire sat in Mineral Properties, her eyelids feeling heavy as rock. She'd spent all last night practicing, and now could barely stay awake.

"You're going to poison us?" someone asked.

Claire's head jerked up, snapping her out of her daze. What had she missed? Looking around, she saw Zuli frowning at Scholar Terra—who frowned right back at her.

"No," Terra said, huffing out slightly. "*You* will be poisoning *yourself*."

Claire's mind scrambled as she tried to remember what today's lesson was. Something about kneading the clay at room temperature? She squinted at her slate. At the top, written in bold letters were the words: CLAY PROPERTIES. Below it was half a sentence: *Clay is . . .*

Blinking, Claire stared in dismay. She sat up tall in her chair, trying to catch a glimpse of the very full slate next to her. But unfortunately, Beryl, the tallest, but also the quietest apprentice, noticed. Shooting her a dirty look, he curled his arm around his work.

"But what if our Grail doesn't work?" Zuli pressed, her mouth a thin line.

A Grail. All right, so they were supposed to make some sort of a clay cup.

Terra pulled out a vial from her skirt pocket. "I have the antidote to the poison, of course. Really, Lazuli, what kind of monster do you think I am?"

Zuli blushed, and Claire noticed that her hair, which tended to spring out in every direction at once, seemed particularly spring-like today. Zuli caught her eye and Claire gave her a shy smile. The girl smiled back.

"When are we ever going to use this?" Geode complained from his pottery station.

Terra threw up her hands, her dangling emerald earrings clinking together as she shook her head. "There are many times a Grail would be useful. Beryl, how about you give us an example?"

Beryl immediately ducked his head as everyone turned to look at him. "Well," he mumbled to his tabletop, "if you were traveling and you couldn't start a fire, the Grail would let you drink water safely without boiling it."

Terra nodded. "Good. And who can tell me the theory behind the Grail?"

Claire kept her own head down, hoping Terra's eyes would skip over her and settle on someone else. No such luck.

"Claire?"

"Um," Claire stalled, looking around the room for some inspiration—that was it! "Inspiration, dedication, courage?" she offered hesitantly.

Terra narrowed her eyes, then slowly nodded. "True, those are the rules behind the theory of *all* craft. You do need to feel inspired to create a Grail, and you must be dedicated to keep working the clay, even if it crumbles beneath your hands. And, of course, you need the courage to try to make one, even when you might fail . . . But what *specific* property of rock are we using to filter poison from water? Lapis, can you tell me?"

So that's what they were supposed to be doing: crafting a clay mug that would allow them to drink poisoned water safely—somehow, they had to make the clay recognize the poison, and filter it out of the liquid. But even though Claire now knew *what* she was supposed to do, she still had no idea *how*.

When Terra was finally convinced that the apprentices properly understood the assignment, she plopped a handful of wet clay onto each of their desks. Geode immediately began to pound his mound flat with large whacks of his fist, but Zuli shaped hers into tiny balls first. Glancing behind her, Claire saw Lapis had rolled his to look like a long, skinny snake.

Claire stared at her clay. She really, *really* didn't want to poison herself. Tentatively, she stuck her fingers in, and got to work. She kneaded with as much concentration as possible, trying to listen to the shape this particular lump of clay might like to take, but apparently her clay wanted to be a lumpy pancake, because it kept falling apart in her hands.

"Time's up," Terra declared an hour later. Claire groaned and desperately tried to shove her handle onto the mug. For one blink of an eye, her Grail had a handle . . . and then it bowed inward like a clothesline and slowly fell off. Claire glanced enviously at Zuli's desk, where a perfectly formed clay teacup sat.

"I said, 'time's up!'" Terra repeated. "Put everything down, please, and place your Grail in the oven for some quick drying."

Claire made one last desperate attempt to squash the handle

on, but it was no use. She hoped the handle wasn't key to filtering poisons.

Hands shaking, not from magic, but from nerves, Claire set her Grail on the drying rack as Terra instructed. Minutes later, Terra carefully removed the dried, hardened Grails from the oven. They all were the same flat red-orange of flowerpots. Only one looked different from the rest. Not just different, but pathetic: Claire's. Her handleless Grail had collapsed in on itself, looking like a stiff, crumpled handkerchief. Behind her, someone giggled. Claire's neck burned hot.

One by one, the apprentices lined up in front of Terra. Zuli went first. Accepting the vial from their scholar, Zuli let a drop of a bright green liquid—*poison*—into her Grail. Cautiously, Zuli swirled the green stuff into the water in her cup before taking a sip.

Nothing happened.

"Well done, Lazuli," Terra said, nodding her head in approval and making a mark on her slate. "Perfect results." Zuli smiled happily.

Lapis went next, his trial going similarly except for a slight hiss of steam that had been absent in Zuli's. Terra kindly pointed out that there was a hairline fissure in his clay.

Claire's stomach twisted and rolled as, one by one, the apprentices drank water from their Grails. Even Geode managed not to poison himself, though after sipping from his vessel, he'd gotten a nasty case of hiccups.

By the time it was Claire's turn, her stomach hurt so badly

that she wasn't sure she would even be able to tell if she were poisoned or not. With trembling hands, she accepted the vial from Terra. The poison was a bright green, the same shade as one of the poisonous frogs Claire had seen in the zoo's rainforest exhibit. Carefully, she let one droplet fall into her Grail.

Pop! . . . Popopopopop!

People screamed as Claire's goblet exploded in a shower of hissing water and clay shards. Zuli dashed under a desk while others ran to the back of the room. An acrid scent lingered in the air, something similar to the smell of plastic too close to the stove.

Terra ran to a window and flung open the shutters. Soon, a cool mountain breeze whisked in, clearing away clouds of red dust to reveal the blackened, twisted remains of Claire's failure.

That night, Claire could barely keep her head lifted as she ate her stringy stew in the dining hall. All around her, Gemmers munched, scraping their silverware against the bottom of their bowls, but even during meals, they were still working. Dusty quarry workers spoke with an anxious group of architects Claire had spotted earlier that day dangling from flying buttresses. Scholar Pumus, too, barely picked at his dinner as he conversed with a man still holding his pickax and measuring tape.

But while the grown-ups always seemed worried, there was constant movement in the hall. The young preambles roamed from table to table, seeking leftover dessert, and the older apprentices gobbled their meals next to their parents before rushing off to join their friends, always giving a wide berth to the rickety table the Martinson sisters had claimed for their own.

Not that they were ignored; that would have been preferable. No, instead they were watched from a distance—as if there were a glass wall between them and everyone else—and Claire couldn't go anywhere without hearing a whispered "*princess.*" Occasionally, she thought she saw a parent nudge their kid toward their table, but no one ever came to sit with them. Claire guessed it was because they didn't want Sophie's lack of magic to rub off on them, but she kept that thought to herself.

After helping in the kitchens, Sophie was allowed to eat with her. Usually, Sophie had a story to tell about what she'd learned (eavesdropped), but today Sophie was looking just as burned out as Claire felt. Her sister rested her head in her ink-stained hands.

"How was your day?" Claire asked

Sophie sighed. "I was forced to help Cook Koal take inventory of the kitchen supplies. There are"—she yawned—"exactly 524 clay mugs with handles, and 1,276 without. In case you were wondering."

"Better than *my* day," Claire said. She told her about the clay Grail and how it had exploded all over the classroom, leaving a hard little round of blackened clay instead of a poison-canceling drinking cup.

"Hmm," Sophie said, looking thoughtful all of a sudden. Which, Claire knew, was not always a good thing.

"What?" Claire shifted and swallowed more of her stew.

"Oh nothing. It's just . . . do we really trust these scholars? Poison? And what about those Hypnotizing Opals you were telling me about?"

"Mesmerizing Opals," Claire corrected automatically, and shuddered. That had been Identification Class, which Claire thought might be easier, since it didn't involve direct magic, just a sharp eye for detail. Which, her art teachers had always said, she had. But as Claire had picked up a seemingly harmless black stone, it began to flicker with different colors. She had paused, unable to look away from the shifting rainbow that darted just beneath the rock's smooth surface. The rock seemed to be winking at her, calling her to follow it . . .

Claire. Claire!

She had not wanted to look away. She *could not* look away.

Somewhere deep within her, Claire had known that this was strange, but she had not cared. The rock had been enough. The rock had been everything . . .

"Claire!"

Suddenly, the rock had been pried free from her fingers, and the spell had broken. With increasing horror, she had learned that she'd fallen into the entrapment of a Mesmerizing Opal, a dangerous bit of Gemmer magic that allowed the gem's wielder to ensnare the mind of whomever looked directly at it. A horrified Master Pumus hadn't known how the opal had ended up in the apprentices' training stones, claiming that the Citadel had banned them a hundred years ago.

For the rest of the day, the apprentices hadn't been allowed to touch so much as a single jeweled button and had instead spent the remainder of the afternoon reviewing the more dangerous and deadly gemstones. Claire hadn't had a full night's rest since.

"Yeah, Mesmerizing Opals, S.A.S. Class—that's scary stuff, Claire." Sophie chewed on the end of a carrot stick but her voice had taken on a familiar, ominous tone. "I just wonder what else they've got planned."

Claire sighed. "Is this about the battle plans again?" Sophie hadn't been able to let that go.

"I don't know why you don't believe me." Sophie took a sip of goat's milk. "Just today, the Wraith Watch was crafting arrowheads that are supposed to pierce through metal. I saw them come into the kitchens for extra silverware to use as targets."

"So?"

"So, the *Wraith* Watch is supposed to only protect against the *wraiths*," Sophie said. "These arrows are specifically made for targeting metal. And metal means—"

"Forgers," Claire said. "So?"

"*So,*" Sophie hurried on quickly, "yesterday I also saw one of the guards try to make a stone arrow—no wood on it at all. Which was something they did back during the Guild War, so that the Tillers wouldn't make their arrows burst into bloom midflight. I wish there was some way we could let Aquila and Anvil know. I'm telling you, Claire, the Gemmers are up to some—"

"Sophie, stop." Claire dropped her spoon. She was so tired she thought she might cry. "I know what this is about."

"It's about the Gemmers plotting something!" Sophie exclaimed.

"No, it's about you being bored. And I'm sorry, but I need to concentrate or I'm never going to wake the moontears, and we'll never go home."

Home. Mom. Dad.

"Claire," Sophie put down her carrot. "You don't have to do this alone."

Claire sighed. Sophie just didn't understand. Even though she tried to give Sophie magic lessons every night before bed, sharing what she'd learned from the day, there hadn't been the tiniest crumb of change in Sophie's Gemmerhood.

And now, it was time for Claire's nightly meeting with Terra, where, once again, they would try something new with the moontears.

"I have to go," she told Sophie, and grabbing her tray, left the table.

By now Claire had a better sense of her way around the echoing halls of Stonehaven, but she still couldn't shake Sophie's unsettling words as she made her way alone down the passageway that led to the stairs in the north tower, which housed Terra's study.

When she finally arrived outside the door, Claire automatically reached for the knob—the study had become familiar enough by now that she didn't need to knock anymore—but something stopped her from turning it.

There were voices coming from inside. Angry voices.

She leaned closer to the door to try to hear.

"She's dangerous," a man's voice scratched out. Claire's heart flipped upside down. It was Jasper's voice.

"She's a child," Terra admonished, and Claire's pulse slowed a little until she heard a third voice.

"If she can't prove herself soon, we will do what we must." *That* was Grandmaster Carnelian. Claire heard a *rat-a-tat* and imagined him tapping his large cane against Terra's desk. "We can't have people pretend to be royalty every day. If this gets out to the lowlands, they may think we're trying to crown a new queen of Arden, which would mean . . ." Carnelian trailed off, but Jasper finished the thought:

"War."

CHAPTER 9

Claire's stomach practically fell to the floor. So Sophie was *right*. They *were* preparing for war. Or at least, that is what it sounded like! And it was all because they didn't believe in Claire—they thought she was a fake.

She turned to run back down the stairs and find her sister when there was the scrape of a chair being pushed, followed by Terra's voice, "Gentlemen, I'm afraid I must end this meeting. We're scaring Claire."

Claire swiveled around just as Terra swung open the study door. Claire looked up into Terra's magically magnified eyes. Had she been able to see Claire *through the door*? What could those odd spectacles *see*?

Behind Terra stood Jasper, scowling, of course, along with Carnelian, the wrinkles of his face folding into amusement.

"Hello, Claire," Terra said calmly, pulling the door open wider so that Claire could enter. "Gentlemen, I'm afraid I must attend to my next appointment."

"Very well," Grandmaster Carnelian said as he leaned on his cane. "I have my own appointment with that delightful-looking pudding Cook Koal created. Commander, will you join me?"

Jasper's eyes glittered, and Claire had the sensation of tiny beetles crawling over her skin. There could be no doubt about it: the commander did not like her. The line of his jaw locked, but finally he nodded. "If you insist, Grandmaster."

Without one last glance at Claire, the two men left. Terra walked to her desk, the layers of her amethyst dress fluttering out behind her like purple smoke.

And then, just as she did every night, the scholar opened her desk drawer and removed the moontears.

"Tonight," she said, placing the necklace in front of her, "I thought we'd try—"

"What's the point?" The words burst from Claire just as her Grail had this afternoon: unexpected and all over the place. "Why do you keep making me try if Stonehaven doesn't believe me?"

Peering over her spectacles, Terra fixed a stern glare on her. Claire shrank back. She knew better than to talk to grown-ups that way, especially teachers. She waited for Terra to announce her punishment—lines, more homework, an hour helping Sophie clean the goat pens—but instead, the scholar folded her hands in front of her and said, "What makes you think it matters if Stonehaven believes you or not?"

Taken aback, Claire scowled down at the book in front of her. This one was entitled *Ivory and Mud: The Rise of the d'Astora Family.* "Please don't tell me something cheesy about needing to believe in myself."

"I would never."

Claire looked up, unsure if Terra was teasing her or not. "How am I supposed to believe in myself if I can only make things explode?" she demanded. "No matter what I do, I'm doing it wrong. I have magic, it just doesn't listen to me. Sophie—"

She broke off.

"Sophie, what?" Terra asked, bowing her head toward Claire. Tonight, the scholar had offset her evening lavender dress with ten or so tigereye chokers that wrapped around her neck like a turtleneck. And though Claire's neck was bare, her throat felt tight, as if *she* were the one wearing all the necklaces.

"Sophie should be the Gemmer princess," Claire said quietly.

"Why do you say that?"

Claire opened her mouth to respond, then stopped, unsure how to articulate her sister. Sophie was everything Claire was not. She was brave. She never gave up. She liked adventures. And it was Sophie who had first figured out Prince Martin's riddle. Sophie cared deeply about Arden's history and its unicorns. While Claire . . . well, Claire just wanted to wake the moontears and bring her sister home.

"Because she wants it," Claire said, looking Terra in the eye. "She came to Arden looking for an Experience. For *magic*. I only came here looking for her."

Terra sat back in her armchair. "Have you ever considered that's why the magic chose you?"

Surprise jolted Claire like an electric current. "What do you mean?"

"Sophie doesn't need magic to make her try new things, while you, Claire, might wait around forever hoping everything stays the same."

Claire blinked, uncomfortable again under the spectacles' gaze. There was such a thing as seeing a little *too* much.

The funny thing was, though, Sophie had needed the magic. Unbeknownst to Claire, Sophie had first run away into Arden seeking a cure for a mysterious disease. And when the unicorn had healed Sophie's chest wound on the Sorrowful Plains, he seemed to have also cured the rest of Sophie as well. Sophie had even said as they journeyed with Anvil that she felt even better than she did *before* that awful summer—and Claire believed her. Her sister had never seemed stronger, or more *Sophie*. Maybe Sophie wasn't a Gemmer because she generated her own brand of magic, a mixture of strength and courage.

Wanting to break Terra's gaze, Claire asked, "Do you believe us?"

At that, the scholar smiled and tapped the manuscript in front of her. "From what I've been reading, I believe that you and your sister are both stubborn enough to be d'Astoras."

"I'm not stubborn," Claire protested. "Mom always said I'm the easy one."

Terra raised her eyebrows. "So it's not stubbornness that makes you keep coming to me evening after evening even though we're no closer to waking the moontears than we were before?" She paused. "It's not always a bad thing to be difficult."

Claire wasn't so sure about that, but she didn't want to tell the scholar she was wrong, so she stayed quiet.

"All right, then," Terra said, picking up the necklace and putting it in her desk before standing up. "Follow me."

"What about the moontears?" Claire asked, still in her armchair.

"They don't seem to be in much of a hurry," Terra said with a glittery shrug. "They can wait another night."

Left with no choice, Claire stood and followed Terra.

At night, Stonehaven seemed to be carved from moonlight rather than stone. Tall candelabras bedecked with glowing diamonds lined the larger halls, while the tiny corridors were left in indigo darkness. Claire shivered slightly. A breeze had found its way inside, and it seemed to be brushed with the scent of autumn. She couldn't help but feel that she was at the end of something, but she wasn't sure exactly what she was at the end of . . . or what the new beginning would be.

As Terra swished through the hallways, mostly empty except for a pair or two of drifting Wraith Watch on duty,

Claire heard a hum. It was different than the hum of magic that would surge through her bones while she crafted, but nevertheless, it seemed to settle deep in her chest. The hum grew louder, and as they turned a corner, Claire could make out a distinct melody. A few steps later, the hum turned into words.

Spring in its steps,
And flowers of snow,
There the unicorn goes.
Hey diddle dee
And hey diddle low.

Terra opened a door, and Claire found herself in a cozy chamber filled with the Gemmers of Stonehaven. But they were far from the tired, solemn people Claire had grown used to seeing at dinnertime. The men and women she usually only saw in clay-splattered smocks or carrying pickaxes from the quarry now lounged about the chamber, some on benches, some on pillows set out on the floor. Many held clay mugs in their hands, from which steam wafted up like a careless thought. And all of them were singing.

Song in the crystal,
And stars under falls,
There the unicorn calls.
Hey la de lome
And hey la de la.

They sang without hesitation, each voice blending into the next. And as she took in the crowd of Gemmers, Claire saw the familiar faces of the apprentices scattered throughout the room, sitting with their families. Even obnoxious Geode, sitting between a freckle-faced woman and a man with a big furry beard, seemed to be actually enjoying himself.

"What song is this?" Claire asked.

"The Unicorn Song," Terra whispered back. "It's one of the most popular. They've been singing it every night since your arrival. And do you know why?"

Claire shook her head.

"Because Gemmers know the secret in stone is *pattern*. Rocks are made up of crystal structures that repeat over and over and over again." Terra raised an eyebrow above her spectacles as she looked down at Claire. "We are like rock. Patterns form in rock and in us. Our lives are made up not from crystal structures but from stories, and stories—*history*—often repeats. And so when we sing this song, night after night, we remember that stories repeat, which lets us hope that one day, the unicorns will return." Then Terra joined in, her voice low and round like the notes of a cello.

> *Bridle of gold,*
> *Beneath doors of fate,*
> *There the unicorn waits.*
> *Hey diddle lee*
> *And hey la de lome.*

As the song wound its way to the end, Claire watched Zuli whisper something to Lapis, who burst into quiet giggles. Grinning, Zuli glanced up and caught Claire's eye. A smile broke across her face, and she waved for her to come over.

Terra leaned down and whispered, "Go. Join Lazuli and the others. Princess or not, you are one of us. Stories repeat. Don't forget it."

With gratitude, Claire crouched and hurried to sit next to the twins.

"It's good to see you here," Zuli said with a grin.

"It's not good, it's excellent," Lapis corrected.

"It's *stupendous*," Zuli shot back, crossing her eyes.

An older woman with pearl-white hair stepped into the center and began to sing a soldier's farewell to his lover, who vowed to transform into rubies and smoke if he never returned. As Claire listened to the song, Zuli gave her a nudge.

"Lapis has something to give you," she whispered, and her brother reached into his pocket and pulled out what looked like a charred clay marble.

"Is that—"

Lapis nodded. "Yep. All that remains of your Grail. On the mountain, we say that your first piece of a new craft holds special luck."

"Some luck," Claire muttered.

"It is," Zuli said earnestly. "Didn't you see Geode's dive under his desk? He was literally hiding from some clay dust!"

She smiled and Claire felt the corners of her mouth tug in response.

The singer's voice grew louder as the soldier in the song approached the battlefield, and his lover cut her hair to prove her dedication.

"I wish it was that easy," Claire sighed. And when Zuli and Lapis looked at her quizzically, Claire hurried to explain, "to prove myself." Even here, encased in diamond light, she couldn't shake Carnelian's doubt or Jasper's accusatory stare. While Terra's words were nice and all, they were just that: words.

"I just want to get one thing right," Claire said, and Lapis patted her knee sympathetically as the song soldier and lover died a spectacular death on the battlefield, all that whining and promise-making for nothing.

The chamber burst into applause and the woman curtseyed. "Quarrel in the Quarry!" someone shouted out, and the rest of the Gemmers cheered in agreement.

"Oh, I like this one," Zuli said, leaning forward. Two journeymen with fiddles struck up a bouncing melody and the whole chamber joined in. The whole chamber, that is, except Claire. For a few lines, she tried to sing along, guessing the words, but it was like they were speaking a whole other language that Claire couldn't grasp.

Slowly, she stood up from the cushion.

"Where are you going?" Lapis asked.

"I'm tired," Claire said, and it wasn't a lie. She was—plus she needed to practice. Maybe if she worked a little harder on polishing, she'd be able to finally wake the moontears. Squeezing the clay marble in her pocket, Claire hurried out.

The music and warmth of the sing-along faded, but Claire could still make out the deep-voiced men as they sang a song of the mountain. Though she could no longer distinguish the words from one another, the melody resonated within her, sending shivers up her arms. She wished, for a moment, that she could be in there, sure of herself and belonging to Stonehaven instead of just being a strange little nobody who had Gemmer magic, but could not make it work.

When she arrived at their room, it was empty. Where had Sophie gone? It wasn't possible that Grandmaster Carnelian had called on her for more errands, was it? But Sophie could take care of herself, she always had, while Claire needed to practice. The misshapen marble in her pocket dug into her thigh as she sat cross-legged on her bed.

The sooner she could control her magic, the sooner she could wake the moontears, and the sooner they could go *home*—to a place where Claire knew her spot at the dinner table between Mom and Dad. To a place where she could sing along with the music Sophie always blasted when it was her turn to do the dishes.

Fighting back exhaustion, Claire dutifully took out the ruby earring and a polishing rag. Her bones began to tingle as pink light trickled out between her fingers—but she needed to make it brighter. *Stronger.*

Biting her lip, Claire scrubbed harder.

"You can do it," she urged the glow, as the hum of magic swelled inside her. "Come on, you got this!"

The glow stayed dim.

Her magic, after flaring up today, seemed to have gone out. Her shoulders slumped, and the door slammed open.

"Claire!" Sophie burst out as she ran into the room, a threadbare blanket wrapped around her shoulders. "*Finally!*"

"Finally what?" Claire asked, letting the earring drop onto her bed. Its light was out before it even touched the mattress.

"I have proof!" Excitement radiated from Sophie, as the blanket fell from her shoulders and tumbled to the floor in a graceful sweep. She looked as lit-up as the gems Claire was supposed to be focusing on.

"Proof of what?" Claire asked. A headache was beginning to throb behind her eyes.

"That I'm right," Sophie said impatiently. "That we can't trust these Gemmers. They had something to do with Queen Rock!"

"Sophie," Claire began.

Sophie's face suddenly loomed over hers, her dark hair falling forward and tickling Claire's nose. "I know what you're going to say. To stop with the theories. But this is *proof.*"

"That's *not* what I was going to say, actually." Claire swallowed. "I . . . overheard something tonight, after I left you at dinner."

"What did you hear?" Sophie stared at her sister expectantly.

"I heard Jasper saying something about a . . ." She hated to admit it, but it was the truth. "About a war."

"Claire," Sophie said, sitting down hard on the bed across from Claire's. "This is serious . . . Because I heard something, too—something I didn't want to tell you, but . . ."

"Sophie, *tell me!*"

"I heard Commander Jasper talking to someone and he said, 'She's our secret weapon.'"

She looked at Claire triumphantly, but Claire frowned.

"Who's a secret weapon? Queen Rock?"

Sophie shook her head emphatically. "No, not Queen Rock. Claire, you know you're the only one who could have woken her. I think they're talking about . . . *you*."

Claire opened her mouth to say that that was ridiculous— she couldn't get a rock to glow brighter than a single fairy light. How was she supposed to be a secret weapon?

They may think we're trying to crown a new queen of Arden . . .

Carnelian's words from earlier that evening came floating back to her, and Jasper's reply.

War.

"Who was Jasper speaking to?"

Sophie shrugged and shook her head. "I didn't get a chance to see! He was behind a fallen block and I was trying to get the goats back into the Citadel."

"You mean," Claire said, her anxiety receding, "you didn't even *see* Jasper?"

"Well, no, but—" Sophie hurried on at the look on Claire's

face, "I know what Jasper sounds like. I can always tell when someone's got a secret, and I just know Jasper is hiding something. And as I said, I have *proof.*"

Claire looked at the determined set of her big sister's jaw. She shouldn't have been surprised: whenever Sophie got something into her head, she wouldn't let it go until she'd seen it through, like the time she'd insisted they had to hang a newly discovered pack of tinsel in all the corners of Great-Aunt Diana's mansion to scare away any ghosts.

That had only been a few weeks ago, but it felt like a lifetime ago. Like Claire and Sophie had been the ghosts, revisiting a former life, while their *real* lives were here, now, in this world.

And very likely to end in a whole lot of trouble.

"All right," Claire sighed. "I'll come with you." Because no matter how much trouble they might get into, she knew she couldn't say no to Sophie.

After all, Sophie was why she was here in the first place.

CHAPTER
10

Sophie grabbed a candlestick and yanked Claire through the doorway, their footsteps echoing in the cavernous halls.

The sisters hurried by the pottery room, the polishing chamber, and then Terra's office, where Claire saw soft diamond light trickling out. Her chest constricted. She really should be practicing—or sleeping. They continued to wind through the labyrinthine hallways, descending one marble staircase, then another, until finally they reached a wide door with a simple red rope tying the handles together: a forbidden wing.

For one moment, Claire thought that Sophie would turn away from the doors and duck down the brightly lit corridor to their left. But she knew her sister better than that. Sure enough, Sophie reached out, and tugged the bow.

"What are you doing?" Claire whispered as the rope slithered to the floor.

"I said I'd show you," Sophie said, voice equal parts irritation and excitement. She pulled open the doors to reveal—*more* stairs. Sophie pulled a tiny lamp out of her tunic's long sleeves and lit it.

An orange flame sparked in the blue darkness. It had been such a long time since Claire had seen someone make light without magic that, in this world of miracles and wonders, the ordinary seemed extraordinary. Even the outline of her sister's form a few paces ahead of her seemed special, as though Sophie were a living flame dancing just out of her reach.

Claire wasn't scared of the dark anymore, but still . . . unease prickled across her skin. As they spiraled down, she had the sense of walking into a cobweb—the sense of touching something obviously there, but impossible to see.

Soon, the air turned musty. It was an old and ancient smell, one that Claire had only caught once before, in Windemere's dirt floor cellar. She breathed in deeply, remembering the time Dad showed her where he'd etched his name on a wall stone when he was her age and telling her that once, he had found an arrowhead from a time long gone not far from where she stood.

Dad. She missed him. She missed him so much that it hurt.

"All right," Sophie whispered a few moments later. "Now don't be scared."

"Scared of w—*oh*." Claire let out a soft cry.

They'd entered a large, circular room made of an inky black stone, twice as tall as the arched ceilings many floors above.

But though they were so far beneath ground, it wasn't empty. It was filled with people. Hundreds of them standing at attention, all facing the center of the room. Claire froze, her breath stuck in her chest as she waited for the people to turn around and spot them.

But they never did.

"They're statues," Sophie said, grabbing Claire's hand and pulling her through the silent regiments. "It's an entire army made of stone."

Claire let out her held breath. The stone was an orangey-red color—a color that should have reminded Claire of desert sunsets, and cozy houses with orange roofs tucked along the seaside, but ever since that awful night in the Sorrowful Plains, when Claire had been forced to see her sister's blood dry, the color had reminded her of terror and loss.

The soldiers were all in uniform, too, each one wearing a version of armor and holding a black stone spear. *Obsidian*, Claire recognized from her Gemmer lessons. It was a shiny rock that came from a volcano and could hold the sharpest edge. It was the rock that Commander Jasper and the rest of his Wraith Watch used to tip all their spears.

"Do you really think they're planning something awful?" Claire asked. She stared uneasily at the standing warriors. In Rock History, Scholar Fossil had taught them that during the Guild War, everything within Stonehaven was made to serve two purposes: to provide beauty and protect the Gemmers. Claire had witnessed firsthand the strength of the Stone

Knight . . . what would an entire *army* of stone knights look like? A deep chill moved through her. If these statues began to march, their stone feet would crush anything in their way. Wooden Tiller houses. Spinner boats. Human bones.

Sophie reached out to one of the warrior statues, tugging the stone sword from his hip. "Why else would anyone carve an army if they weren't planning on starting a war?"

"Why else indeed," a new voice said from the darkness of the stairs.

The sisters turned just as Jasper stepped off the landing and into the cavern.

The Commander of the Wraith Watch walked toward them. In the weak light, he looked taller than ever, and it took Claire a moment to realize he hadn't grown, just merged with his long, skinny shadow that streamed out behind him and up the chamber's wall.

"How dare you betray our hospitality? No, don't say a word," Jasper warned as Claire opened her mouth. "How *dare* you disturb the Missing? How dare you spy on Stonehaven?"

"We're sorry," Claire squeaked, her heart pounding against her chest so hard that she thought that maybe it was trying to escape. "We didn't mean—"

"Stop it, Claire," Sophie commanded, every inch the big sister. "You don't have to explain yourself. We're not the ones with a secret stone army!"

Jasper banged the spear butt on the ground, and previously hidden Gemglows flared. Claire's eyes watered in the unexpected light. She squinted as Jasper hissed, "This is no army. This is the Missing, a war memorial commemorating all the Gemmers whose bodies were never recovered from the battlefield."

Claire looked around at the warriors, repeating and repeating and repeating, like lines in a dictionary. All these people had died in the Guild War? Her mind swam. And this memorial only represented the Gemmers—what about the Tillers, Spinners, and Forgers?

"History," Jasper said, voice as hard and cold as hail, "is not always pretty. Come with me."

Silently, they followed Jasper back through the clay warriors and to the stairs, the tip of his obsidian spear glittering in the dim light like an eye.

No one saw them sweep through the Citadel's halls. The evening bells had tolled long ago, and everyone was now sleeping. Claire wondered how long they'd been in the memorial . . . and how many hours were left before the morning chimes sounded and she was forced to endure another day of Gemmer classes.

But when they reached the door to their room, Jasper swept them past, and up another set of stairs.

"Where are you taking us?" Sophie asked sharply.

"To where you should have gone in the first place," Jasper grunted, his pace quickening.

Sophie halted. "No," she said, shaking her head fiercely as she pulled on Claire's tunic. Claire stopped walking.

"My sister and I will return to our room," Sophie said. "We'll stay there. I promise."

"Follow me," Jasper insisted. "That's an order. You won't like what happens if you don't comply with the Commander of the Wraith Watch."

Sophie grabbed Claire's hand, squeezing hard, but still she did not move. Jasper's eyes narrowed and he slowly lowered his spear's point until it was level with Sophie's heart.

"Jasper?" Scholar Terra's voice cut through the silent halls. "What are you doing with the princesses?"

The spear suddenly lifted as Jasper whirled around to face Terra, resplendent in a garnet bathrobe and matching sleeping cap.

"Taking them to the tower," Jasper said gruffly.

Terra's eyes grew larger behind her spectacles. "Who gave the order?"

Jasper shifted slightly. "Well, I did."

Terra's nostrils flared slightly. "Only Grandmaster Carnelian can give that order," she said tightly.

"These girls were in the Chamber of the Missing," Jasper yelled, apparently no longer able to contain his temper.

Terra swept forward, her eyebrows looking extra thick as they dipped beneath her spectacles. "And why was that, girls?"

"They were obviously searching for alternate ways to breach the Citadel!" Jasper exploded.

"We were not!" Claire said hotly.

"Then what were you doing?" Terra asked.

Claire didn't know what to say. It wasn't *her* idea to go

sneaking around in the dark. She looked at Sophie, and the Gemmer adults followed her gaze.

Sophie looked back defiantly. "Claire heard Jasper talking about war, and then—"

"As Commander of the Wraith Watch," Terra said, sounding weary, "Jasper is also the keeper of the memorial. No one else is allowed down there, except on the longest night of winter, when the Gemmer Guild mourns all that were lost. A time to again remember why the Gemmers shall *never* march to war again."

"But," Sophie protested, "I heard voices, too!"

"Terra," Jasper said, turning away from them. "These girls are clearly trouble. Here they are admitting to spying on our conversations."

"Be that as it may," Terra said, "it is still the grandmaster's decision, and we will trust him to make the right one. Go to bed, Jasper. I'll see that the girls go back to their rooms."

"Trust can be a dangerous thing in times like these," Jasper warned.

Dangerous times—times when magic wasn't strong enough to keep things from falling apart and Queen Rock was missing. She shivered.

"I see no reason to go against protocol in this instance," Terra replied, calmly but firmly.

Finally, Jasper relented. "As you will, Scholar. Carnelian can make the final call in the morning as to whether the intruders will be exiled. But rest assured that as soon as he gives the command, I will personally make sure they are dumped outside the

Citadel's wall, never to impose on us again." He walked quickly down the hall, and Claire didn't breathe until he'd gone.

"Thank you, Scholar Terra," Sophie said.

Terra turned to Sophie, her eyes bright with anger. "I don't want to know why you were in the forbidden sections of the Citadel, but there is a reason those wings are off limits."

"We won't do it again," Claire said, feeling bad for Sophie, even though it *was* her fault.

"You won't have an opportunity to anyway," Terra said. "I'm sorry to say this but Jasper is right. It is almost certain that Grandmaster Carnelian will support his motion to exile you both."

Shame and panic collided in Claire's chest. She *knew* she should have stayed in her room and practiced more! Instead, she'd wasted time, and now they were in trouble, and might, as soon as tomorrow, be kicked out of apprentice lessons forever. Her lip trembled and she tried not to cry.

Even Sophie, it seemed, was out of words.

Unable to meet Terra's eyes, Claire looked down at the floor, staring at the veins of blush pink that swirled through the marble. "I'm sorry," she whispered.

The trip back to their bedchamber felt twice as long.

As soon as their door clicked shut, she whirled on Sophie. "What were you thinking?" Claire shouted.

Sophie crossed her arms, her face defiant. "What?"

"I told you I had to practice!" Panic made Claire's voice rise, skidding out of control. "We came here to wake the moon-tears, not to spy on Jasper . . . and now I'm not sure if I will ever be able to, and maybe I'm not even a Gemmer princess after all!"

"Claire—"

"Calling a faint light from a ruby isn't really progress, and all I made today was this lumpy ball of clay." She thrust her hand into her pocket and shoved the misshapen marble under Sophie's nose. "And no matter how hard I try, I just can't—"

"*Claire.*"

Claire felt the pressure of Sophie's hands on either side of her shoulders.

"You don't have to worry about proving you're the princess or not because you *are*," Sophie said. "You woke the last unicorn. You saved my life."

Sniffling, Claire took a few deep breaths, then nodded. Sophie let go of her shoulders.

"Claire . . . you *did* create something." She plucked the clay ball from Claire's palm and held it up. "It might not be a Grail, but it's a perfect little clay egg."

Claire rolled her eyes. Sophie thought she was helping, but she wasn't. Not one little bit.

"If you like it so much, you keep it," she said, getting into bed. "I'm giving up. Maybe Arden will be better off if we just go home."

"Isn't that what you've wanted, though?" Sophie's words whipped out. "Oh wait, I forgot. Why would you want to go home when you're a *princess* here?"

Claire stared at her sister, mouth agape. "You think it's *fun* to be a princess? You think it's *fun* to have everyone laughing at you and to be the worst in the class? You're the one who got us into Arden in the first place, and now that we're here, I'm just trying to do the right thing! It's not my fault you're not magic—stop being so selfish!"

The skin around Sophie's lips had gone white. "You think I'm being selfish?" Her voice was quiet, but it held all the tension of an oncoming hurricane. "Well then, here's my first act of *not* being selfish. You can have the room to yourself!"

And before Claire could utter another sound, Sophie had thrown the clay egg to the floor and slammed the door behind her.

With the back of her hand, Claire wiped away angry tears. Infuriating Sophie! How did she not understand? How did she not *get* it? And after all that she had been through—riding a wyvern, traveling through a stone forest, facing the Royalists—why did she still let Sophie convince her to do something she hadn't wanted to do? Why did she still care so much what her sister thought?

And now Claire was mad at herself. She would never be able to sleep now. And in the morning, she'd have to face Grandmaster Carnelian and his multitude of rings.

She pulled the covers up over her head, and let her tears fill the hot darkness, hoping upon hope that tomorrow would never come.

CHAPTER
11

Tomorrow, it turned out, was here already. Claire's eyes itched from lack of sleep and she rubbed them as early morning sunlight streamed into their room.

It was their last morning in Stonehaven.

She had spent the short amount of the night left tossing and turning, and when she wasn't trying to count sheep—or goats, as it was nowadays—she'd been full of thoughts of Mom and Dad. She missed them. She had remembered what her parents had told her before fifth grade graduation, not so long ago, when Claire had been consumed with worries about middle school and leaving elementary school behind forever. Dad, who'd met her eye in the rearview mirror and smiled, said that if she was so worried, he could help her create a disguise so she could sneak back into fifth grade in the fall. Mom had reached behind from the front seat and patted her knee. "The end of one thing always means the birth of something new," she'd said.

But something new didn't necessarily mean something good. And in this particular case, Claire couldn't see how it could be good. Not when she and Sophie were being exiled from Stonehaven in disgrace.

Glancing at Sophie's bed, she saw that it was empty. Her sister hadn't come back.

Misery filled Claire and mixed with her fear of being outside Stonehaven's wall—without Anvil's or Aquila's protection. Her stomach clenched. How long would it take them to find Aquila? And when they found her, would the woman take them back to the old stone well, or would she be too disappointed in Claire's failure to help them?

Claire groaned out loud. She needed to get up. She needed to plan. Taking a deep breath, she swung her legs out of bed and began to walk to the wardrobe where their traveling packs and Kompass had been stashed.

"Ow!" A sharp pain jabbed her foot, and tears sprang to Claire's eyes. Looking down, she saw she'd stepped on the little clay egg that Sophie had thrown last night. But it wasn't an egg. It was just a ridiculous marble that hurt even worse than stepping on a Lego. And now it had a crack in it.

Annoyingly, though, she could practically hear Sophie, "See? Now it looks even more like an egg!"

If only it was as easy to crack the moontears as it was an egg.

An *egg.*

And suddenly, there it was. A thought. An idea, one that could let them stay in Stonehaven . . .

Holding the clay egg tight, she ran out of her room and sprinted down the hall to Terra's study, where she burst in.

"Claire!" Terra looked up from a tapestry, startled. "If you're here to discuss your exile, I'm afraid we must wait for—"

"An egg!" Claire cried. "We've been going about the moontears all wrong. We've been treating them like rocks, when we should be treating them like *eggs*. They don't need to be polished or molded or melted—they need to be *hatched*!"

She set the clay egg on the desk, and looked up at Terra, expecting her to exclaim, too. But instead, Terra sadly shook her head, her long aquamarine earrings brushing her shoulders.

"It's a good thought, Claire. In fact, I've played with the same idea myself." Sorrow entered Terra's magnified eyes. "But to hatch an egg, you have to understand so many things about it: how warm it must be, what it needs, how long it needs. In the case of unicorns . . . Well, there *is* a theory I've read about. Instead of sitting on an egg like a chicken or birthing a colt the way horses do, some of my research suggests that a living unicorn must touch its horn to the moontears when they're ready." She sighed, and her earrings glistened like unshed tears. "But that's only a theory. And besides, as we know, there are no unicorns—not anymore."

The sadness in her eyes seemed so deep at that moment that Claire felt afraid of falling into it, like an endless well. Of not being able to fix it.

"That's why I've had you try alternative magics," Terra

explained. "Only a unicorn, I think, would truly be able to answer these questions. And as you know, the last unicorn anyone ever saw was three hundred years ago, at the end of the Guild War."

Claire started to nod in understanding, but then stopped.

Because what Terra had said wasn't *technically* true. Not anymore.

Anvil had told Claire not to tell—had made her promise, for both her sake and the sake of the last unicorn. It would be a very dangerous thing for anyone to know the truth:

That she had freed the last unicorn from the stone.

And in fact, hardly anyone would even believe her if she did tell.

But Terra had only ever been kind to Claire. And looking around at the unicorn-filled room, Claire knew that no one in all of Arden would be more delighted or adoring of a living, breathing unicorn than Terra—and no one would be more likely to believe Claire than her.

The Malchains would understand. She hoped.

Taking a deep breath, Claire said, "Scholar, I have something to tell you . . ."

And so she did. It all came tumbling out of her, sounding like some beautiful bedtime story that had been read to her before she could remember. She told her about Unicorn Rock and her role in its disappearance. How she'd managed somehow to use her blood and her magic to free the unicorn, just in time to save her sister's life, before the unicorn fled.

When she was done, Terra sat very, very still. Then she flipped through several lenses of her magnifiers, lingering a minute or two on each one as she peered at Claire.

Claire wondered if she'd done the right thing. If she should have listened to Anvil. If she had ruined it all. Finally, she couldn't take it any longer. "Do you believe me?" she asked.

Pursing her lips, Terra finally nodded—and then she did something even more amazing: she smiled. "My spectacles can see the truth in you, but I would believe you anyway."

She stood. "This is exciting. This is an incredibly important piece of information. In fact, this changes everything." She began to pace the short length of her office. "I'll have to speak to Carnelian, you understand. But I should warn you . . . if I can convince him of the veracity of your tale, then there will be much more work ahead. For starters, there will be another test."

Claire's stomach sank. "What kind of test?"

"The Grand Test," Terra said. "A test that proves your word, once and for all. It will require the Throne Room to be prepared, and I'm sure most if not all of Stonehaven will want to witness it. Please stop chewing your nails."

With a start, Claire removed her fingers from her mouth. "But Scholar," she said, "what if I make something *else* explode?" She nodded at the clay egg still on the desk.

Terra tilted her head. Her shoulder-length earrings gently knocked together, sounding like wind chimes, a random melody playing against the steady drip of sapphires in the desk hourglass. Finally, she nodded and, reaching into her drawer, pulled out . . .

"A pencil!" Claire exclaimed as the scholar gently pushed it into her hand.

"This once belonged to the great Gemmer artisan Charlotte Sagebrush. That's her sketch up there," Terra said with a nod to one of the many drawings of a unicorn hanging on the wall. "With that pencil, she supposedly invented Arden's first alphabet. I want you to have it."

"Wow," Claire said. It didn't look like any of the yellow pencils she had at home. The wood around it was unpainted, with little nubby knots where leaves might have once sprouted. It was little, too, only the size of her pinkie. "But why me?"

"You have worked hard, even if the moontears have not yet been woken. And it could be helpful for you if . . ." Terra trailed off, but Claire knew what she meant.

If she failed this Grand Test.

If she was sent beyond the walls of Starscrape Citadel.

If they ran into wraiths.

Still, Claire clung to the pencil and clung to her hope. Maybe the pencil, along with Claire's new understanding of magic, could help keep her and Sophie alive until they made it back to the old stone well. And maybe they wouldn't need it.

Maybe she would pass the test, like everyone wanted. Maybe she could still bring back the unicorns.

She gripped the pencil so tightly that her knuckles turned white.

"If you are who you say you are, all will be well," Terra said, as if once again reading her mind. Closing the drawer, she turned to look Claire in the eye one last time. "You will be able to call the unicorn that you freed from the rock. I believe in you. And when the unicorn comes, it will wake the moontears for everyone to see. Then everyone else will believe you, too."

She paused. "But Claire, I would be remiss not to warn you. If you fail . . . the grandmaster doesn't believe in *third* chances."

CHAPTER
12

The only thing louder than the crowd in the Throne Room was the pounding of Claire's heart. Any minute now, the trumpets would sound. And when they did, Claire would push open the door of the waiting chamber and step out onto the dais for the Grand Test.

She wished she hadn't fought with Sophie last night. Even though she didn't want to be distracted by any more Sophie-shenanigans on this most important of days, she wished that her sister was beside her to squeeze her hand and tell her that it would all be okay. Instead, Sophie was likely pouting somewhere in the kitchens. Did she even know Claire had been given one last chance to prove her worth? From the sounds of it, everyone in Stonehaven had heard about the Grand Test and had gathered to witness it, just as Terra had predicted.

Claire's hands were sweating. Maybe there was some small chance Sophie hadn't heard, but if she had, she kept away anyway. Sophie hadn't shown up when Terra helped Claire into a new gown, one more appropriate for the occasion. Or when Zuli had fixed Claire's hair, and Claire had wished for Sena's clever fingers, or better yet, Mom's.

And when Terra had led Claire to the waiting chamber, Claire had been cautious when she peeked behind the window drapes, thinking Sophie might be hiding there, waiting to jump out and scare her.

But she was not.

Claire tried to remind herself that it was for the best. She was still angry with Sophie for getting her in trouble. She let herself touch the pencil she'd insisted Zuli tuck into her updo. It made her feel a little better, but not much.

Claire began to pace the small waiting room, her dress whispering behind her as she walked. The gown Terra had chosen for her was a relic saved from the days of the d'Astora monarchy. It was a simple dress of Gemmer blue, with long sleeves tumbling to the floor in a shimmer of silk. The only luxury added to it was a silver belt encrusted with sapphires that cinched around Claire's waist and flowed down the skirt. Between the belt and yards of fabric, the outfit should have been heavy, but Scholar Terra had done something to the stones to make them feel as light as feathers. Or maybe, Claire thought, her newly trained Gemmer magic was helping her carry the load.

There was a cheer from behind the door, and then a burst of applause. Claire's heart sped up and she turned quickly—too quickly.

There was a loud *rip!* as Claire lurched headfirst toward the floor, her gown's train caught under her own heel.

She barely stopped herself from landing on her knees, just as, beyond the doors, a set of trumpets played.

It was time.

Nervously, Claire stood, brushed her skirts back into place, and with one shove, pushed open the heavy door.

Her breath caught as she stepped into the Throne Room. Unlike the rest of the Citadel, the Throne Room was not made of marble skimmed with pink. Instead, it was constructed entirely of amber—a gift from the Tiller Guild hundreds of years before the Guild War, as a thank-you for the hearthstones that never lost their warmth, even in the depths of winter.

It was an acknowledgment of friendship between the two guilds, for though the amber was now stone, it had begun its life as tree sap, catching insects in its sticky sweetness along with, legend said, the many secrets of this place. The amber's translucence let the sun sweep in, turning everything the warm color of maple syrup—a shifting color that was as red as an autumn leaf and warmer than gold.

The voices of the Stonehaven choir swelled to the rafters as Claire made her way to the center of the dais where Grandmaster Carnelian stood. As always, Stonehaven's grandmaster hunched over his ram's head cane, but though he seemed tired, his dark eyes sparkled with a ferocious energy as Claire approached. She was reminded, for the thousandth time, it seemed, that this was her one and only last chance.

Shaking with nervousness, Claire's gaze slid to the pedestal. Her head felt light and her ears popped. On the plump purple cushion lay what looked like a long icicle, glimmering in the sunlight. Was it some kind of wand? What were they going to ask her to do? In her time at Stonehaven, Claire had never heard of any crafting that needed a wand! It felt as though someone had hollowed Claire out with a spoon, and now all that was left was her heartbeat rattling around inside her. What if she made something burst or blow up, like she had with the clay Grail?

Her eyes must have looked wild, because Grandmaster Carnelian gestured her onward. Claire arrived at his side just as the choir finished its song.

"Claire Martinson," Carnelian rumbled into the stillness, "we are gathered here today because of a story you shared with Scholar Terra of the return of the last unicorn, recently freed from rock. By you."

Fear rose in the back of Claire's throat, acrid and bitter, but she nodded, and Carnelian continued. "And so, before the Grand Test might be given, we the people of Stonehaven ask that you now listen to our story. Patterns form and stories repeat. Will you listen?"

Uncertain, Claire nodded.

"Very well," Carnelian said, both voice and face expressionless. He stepped aside, and Claire saw Scholar Terra climb the steps of the dais. She had changed her own outfit after leaving Claire in the waiting chamber, and was now resplendent in rubies and topaz, and every time she took a step, her gown winked a cold fire. The formality of the outfit only sealed the deal in Claire's mind: this was more than the other little tests she'd tried in Terra's study over the past weeks. This was *completely* different.

And Claire had no idea what this test would involve.

As Terra flipped through gold-leafed pages, Claire looked out into the crowd.

A group of apprentices in their blue uniforms sat near the front, and behind them were the teenage journeymen, in white tunics trimmed in blue. The rest of the room was filled with all manner of people who worked with the rock: potters, glassmakers, sculptors, quarry workers, and more. But though there were enough eyes on Claire to make her knees knock together under her gown, she could not find Sophie among them.

"Time before memory and time before blood," Terra read out loud, her voice carrying easily throughout the Throne Room, "a lonely, widowed king ruled Arden. His sole joy was watching his only child play upon her crystal flute."

Flute. Claire's eyes fell to the pedestal before her, and now she could make out three small indents along the icicle. But it wasn't an icicle at all; it was a crystal flute.

"The king's daughter," Terra continued, "was enough to keep him attached to this earth. But then, one dark day, his daughter fell sick. She stopped playing her flute, and though many tried, no one knew the cure."

Terra's voice seemed to echo the words of another story—one that Claire didn't want to remember. Because it hadn't been so long ago that Mom and Dad had sat Claire down and told her that Sophie would be in the hospital for a little longer than they had first thought because the doctors weren't so sure how to fix her. How to cure her.

Claire shuddered slightly, as though throwing off the memory, and she forced herself to pay attention to Terra.

"Then one day, a messenger told the king that there was a wise woman in the woods who lived under a waterfall and in the stars. She might know the cure. So the king set off, and when he finally came upon the woman under a waterfall and in the stars, he offered her all that he had for his daughter's health.

"'I have no need for the wealth of a king,' the wise woman said. 'I have all that I need here, though I can no longer see the stars.'

"So the king gave the wise woman his eyes, and she told him that only a unicorn could save his daughter. The king returned to his palace, but though he sent many forces out, they could not capture a unicorn. The king returned to the wise woman under a waterfall and in the stars, and asked her how he could catch a unicorn. He offered all his power to her.

"'I have no need for power,' the wise woman said. 'All I

need is here. Though I would like a stronger voice so that I can sing in harmony with the waterfall.'

"And so the king gave the old woman his voice, and she told him that a unicorn always comes to the rescue of an innocent about to be sacrificed."

Panic spiked in Claire's throat. *Sacrifice.* What were they going to ask her to do?

"And so," Terra said, no longer looking at the page in front of her, but instead staring straight out into the crowd of Gemmers, "the king took his ailing daughter to a glade, and slipped a dagger into his only daughter's heart. And as her royal red blood spilled onto the grass, a unicorn did finally appear.

"Weeping, the king threw himself before the noble beast, begging the unicorn to save his daughter. The unicorn reared in rage, in horror, in fury. As diamond hooves slammed down, the unicorn lowered his head, the sharp point of his horn aimed directly at the king's chest."

Claire gasped.

"But!" Terra voice flicked out. "Before the unicorn plunged its horn into the lonely king, he approached the princess. And in the princess's dying heart, the unicorn sensed a great wish—a wish that her father would be forgiven.

"Humbled by the girl's thoughtfulness, the unicorn granted the king's wish. He placed his horn to the daughter's heart. The wish seed within the king's daughter sprouted and blossomed, until the princess was nothing but a bright and burning wish. With a cry of delight and a cry of change, a light enveloped the king's daughter. And when the light had finally dimmed, the king saw what he had done: his daughter, his only child, the apple of his eye and light of his life, had transformed into an immortal unicorn."

Terra paused. "While the king saved his daughter, he had also lost her, for a unicorn belongs to no man, only the wind and sky. The king had to let his daughter go in order to save her."

A soft sigh escaped Claire's lips. The image the scholar's words had painted was beautiful, and her fingers itched to sketch, right then and there, the unicorn princess in transformation. She wondered if there had been a moment when the girl had just been a girl with a pearly spiral horn. Or maybe, her hair had first turned a milky white.

Terra paused another moment, gathering herself. "When the king returned home, he tried to play his daughter's crystal flute, but no sound came out. He wandered the halls, sad and lonely as ever . . . until one night, he heard the sweet notes of the flute."

Claire pulled her gaze away from Terra and looked again at the flute before her with fresh wonder. Her hands had gone clammy, and nervousness buzzed through her whole body. Again, she scanned the crowd for Sophie's face. Why wasn't she here?

"Jubilant, the king ran through the halls, searching for his daughter," Terra went on. "He followed the song to the kitchen garden, where he heard a young serving boy playing his daughter's flute—and a unicorn was standing there, listening. A unicorn who, he was told, had his daughter's wish-filled eyes."

Terra closed the book, clearly reciting the rest from memory. "The king adopted the boy and made him his heir. And ever since that day, the flute would be silent for all but Arden's heir. And if the heir so chose to play upon it, a unicorn would always arrive to give counsel."

Terra bowed her head, as if giving the story a chance to circle three times, then burrow into listeners' hearts. Taking advantage of the silence, Claire glanced at the flute. Where the sun hit it, tiny rainbows danced just beneath its surface. She wondered if that was what magic looked like, if one could see it. Something vibrant and bright just below the surface of things. Maybe her Gemmer abilities had always lingered within her, even in Windemere, hiding like these tiny rainbows until just the right time or angle of sun.

Then Terra stepped away, and all attention turned back to Grandmaster Carnelian. He leaned so heavily upon his cane that Claire worried that it might snap beneath his weight. But when he spoke, his voice was strong. "Claire Martinson, know that if you deceive us now, your life and your sister's will be at peril, and you will be tried for the destruction of Unicorn Rock and Queen Rock. You claim to be a descendant of Prince Martin d'Astora, yes?"

Claire swallowed, then nodded.

"Claire Martinson, you claim to be Prince Martin's oldest descendant with Gemmer blood, yes?"

Again, Claire nodded, but this time she had to bite her lip from crying out, *Sophie's the oldest! She should be heir!* She scanned the crowd frantically but still there was no Sophie. She was scared *and* hurt—no matter how bad their fights had been in the past, the sisters always forgave each other. Why hadn't Sophie come?

Carnelian fixed his eyes on her. Without blinking, he asked the final question, "Claire Martinson, you claim to be the one true princess to inherit all of Arden, yes?"

The word on the tip of Claire's tongue was small, no larger than a pebble. But even a pebble could be the base of a mountain.

She squared her shoulders and took a breath. After all, there was no going back now. "Yes," Claire said. Though her voice was barely above a whisper, it ricocheted off the amber walls, repeating endlessly, as if she were saying yes for each and every person gathered in front of her.

Inclining his head ever so slightly, Carnelian waved Claire forward. She saw now that in his other hand was a small glass box—and inside that box was Sophie's moontear necklace. "Then we, the people of Stonehaven, invite you to sound the crystal flute and call a unicorn into Stonehaven."

Claire blinked in surprise. "Is that all? But what . . . what about the moontear necklace?"

Carnelian's lips pursed. "As Terra has likely explained to you, a unicorn is likely required in order to help birth more unicorns. If our theory is correct, and the moontears are like eggs, then it is the unicorn, and not the princess, who must awaken them. And if what you told us is true, there's still one last unicorn out there in Arden, and he is our final hope."

Claire swallowed hard. Carnelian's face was stern. Did he truly believe what she'd told them? That the pink star-shaped scar on Sophie's collarbone had come from when a unicorn's horn had saved Claire's sister from dying?

Either way, this test would prove that she'd been telling the truth.

It had to work.

The unicorn she'd awoken from rock—the last unicorn in Arden—had to come to her. This was the only way. She'd tried everything else. She had to be right. Because if she wasn't . . .

No, she couldn't think about that now.

Taking a step toward the pedestal, Claire noticed a hum in the room. Not the hum she felt when she crafted magic, but an energy that seemed to pass from Gemmer to Gemmer as they looked at the flute in anticipation. It was the hum of hope.

Inspiration. Dedication. Courage. The rules of magic popped into Claire's head before she took the flute with both hands. It was as cool as creek water and as smooth as a sea-worn shell. Her fingers slid easily into the holes, as if the flute had been carved for her. A trill of anticipation sang through her veins. She looked at Terra, who nodded encouragingly.

Patterns form and stories repeat.

She recalled once again the breathtaking beauty of the unicorn she'd seen on the Sorrowful Plains, when it had emerged in a flame of white light from stone. She'd never before witnessed anything so glorious—the sight of it had moved through her like a song, like the clearest form of joy she knew.

Claire held the flute to her lips.

There was no question about it now; the excitement in the room was palpable. In the amber light, the edges of the flute glittered like a comet's tail, as if it, too, had been dragged through the night sky, collecting moonbeams and starlight.

Taking a breath, Claire closed her eyes . . . and blew.

In her exhale, she felt something rush from within her and into the flute: something wild, unknown, and untamed. Something like hope. Something like a unicorn. She wanted to cry from the sheer happiness of that feeling, the purity of it, the wonder.

But the crystal flute stayed silent.

Claire gasped for breath, her lungs empty. The Citadel remained

quiet,

quiet,

quiet.

Gripping the flute tighter, Claire blew again, harder, too. But not a sound—not even the dream of a whisper—leaked out. She blew again, pushing air out until she felt heat rise in her cheeks, until she felt dizzy, pulled under and drowning in disappointment.

A loud drumming pounded in her ears, and for a second, Claire thought it was the sound of a hundred feet stomping

toward her. Then she realized—it was the sound of her panicked heart.

What had she done wrong?

Instinctively, Claire looked back at the door, and there, in
that very moment, Sophie burst through. She was wearing a
flowing, pale purple gown. Her hair, for once, was down, held
back from her head with a headband and sheer veil.

Her sister took in what was happening and her hands
immediately covered her face. She'd come at last, just in time
to witness Claire's utter disgrace.

Claire had failed.

There was no unicorn.

She could feel the incredible disappointment of the room,
the shuffle of restless feet like a roll of thunder.

"But Grandmaster, I felt the magic!" Claire blurted out as
she whirled to face Carnelian, his face as impassive as a lake.
"What . . . what does it mean?"

She looked wildly into the crowd. Where was the unicorn? All she could make out were faces both mournful and
furious. Amid them, she spotted Lapis and Zuli, who looked
back at Claire with pity in their eyes. Carnelian shook
his head, and from somewhere near the front, Claire heard
weeping.

Master Jasper strode down the aisle, his obsidian spear glittering like an eye. When he reached the dais, he lowered its
point and aimed it at her chest.

"It means," Jasper said, splitting the silence into halves as easily as a foreman breaks a rock, "that you are not a princess. And that you have lied."

Sophie darted toward Claire, wrapping her arms around her sister protectively. "It's okay," she whispered into Claire's ear.

But it wasn't.

"Imposters, just as I thought." Jasper banged the butt of his spear against the floor. "Wraith Watch, seize them!"

CHAPTER
13

$\mathcal{N}$ot a princess. *Not a princess.*

Jasper's proclamation rolled over Claire again and again, like waves pushing her under. And just as relentless was the Wraith Watch itself, their black spears surging toward her and Sophie.

Claire's throat felt coated in peanut butter. She couldn't breathe, she couldn't run. She could barely get her eyes to *blink*.

"Stop! Where will you take them?" Lapis asked, stepping forward from the crowd.

Immediately, Zuli reached out and pulled Lapis back, out of the way. But the grandmaster had heard him. He turned toward Claire and Sophie. The look on his face—part anger, part disgust, tinted by disappointment—made Claire recoil.

"They will stay in the prisoners' tower," Grandmaster Carnelian ordered, loudly enough for all to hear. "To ensure the safety of all Gemmers."

The guards prodded Claire and Sophie down the aisle, the crowd splitting. For the second time in a single day, Sophie and Claire were marched past their bedroom door and up—up to the highest point of the Citadel. This time, no one was coming to rescue them.

The guards pushed the girls in, Claire stumbling a bit on the uneven flagstones. It was dark in the tower, with only a slice of light coming in through the small slit window on the wall and the tiny open square on the door. A horrible screech reverberated as the door's window slid shut.

Silence filled the small cell. A suffocating silence that filled Claire's ears, eyes, nose, and mouth the way darkness fills a room.

"Claire?" Sophie's voice reached out to her in the dark. A moment later, she felt her sister's hand on her back. "What . . . what happened?"

"I don't know." Claire shook her head helplessly. She pulled her knees up to her chest and let her head sink on them. "I thought I was the princess . . . I *thought* I woke the unicorn from Unicorn Rock, but maybe . . . Maybe it didn't happen like that after all."

"What do you mean?" Sophie asked, and though Claire could only see the outline of her body in the darkness, she could tell her sister was listening intently.

"I mean," Claire said in a rush, "I was scared! The Royalists were there, you were bleeding everywhere, and the wraiths— when they come near you, it feels like they freeze your body, but not just your body. Every part of you: thoughts, secrets, you—your *soul*. What if . . . what if they froze my mind and I made the whole thing up? What if it was just a nightmare I dreamed?"

She hugged her knees to her chest harder. The deep fear that had been needling her since her failed Gemmer classes twisted into her even deeper. Had she let the idea of being a princess, of being special, get the better of her?

"Oof!" Something hard poked between Claire's ribs, making her uncurl. "Hey!'

"You're feeling sorry for yourself, Clairina, and I'm not going to put up with it." Sophie's hands grabbed for Claire's wrists, and Claire felt herself being yanked to her feet.

"If you start doubting yourself, then all really *will* be lost. Now let's go over what we know."

In the dim light, Claire could just make out Sophie holding up her finger. "First, we know you woke a unicorn from the stone. That's a fact. Unicorn Rock was there and then it was gone. The only explanation is the one we know is true." She held up another finger. "Second, you definitely talked to— *rode on*—a wyvern. Third, you've drawn pictures that come alive. Fourth, you made those gems glow."

"Not very brightly," Claire said miserably. "And I exploded my Grail."

Sophie shrugged. "I think you're definitely a Gemmer, Claire, and a very powerful one at that. That's probably why your projects keep blowing up. You're *too* powerful."

Claire shook her head. "I don't know. I'm so confused. Even

if that's true, I still failed the test. I'm not Arden's heir. I can't call the unicorn, which means we still can't wake the moon-tears. So it's all for nothing, isn't it?"

Sophie shrugged. "Maybe, but the least you could do is give us a little light in here." She nudged Claire.

Claire tried to huff out a small laugh, but there was no heart in it. Still, Sophie had a point. With the silk of her long sleeve, Claire began to polish the face of a sapphire facet on her dress-skirt. Almost immediately, she felt a tingle in her fingers, and a hum in her bones that echoed the tiny song of the sapphire's crystalline structures. A true smile lit her face as light flowed out of the stone.

"Wow," Sophie breathed. "See? That makes things much better." The light that spilled from the sapphire was clear and soft, and now Claire could see her sister, still in the pale purple gown embroidered with silver leaves, as well as the rest of their tiny stone cell.

A thin straw pallet was in one corner, and a wooden bucket in the other. The rock walls were bare, and as she took them in, Claire's heart sank even further. There was not an opening to be seen—not a mouse hole, not even a hairline crack except for where the door was locked shut. Without some Gemmer tools, there was no way they'd be able to break out of here.

She groaned softly. The light, instead of making her feel better, had only revealed how bad their situation really was.

"Hey." Sophie reached out and touched Claire's shoulder. "It could be worse. They didn't put us outside the walls for the wraiths. I bet Anvil will hear about it and come for us. Maybe Aquila has already found the unicorn, and that's why it didn't show up when you called!"

Claire nodded. Not because she believed Sophie, because she didn't. But she also knew that Sophie still thought it was her job to take care of Claire, just as it was Claire's job to take care of Sophie.

"I bet you're right," she said, going over to sit on the pallet. Sophie nodded. "I know I am."

Hours later, Claire was woken by the screech of the door's window opening again. There was a muffled thud of something hitting the ground, and then the window clanged shut again. Quickly, Claire repolished the sapphire as Sophie walked over to the little cloth parcel that had just appeared.

"Sandwiches," she said, handing one to Claire. "Goat cheese and goat meat and . . . some sort of green stuff."

Claire sat down next to Sophie and took a bite of her sandwich. The bread was only a little dry. Next to her, Sophie carefully smoothed out the napkin the sandwiches had been wrapped in and laid it out on the floor. Then, she proceeded to carefully unmake her sandwich. For some reason that always drove Mom crazy, Sophie liked all the parts of a sandwich; she just didn't like when they were all stacked together.

"Claire!" Sophie said suddenly. "What do you think this is?" She pointed at a stain on the napkin. No, not a stain. Claire held up the sapphire and gasped. Drawn onto the napkin, in the same chalk the apprentices used on their slates, Claire could make out thin lines that looked like . . .

"It's a map of the Citadel!" Sophie said triumphantly. "And it seems that there's a passage that leads right out of this cell." She tapped a line. Sure enough, two doors were marked on their tower cell. Dash marks led from their cell, and through the walls to what looked like the kitchen cellars. "It's a way out!"

"But who drew this?" Claire demanded. "Who'd help us? It could be a trap."

"Look, there's something else scribbled here . . ." Sophie pointed at the corner of the map.

Claire took it up and peered closely. "It's an *L* and a *Z*. For . . . Lapis and Zuli!" An image of the twins' bright expressions when Claire had sat beside them during the sing-along flashed through her mind. Gemmers, Claire had heard before, were loyal to the point of stubborn. She wasn't entirely sure what she'd done to gain their friendship, but she was grateful for it.

Looking back up, Claire saw Sophie had already lunged to her feet and had started tapping the stone blocks.

"I think we can trust them," Claire said. "They were always nice to me in class . . ."

"Good. Because we either stay here, caught, or we go out and risk being caught. There's not really a choice, is there?"

"What are you doing?" Claire asked, ignoring her question.

"Looking for the secret tunnel's entrance," Sophie said. "This is what they do in the movies. If there's a passageway behind it, it'll sound hollow."

"You're not going to hear if something is hollow behind rock," Claire pointed out.

Sophie's fist froze midair. "Then you try something!" she snapped. "We don't know how much time we have before Jasper returns. We need to get out of here."

Looking around, Claire's stomach twisted. There were so many rocks—how would they figure out where to look? She glanced down at the cloth map again. There didn't seem to be any clue as to how to get out of the tower in the first place. Squinting at the cloth, Claire wondered if the napkin was a map at all. Maybe they wanted to see a map so badly that they'd used their imaginations to make the lines add up to something greater than they were. Maybe it was just that—some lines.

Some lines.

"Hang on," Claire said, standing and extinguishing the sapphire. "I have an idea."

"What are you doing?"

"Give me a second," Claire replied, running her hands along the mortar, tracing it up and over. Good. The paste holding the blocks together was a form of stone, too. Gemmer magic controlled *all* types of stone. And the cement was all connected, creating one single grid along the walls. Taking the napkin, Claire began to polish.

It wasn't as easy to call light from the mortar as it was from the diamond or even the sapphire. The mortar needed to be coaxed and reminded of the time that it had once been sand and lime and water all mixed together—before it had hardened.

Slowly, a faint glow, barely as bright as a birthday candle, began to follow the path of the mortar, outlining every single block and flagstone.

"I don't get it," Sophie said, coming to stand behind Claire. "What are you doing?"

"Mortar glues all the rocks together," Claire explained, still rubbing the napkin over the walls. Her arms were getting sore and her fingers felt like they were falling asleep. Still, she kept polishing the walls and floor. "If there *is* a secret door, though, that won't be glued down to others, would it? It would be fitted in tightly, but there would be no mortar outline. So I'm looking for a big stone with none of these lines around it."

"Like that flagstone?" Sophie pointed to a large swath of darkness on the floor.

The flagstone was the only one in the entire cell that had no glowing outline. Claire grinned at Sophie. "Exactly."

Sandwiches forgotten, the sisters spent the next hour trying to pry up the door with their fingertips . . . to no avail.

"Nothing's easy," Claire told Sophie, who was beginning to complain.

"I know, I know. That's what Mom always said before we went to the hospital."

"And what did you say to that?"

Sophie snorted. "That she was welcome to get stuck with needles instead of me."

Claire smiled slightly. She used to hate talking about that time, the time when Sophie was first sick, but now it seemed so far away that maybe it was okay to laugh about it. Their old world, the world they had come from through the chimney, was beginning to seem hazy, while Arden was so alive and so real. And though Sophie had started to get sick again in the real world, the unicorn from the rock had healed her. Arden had healed her. Anyone could see it.

Mom and Dad would see it, too, just as soon as they got back home.

Claire turned back to the flagstone trapdoor. "If only there was a handle . . . ," she muttered.

"I wish you still had your pencil," Sophie said with a groan.

"Oh!" Claire reached into her hair, which was now somewhere between a beehive and a nest rather than an updo, and withdrew the pencil. "Terra gave me this—but how would it help us?"

"Excellent," Sophie said. Still on her hands and knees, she tapped the flagstone. "Why don't you draw a doorknob right here?"

"What?"

"Yeah," Sophie said. "I've seen how good you are with a pencil. You know how to make things look all realistic, like a photograph. If you draw a doorknob, maybe it'll become real, too."

"I don't think that's how it works," Claire said. "If that were true, I'd be able to draw unicorns into existence. Or maybe a way to get home."

Sophie tilted her head, but didn't say anything. And Claire knew she wouldn't until she'd tried. Sketching in an arc, Claire tried to think of how doorknobs looked at home. And what one would look like in the mortar's dim light. This pencil didn't fit in her hand as well as the one she'd lost in the wyvern's cave, but it still felt good to draw again. This was a kind of magic she understood.

"Don't forget screws," Sophie said, leaning in so close that tips of her hair brushed the floor. "It won't turn without screws."

Claire rolled her eyes, but added them in.

"Hey, that doesn't look bad," Sophie said a few minutes later. "Try now?"

Sticking the pencil back into her hair nest, Claire sat back on her knees. She tilted her head. Sophie was right. The handle didn't look bad. In fact, if she squinted a little, it even looked pretty real. Reaching out her hand, she tried to grab the smooth handle—but her fingertips just scraped against bare rock.

"It doesn't work," Claire said. "I *told* you it wouldn't."

Sophie elbowed her over. "Let me."

Claire scooted back, her silk skirt catching. Miserably, she looked at the billowing fabric. This dress was meant for sitting at a banquet table holding a goblet. It was not meant for a prison break.

"I got it!" Sophie whispered triumphantly.

Claire's head jerked up. "Really?"

"Yeah, it's kind of flat, but if I pinch it—get back!"

The flagstone beneath them groaned, then slowly rolled back to reveal a stone staircase that spiraled down into the darkness.

"How did—did I really do that?" Claire gasped.

"Not without my help," Sophie said. And as she said it, Claire realized it was true. Her magic may have made the door handle, but she'd never have thought of it without Sophie. It was like Sophie had a magic all her own, a kind of magic that inspired Claire's, that made Claire's magic clearer and stronger. They were a team.

Standing up, Sophie shook out her skirts, took a breath, and then studied the map in the glow of Claire's sapphire light. "I think I know where this leads. There are some chutes in the kitchen cellar that were once used to send war supplies down the mountain quickly." She grimaced slightly. "I thought it was a garbage chute at first. Cook Koal fixed that mistake."

"Then let's go," Claire said. "The faster we can get out of Stonehaven, the sooner we can find Anvil, and go *home*." The image of Mom and Dad popped into her head. She wondered how much time had passed since she and Sophie had last gone up the chimney, and whether they were worrying about them even now.

"Home," Sophie repeated softly. "But what about the moontears? Are we just going to leave them behind?"

The white stones flashed into Claire's mind. The moontears. Unicorns. Maybe they weren't ever supposed to be woken. Maybe Prince Martin hadn't meant for them to be given back.

"The moontears are better off here, in the hands of the Gemmers," Claire said quietly. "I'm not the princess. And if only the true princess can awaken the unicorns, then there's no use in taking them."

Sophie was quiet, thinking. "There's so much I'd miss if we went home," she said at last.

For a moment, Claire thought of the friends she'd met here: Nett and Sena. Aquila and Anvil. Even Zuli and Lapis. But she and Sophie were now wanted people in Arden. Not only did the Gemmers think they were spies, but the Tillers believed they were thieves, and the Forgers knew they had broken guild laws. It wasn't safe for them.

And now that Sophie had been healed, there wasn't any reason, really, why they should stay. But still, she didn't want to seem like a coward, not after everything they'd been through.

"Where else could we go to be safe?" she asked.

Sophie shrugged. "We'll be safe if we can call the unicorn back. That's why I grabbed this." From her gown's long sleeves, she pulled out something long and delicate: the crystal flute.

"Sophie!" she gasped. "Why did you do that? The flute doesn't work. And they're going to know it's missing!"

"They're going to know *we're* missing, too. That's why we've got to hurry, silly," she said, grabbing Claire's hand.

Claire looked at the steps. "But we don't even know the way!"

"Obviously, I remembered this, too. Just in case." Sophie pulled the bronze Kompass out from her gown's pocket. "You may be the one with magic but I'm obviously the one who plans ahead. Now, let's go."

CHAPTER 14

The stairs and tunnels were completely dark, except for the glimmer of light that seeped through the cracks between stone blocks. With regret, Claire had extinguished her sapphire. If light could get in, it could also get out.

It felt like they'd been running for hours, though it could only have been minutes. Claire and Sophie had taken off their shoes to make less noise, and now Claire's feet were beginning to ache from running along the stone floors of the secret passageway, and the silence around them, except for their panting breath, had begun to close in on Claire. It was as though they were moving through the internal organs of the Citadel—the dark was so dense that it sometimes seemed like the walls themselves were breathing.

And then, suddenly, the passageway wasn't silent anymore.

A man's voice drifted toward them. Was someone else inside with them?

But no, the voice was coming through a crevice in the wall. Clutching her skirts, Claire walked forward as quickly as she could, hoping that the tinkling clatter of sapphire against sapphire would be mistaken for old pipes rattling.

A line of light filtered through the crack.

"And what do the Tillers say?" the man's voice asked.

Claire froze. It was Jasper!

"The Tillers don't want to be involved, one way or the other," a second voice, female, trickled through the wall in answer to Jasper's question. Claire frowned. There was something familiar about that voice . . .

Sophie stopped short, and Claire nearly ran into her. She had obviously recognized the voices, too.

"One week from today," the female voice continued, "you will be Grandmaster of Stonehaven—the head of all the Gemmers. You just need to do your part."

"I've already done my part," Jasper said sulkily. "I've locked up the imposters. I don't know what else the Royalists need from me."

Mind spinning, Claire pressed fingers to her temple. Sophie had been right! The Gemmers—or at least Jasper—*had* been planning something. She tapped Sophie on the shoulder, wanting to let her know how sorry she was for not believing her. But Sophie, instead of looking at her, sank down onto her knees, and pressed her eye to the crack.

Curious, Claire leaned over her crouching sister, and peered through, too.

She was staring into a small office with a checkerboard floor and austere fireplace that had been lit with something that made the flames cherry red. The only decoration, as far as Claire could tell, was a display of obsidian spears fanned out like turkey feathers above the mantel.

Jasper was seated behind a desk, and a white-haired woman in a blue cloak sat opposite. The same woman who haunted Claire's dreams: *Mira Fray.*

To most in Arden, Mira Fray was a renowned Spinner historian who spent much of her time along the Rhona River collecting stories and was respected by all guilds as a woman of truth and honor.

But what most did not know was that Fray—educated, intelligent, *practical*—was also the leader of the Royalists, a secret society that believed Queen Estelle had been turned into a rock, and that when she awakened, she'd defeat the wraiths, bring back unicorns, and magic would flourish again.

It was Mira Fray who had ordered the Royalists to kill Sophie that awful night on the Sorrowful Plains—willing to risk anything, even human life, on the chance that Queen Estelle would emerge from stone, and defeat the wraiths once and for all. Which would have been great if it were true.

But the truth was that the real queen had been evil, and that she'd been the one who'd ordered a massacre on the Emerald Plains, which had ever since been known as the Sorrowful

Plains, now a place of desolation and dust . . . and the home of the destroyed Queen Rock. The space between Claire's shoulder blades prickled. What *had* happened to the monolith?

"Master Jasper," Fray said, her voice a little *too* kind, "do you know why the Tillers will often let whole forests burn?"

Fray didn't wait for Jasper's response. "It's because things that are sickly and weak sometimes can't be healed. Sometimes, fire is necessary to clear away the mistakes of the past so that in its devastation, a new and stronger forest may emerge. Guild magic is weak, and the leadership of the grandmasters has brought us no closer to ridding the land of wraiths or ensuring our children are born with the ability for magic. It is time to return to the past to seek out our former greatness. It is time to tear down, so that we can rebuild."

"Historian Fray, what exactly is the Royalists' plan?"

Fray slowly stood up, the red flames outlining her frame, as though she'd been traced in molten lava.

"War," she said.

"What about the girl?" Jasper asked. "She's only a child."

Fray smiled. "Her death will be the key to our victory. S—"

Sophie's warm hand slapped over Claire's mouth, but she was too late. Twin gasps of surprise filled the tunnel.

"What was that?" Fray asked sharply, interrupting herself. "What?"

"I heard something, from the walls." Fray spun around. "Do you have spies watching me, Jasper?"

"No," Jasper's voice broke slightly, and Claire realized he

was afraid. He should be. She'd once seen the woman crack a grown man's ribs with only a piece of thread.

"The Citadel is old, Historian, and all sorts of mice skitter within its walls."

"Sounds bigger than a rodent," Fray said. "But be warned. If you're lying to me, I have ways of finding out. Bring me to the imposters."

There was the scrape of a chair as Jasper stood. Claire held her breath as she heard their footsteps lead to the door. Then there was a click as the lock shut behind them.

"Go," Sophie whispered hoarsely. "We need to get out of here before they realize we're missing!"

Terror washed over Claire, a relentless punch of fear that would sink her if she didn't start moving. *Now.* She began to run.

As they pounded through the passageway, Claire thought she heard an alarm—and yells of Gemmers in the distance.

Soon the smells of the kitchen began to hang in the air. They were getting close to the edge of the map. They were getting closer to freedom.

Sophie stopped once again, and Claire ran into her, squashing her nose into her sister's back.

"It's here," Sophie said, and grabbed a large lever protruding from the wall. "This is the cargo chute."

"Are you sure it's safe?"

"No."

"*Sophie*—"

There was a loud clanging somewhere above them. There was no denying it. The Gemmers knew they had escaped.

Sophie pulled the lever, and a giant hole opened up in the ground, leading down into pitch blackness. Quickly, she tied the laces of Claire's slippers together and looped them over Claire's shoulders so that her hands would be free. "Sit!" she commanded.

Claire did. Brushing her fingertips against the floor, she thought she recognized the stately hum of marble. Maybe she *was* getting the hang of this Gemmer stuff, after all.

"Keep your toes pointed straight," Sophie instructed. "And don't be scared!"

"What—?"

And then there was a push on her shoulders, and she felt herself slipping . . . and then hurtling down into darkness.

CHAPTER
15

Claire screamed as wind whistled past her ears. She wasn't falling into a void. She was *sliding* into it. She couldn't see a thing, but she was aware of marble all around her, of its cool touch against her palms and the whisper of her gown's silk against stone.

Quickly, Claire squeezed her eyes tight, and tried to focus on the marble. She felt beneath her fingers the fine grain and beneath that, the marble's memory of intense heat and high pressure, of being melted in the furnace of the earth's heart.

I don't need the heat, she tried to tell the marble. *Just your shine—your ability to gleam.*

There was a tingle in her fingers. Slowly, light bloomed around her, emanating from the slippery marble slide as she sped along it, and reflected, flickering, from the sapphires studding her gown. Finally, Claire could see what was happening. She was speeding down a large marble pipe that twisted and turned like a hamster village. Whatever marble her dress slipped past glowed for a few seconds before fading into darkness. She was her own raft of light in a sea of shadows.

"Pretty!" Sophie called behind her. Claire twisted back to see the soles of Sophie's bare feet as Sophie slid down behind her. "Get ready now, the landing might be . . ."

But Claire suddenly slipped around a bend and she couldn't hear her sister. *Might be what?*

The pipe seemed to level, and one more unexpected bend later, Claire shot out of the tunnel, and into—a forest.

She came to a skidding halt on a carpet of moss, stopping just short of a small pool fed by a waterfall. She blinked.

"Move!" Sophie's bellow echoed out of the tunnel, and Claire lurched to the side just as Sophie crashed into her landing spot.

Sophie sat there for a moment, looking stunned, then flopped back onto the moss, arms and legs spread wide as though she were making a snow angel, her skirt a crush of lavender and silver threads beneath her.

"That was faster than I expected," she said, between deep breaths.

Claire crossed her arms but remained seated. She wasn't entirely sure her legs could support her right now. "And what, exactly, *did* you expect?"

Sophie moaned and struggled into a sitting position. "A softer landing, for one." She began to pull her slippers back on.

Looking around, Claire saw they were in the middle of a wooded glade. From somewhere far off, a morning dove cooed. Sunrise was just around the corner.

"Where are we, then?"

Sophie scrunched her nose and tilted her head. "I think somewhere on Starscrape Mountain, maybe halfway down." Getting to her feet, she walked over to the reflection pool. Sophie's purple headband had slipped too far back, and her usually sheetlike hair was more like a knotted basketball net.

Standing by the reflection pool, her sister looked like a wilted wildflower . . . a little bit sad and lonely. But at this exact moment, Claire didn't really care. "You don't know?" she asked, her voice rising in a screech. "You didn't want to find out before you pushed me down a slide that was *half the length of a mountain?*"

"Stop being so dramatic," Sophie said, pulling the Kompass from her pocket. "You're all right. At least we're free."

"No we're not," Claire said. "Not really. We're outside Stonehaven's protection. All our supplies are still back there, including anything that could have protected us from the wraiths." She stopped, the horror of her words only sinking in when she spoke them. *Wraiths.*

They would *never* be free in Arden.

No matter where they went, what they did, there was always danger. They'd had the Great Unicorn Treasure in their hands, and now the moontears were lost to them, locked behind the cold walls of Stonehaven. All they had was a flute that wouldn't play. And a princess who wasn't a princess at all, just the Royalists' pawn.

The Royalists who wanted to start another Guild War. The Royalists who wanted *her*.

Dead.

Her death will be the key to our victory.

Fear gripped Claire's stomach and flipped it. She hunched over, thinking she was going to be sick all over the grass.

A warm hand gripped her shoulder. "Breathe," Sophie instructed. "Deep breaths."

Claire obeyed, and after a minute or two her stomach settled, though she couldn't say the same for her thoughts.

"I want to go home," she mumbled, the words coming before she could stop them.

Sophie released Claire's shoulder and pulled the Kompass from her pocket. "I'm not going to let anything happen to you, Clairina, but you need to pull it together. We need to go."

"I know!" Claire said. "We need to go *home*."

Shaking her head, Sophie flicked open the Kompass. "First, we need to go to wherever Anvil and Aquila are. We need to warn them. And once we do that, I promise, Claire, we'll go home."

"But—" Claire's words were cut off by the click of the Kompass snapping shut.

"This way!" Sophie called, breaking into a jog.

And with a sigh, Claire ran to keep up.

She had gone on hikes with her family before, and enjoyed them, especially in the spring when everything smelled clean and freshly green. But running down a mountain while fleeing an angry guild and a murderous secret society was an entirely different matter. Each gentle brush of breeze turned sinister as it shook the pine needles. And as branches clacked against one another, she couldn't help but think they sounded like teeth snapping shut.

Still, they couldn't run the entire time. As they slowed to a walk, Claire wondered what they would tell Mom and Dad. It was possible that they might not have even noticed the girls were missing. Time ran differently in Arden. Sometimes, it ran by so fast entire months had passed here in Arden by the time Sophie returned the next night to Windemere, and other times, when Claire had woken that horrible morning to discover Sophie was gone, it seemed to slow down. It made Claire's head hurt to think about it.

They took breaks, alternating between jogging and walking, and only stopped once to pick some blackberries Anvil had told them were safe to eat. Then they began to run again.

Sooner than Claire thought possible, the afternoon light began to grow long and golden. It would have been beautiful if she didn't know what came next: a cold night filled with even colder shadows. Shadows that bit and tore. *Wraiths*.

Glancing around, Claire wondered where the wraiths hid during the day. She assumed they lived underground, where even a midsummer's sun couldn't penetrate. She supposed it was possible they could live in hollow trees. And if that were the case, maybe they could be hiding right under their noses this very second.

Shivering, she tried to shake off the creepiness. No more bad thoughts. No more worst-case scenarios. She would only think about beautiful things.

Like unicorns—the unicorn they had freed from the stone had driven back the wraiths. For a time, anyway.

"Hey Sophie?" Claire called to her sister as they slowed to a walk. "What do you know about unicorns?"

"A few things," Sophie said, using a walking stick to push back a thorn bush so that they could pass. With her other hand, she consulted the Kompass.

"Like what?" Claire pressed.

"Well," Sophie said thoughtfully, "unicorns can heal. And when they walk, they sometimes leave snowdrops in their prints. They can also unlock anything. Doors, chests, you name it. And," she said with a glance over her shoulder, "I'm guessing, passages between worlds."

Realization dawned on Claire. She knew that Prince Martin had had the help of a powerful Forger in order to craft a passageway between home and Arden, but she had never given much thought to the unicorns' role in the chimney's creation. She wondered if their adventure now would have even been possible without a unicorn.

When Sophie ran out of unicorn stories, she switched to asking Claire questions about magic. How had Claire done magic that first time? What, *exactly*, did Claire mean by feeling a *hum*?

And for the hundredth time, Claire explained how she'd first mistaken her Gemmer abilities for a buzz in her bones—a slight tingle that felt like her fingers were going asleep. And how only later did she realize that it was a sign of crafting. That it was an itch to create.

"I mean, I'm aching to create, too," Sophie grumbled. "It's just not working." She unclenched her fist, to reveal a small sapphire, one that must have fallen from Claire's dress. As they'd run, branches had torn at their dresses. The sleeve of Sophie's gown had completely unraveled, trailing long strands of silver threads, while Claire's dress was missing half its sapphires.

She hadn't realized that Sophie had picked one up. She hadn't realized that her sister had been trying to make it glow this entire time.

"We're going home soon," Claire said, trying to make Sophie feel better. "It doesn't matter if you have magic or not."

"Yes it does!" Sophie said, and Claire took a half step back at the fierceness in her sister's voice. "In the past year, I've missed out on so many things. The seventh grade overnight. The last day of school. Even my birthday . . ." Sophie took a deep breath, her shoulders rising. "I don't want to miss out on this, too."

"I'm sorry," Claire said. "I didn't mean—"

But Sophie seemed to be too caught up in her own thoughts to listen. "You have this great gift—*magic!*—and you're too scared to stay and use it. Of course magic matters." Sophie let the sapphire drop, then flounced ahead, putting space between them.

Claire let her.

Because Sophie was right. Claire *was* scared. She did want to go home. The Royalists wanted her dead. She wasn't being a coward, she was being safe . . . wasn't she? She stooped to try to search for the sapphire among the fallen leaves. Maybe Sophie just needed to try again.

"CLAIRE!"

Claire's head snapped up. Sophie had stopped, and was waving wildly. "CLAIRE, COME HERE!"

Claire ran toward her sister. "What is it?" she panted. "Royalists?"

"I found—oh, just come look!" Sophie pulled Claire behind the tree and pointed to a glittering spider's web lacing together the dead branches of a bush. The spider's silk was incandescent, seeming to shimmer with the same luminosity that she'd seen in pearls, or the underside of a seashell or . . .

A jolt of electricity shot through her spine.

The strings of the Unicorn Harp.

The strings that had once been part of a unicorn's flowing mane.

"He was here!" Sophie said, shouting triumphantly. "The unicorn!" She looked at Claire, her brown eyes shining with a feverish radiance. "Claire, I *know* you want to go home. And we will! But when we tell Anvil and Aquila that the unicorn is so close, do you think—can we maybe stay?" She broke off, and stared hopefully at Claire.

Cautiously, Claire reached out her finger and touched the

hairs. They felt like the silkiest of threads. Something as tentative and thin as moth wings brushed her heart.

Maybe she didn't have to be a coward.

Her heart beat faster.

Maybe . . . she could help Arden after all.

A smile crept across her face, a kind that she didn't think she'd ever felt before, but recognized well. It was a twin to Sophie's own wild grin—and Sophie knew it, too.

"Yes!" Sophie said, giving a little spin that made her underskirt twirl out like the top of a cupcake. "Let's find ourselves a unicorn!"

Claire's newfound confidence lasted until they reached a river she thought she recognized. The sun had turned into a red eye in the sky, slipping ever faster to the horizon. She peered at the Kompass in Sophie's hand. The needle, which had once been as long as her pinkie finger, was now only the length of its nail.

"I think that means Aquila is close by," Sophie said, squinting down at the object in her hand, then scanning the trees. "It's been shrinking all day."

Again, Claire's fingers brushed the unicorn mane in her pocket. "She must be close because the unicorn is close," she said.

"Mmm," Sophie replied, sounding noncommittal. "Does the chimera over there look familiar to you? I think we're near the bottom of the mountain."

Claire looked toward where her sister was pointing, and sure enough, there was the glint of sunlight off metal. She was relieved Sophie had reminded her about chimera—if she hadn't, Claire would have probably mistaken it for the glint of sunlight off sword, instead of the strange, stiff metal beasts that dotted Arden's terrain.

While chimera looked ferocious, Claire didn't feel scared—only sad. During the Guild War, the Tillers and Forgers had worked together to craft these metal monsters to face the Gemmers on the battlefield. But as Arden's magic seemed to fade, so had the chimera. Many slowed down and then finally stopped altogether, frozen where they stood.

This particular chimera clung to a tree's trunk, and was a cross between a lynx and an owl, its sleek, feline body interrupted by a pair of enormous copper wings. The chimera's magic must have run out midclimb, its claws sinking into the mottled bark for three hundred years. No Forger today knew how to make them come alive again . . . except for, perhaps, one.

Again, Claire thought of her friend Sena. Her parents, Mathieu and Sylvia Steele, had been alchemists, illegally combining Tiller and Forger magic together to experiment with possibilities. Sena had told her how they had managed to bring a small chimera kitten back to life, and when they'd been found out, Sylvia had been sentenced with lifelong imprisonment while Mathieu, a Tiller, was sentenced to execution for masquerading as a Forger all those years. And

Sena—poor Sena!—had been taken in by Nett's grandfather, Francis Green.

Claire walked a little faster. She didn't like Francis Green. Not after what he'd done. Not after he'd betrayed them.

Soon, Sophie called out again, and this time, Claire followed her gaze to a small stone hut, complete with a waterwheel that churned slowly in the Rhona's waters. It looked like a cottage in a fairy tale, where Snow White might hide from her evil stepmother. It was—and there was no other word for it—*cute*.

"I can barely see the needle now," Sophie said, clicking the Kompass shut and putting it in her pocket. "I think Aquila must be in there."

Claire felt her rib cage expand with relief. They wouldn't have to spend a night without protection from the wraiths. She glanced back over her shoulder. Still no sign of Royalist blue or Wraith Watch white. But even with Aquila nearby, danger was still too close for comfort.

The girls hurried to the hut, Claire desperately aware of the shadows that grew longer and longer in the sun's wake.

"Aquila?" Sophie called as she pushed open the rotting door. "Hello?"

No one answered.

"Maybe she's out back?" Claire said, looking around. It was difficult to see in the dingy, unlit hut. She stepped in a little more. Grabbing a stubborn sapphire, she began to polish. There was the familiar hum in her bones, then light.

She sucked in a breath.

Traveling supplies were spread in disarray across the wooden floor—small parcels of food, maps, blankets . . . and two twin axes, their tips hooked like eagles' beaks.

Aquila's axes.

They lay on the floor, abandoned like the rest of the house. Claire didn't need any magical craft to know something bad had happened.

"*Claire*," Sophie said, and the tone of her voice sent tingles up Claire's spine. Slowly, she looked at her sister. Her hands were clasped over her mouth, as if holding back a scream. In the hallway, two figures loomed. Two very familiar figures.

"Light," Sophie commanded in a strangled voice. For once, maybe because Claire was scared, the sapphire glowed intensely. As she raised the gem higher, blue light washed over the figures.

It was them.

Anvil and Aquila Malchain.

Anvil's ax was raised above his head, looking as if he were about to chop something, his face snarled in an expression of rage. Aquila's grandmotherly bun had unraveled, and her gray hair streamed out behind her as if she had been running, one hand gripping a knife while the other was clenched into a fist.

And both of them were utterly and completely still.

Still as stone.

CHAPTER
16

The sapphire in Claire's hand clattered to the ground as she leaped back. It spun wildly across the dirt floor, sending circles of blue throughout the room before it swiveled to a stop in front of Aquila's boot.

Claire's stomach clenched and she had to breathe through her nose to choke back the rising bile. A warm, wet liquid dripped from her hands. Looking down, she saw that she'd cut herself on the sapphire's sharp edges.

Sophie, her hands still clapped across her mouth, inched toward the Malchains. Cautiously, she picked up the sapphire and held it closer to Aquila. The Forger's face was twisted into an expression of horror.

Sophie huffed in, then flashed out her hand to the woman's arm. She whipped her hand back. "She's cold," Sophie whispered. "And hard. She feels like . . ."

"Like rock," Claire finished grimly.

But it wasn't as if the Forger had been turned to stone. Her cheeks still blushed pink, her hair still shone a steely gray, but there was no life to her pallor, no sense of the body's ability to change and fold and wrinkle.

Though every nerve screamed at her not to, Claire took a step closer. She couldn't abandon her friends—not again. Nett's mischievous eyes and tufted hair flew into her mind. Everyone who helped Claire ended up getting hurt. The very least she could do was look.

Red glittered on Aquila's arm. Motioning Sophie to lift the sapphire a little higher, Claire saw that Aquila had been injured. A shallow graze that skimmed the skin. But the red was not blood.

"Rubies," Claire choked out. "Her blood—it's been turned to rubies."

"*What?*" Sophie squeaked. She'd sucked in her cheeks, looking gaunt and ghostlike. In fact, as Claire looked at her sister, Sophie seemed to shrink in on herself, regressing back to the pitiful girl she'd been in the hospital. She looked younger. She looked scared.

Claire had the odd sensation that suddenly the tables had turned, and she was the older sister who knew everything. But instead of feeling smug, she felt only numbness.

"Scholar Pumus says there are minerals in the blood that can be crystallized and turned into rock," Claire explained. She took another deep breath to steady the rising nausea. "It must have been a Gemmer who did this to them." She thought for a moment. "Everyone at Stonehaven thinks Unicorn and Queen Rocks were destroyed by Forgers—maybe they blamed Anvil and Aquila. Someone from Stonehaven must have wanted revenge."

Sophie shuddered. "Do you think they've been here, like . . . *this* . . . ever since we entered Stonehaven?"

Claire wished Sophie would stop asking the hardest questions. "I don't know . . . but it's been a while, I think."

An untouched layer of dust covered the floor. If it had happened recently, there would have been footprints or no dust at all. Her own question was at the tip of her tongue. "Pumus said magic like this—*big*, I mean—hasn't worked in three hundred years. Do you think . . . ?"

"No," Sophie said, shaking her head. "Definitely not."

Because the sisters knew each other so well, Claire didn't have to say her real fear: that Queen Estelle d'Astora of Arden was back. Alive and well. And that she was the one who had turned the Malchains into stone. A petty revenge on the descendants of the Forger who had helped her little brother escape with the Unicorn Treasure.

"Are they," Sophie started, "I mean, have they . . . ?"

Claire shook her head. "They're not dead, I don't think. Not yet."

Stepping away from Aquila, she looked at Anvil, who stood next to her and slightly behind. It looked like he'd been shouting something. His eyes stared straight ahead, and maybe it was a trick of the sapphire's light, but Claire had the sense that he could see them.

Tentatively, she reached out a hand and patted his side. Unlike Sophie, she didn't flinch away. After her weeks of being an apprentice at Stonehaven, she knew that rock, too, was alive in its own way, capable of transformation.

"How can ruby blood *not* kill them?" Sophie asked, shuffling forward.

"It will, over time, if we don't do anything about it," Claire said slowly, trying to remember exactly what Scholar Pumus had said in class. "But I have an idea."

Grabbing a mug that had rolled away on the floor, Claire hurried to the back door and to the edge of the Rhona River. She dipped it into the water until it was full. Hurrying back inside, she sprinkled some water on Aquila's hand.

"Every living thing needs water," Claire said as Sophie looked at her dubiously. "And when you sculpt clay, you add water to help shape it."

"You think you can *mold* her back to herself?" Sophie asked.

"Usually I wouldn't," Claire said. "But we don't have the usual help." From her pocket, she pulled out the knot of unicorn mane. "Unicorn artifacts help make guild magic stronger, so this will make mine stronger, too."

Claire dipped her fingers into the mug again, and ran her wet fingertips over Aquila's hand. It was cold, but Claire remembered how Aquila had used this same hand to teach Claire and Sophie how to sharpen a sword with a whetstone.

And when they'd separated—Aquila to search for the unicorn, and Anvil to escort the girls to Stonehaven—Aquila had flashed a smile, her teeth as shiny as the two battleaxes strapped across her back.

"The cautious never leave, but the restless don't get far," Aquila had chided a nervous Claire. "Anvil, take care of that blade, will you? And make sure you don't lose any thumbs. I'm tired of sewing them back on for you."

Aquila might have the rosy cheeks of the kind of grandma who baked cookies after school, but she was just as lethal—if not more—as her younger cousin.

As Claire focused on a warm-blooded, lively, teasing Aquila, she began to feel the hum of magic zip through her. But the hum felt wrong somehow, off-pitch and squeaky. It jounced and jittered, instead of flowing through her with ease. Suddenly, it seemed to Claire as if she'd hit an oil slick. Her hum skidded, then scattered into nothingness.

"It's not working," she said, lifting her hand away. "It's like there's some sort of barrier around them that's making my magic slide right off. I can't get her to realize that she's *not* rock."

Claire looked at the gleaming strands of unicorn mane. Dad always said if you were going to do anything properly, don't try to take shortcuts. A unicorn's mane was not enough.

Claire stepped back so she could look Aquila and Anvil in the eye. "Don't worry," she said aloud, hoping that even though they couldn't move, they could somehow hear her and understand. "We think the unicorn is nearby. Sophie found some of its mane. We're going to find the last unicorn and . . . ," she paused, searching for the word, "un-rock you. Right, Sophie?" She looked at Sophie expectantly.

"Er, yes," Sophie said, and she gingerly patted Aquila's other arm. She glanced over at Claire. "We should look around and see if the Malchains have anything that could help us track the unicorn."

"That's a good idea," Claire said, and she wished that the Malchains could have made a Kompass to track the unicorn, too. When Sophie had asked Aquila why she couldn't just forge a Kompass or Looking Glass to find the unicorn, the Forger had explained that something about the strength of unicorn magic made crafted objects not work properly. A Kompass's needle set for a unicorn would always spin, and a Looking Glass would only hold a bright, white light.

"But after that," Claire continued, "we leave. Whoever did this might come back."

They hurried into the main room of the cottage. Sophie began by checking out all the highest cupboards while Claire opened the drawers of a nearby chest. Nothing but cobwebs and spider prints. Shutting its lid, she peered beneath. Something glinted in the darkness.

Flattening her hand as much as she could, she reached under and grabbed something hard: the hilt of a sword. And as she pulled the weapon out from under the chest, she realized it wasn't just any sword.

It was Fireblood.

Sena's sword—the one she had given to Claire.

Delight tumbled over sadness as Claire took in the blade. Delight at seeing something familiar, because in this strange world, anything familiar was a gift. Sadness, because Aquila must not have found Sena yet. She'd promised she would find Nett and Sena and return the sword to the redheaded Forger.

But it seemed Aquila had been attacked before she'd had a chance to do either.

"I found the ReflecTent and their travel rucksacks," Sophie whisper-called from across the room. "I've repacked them and stuffed in some seedcakes that still look okay."

"I found Fireblood," Claire said.

"Oh." Claire watched as the same complex emotions flew across Sophie's face. "Well, good. That'll be useful, too." She opened the door and stepped out, but Claire hesitated. It felt wrong to just leave the Malchains.

"Do you think they'll be cold?" she blurted out.

Sophie's head popped back in, and she pulled out two of the travelers' blankets before hurrying back into the hallway. As carefully as she could, Claire wrapped the blankets around her friends' shoulders.

"Should we lay them down?" Sophie asked.

Claire shook her head. "I think they're too heavy for us. Besides, you know the Malchains. They would rather face danger standing up."

Sophie gave a tight nod. "And I'd rather not face any danger at all, so let's go."

"Where?"

"Anywhere but here."

CHAPTER
17

After traveling a safe distance from the cottage, they set up camp. It took longer than usual without Anvil to help them, but when Claire stood back to admire their handiwork, she was pleased. The ReflecTent only listed slightly to the right, but they had properly placed it in a small clearing where moonlight could find it.

"I thought wraiths were only scared of the sun?" Claire had asked the first night Anvil had silently set up two tents just like this, one for himself and one for the girls.

"True," Anvil had said without elaboration. Sophie always claimed that his long silences made her uncomfortable, but Claire appreciated that he always allowed others room to think. She knew how important uncluttered space was in art.

"So," Claire had said after realizing he wouldn't continue. "How can the ReflecTent protect us?"

"Double reflection," Anvil had replied, and with Claire's promptings, he'd explained that all moonlight was truly just reflected sunlight.

"When the moonbeams hit the ReflecTent"—here he had smoothed out the aluminum foil–like material of the tent— "it turns the beams back into sunlight, driving away wraiths and protecting us once we're inside."

Looking at the ReflecTent now, Claire silently thanked the Malchains for the tent. They had helped the girls. Again.

With the sun nearly set, the girls hurried inside. Carefully, they snapped it shut and placed Fireblood by the entrance. After nibbling at the seedcakes ("At least it's not more goat's milk," Sophie had pointed out), the girls laid out their bedrolls. Claire scooted in immediately, but Sophie stayed sitting up, poring over some of Aquila's maps they'd found in her pack.

"She's marked two spots," Sophie said. Her finger slowly twirled the tip of her ponytail. "Both of them are north, so maybe we should head there?" She ruffled to another page, while Claire fiddled with the knot of unicorn mane and strained her ears. The only good thing about nighttime was that neither the Royalists nor the Gemmers would be wandering around—not with wraiths lurking everywhere.

Still, Claire listened to the night's each and every sound. Back home, it was early summer, the mosquitoes just starting to fly, but here, dry leaves rattled and fell as the unfeeling wind shoved by.

Claire shivered.

"Don't worry," Sophie said, peering over a map toward Claire. "That's just the Forest's Reminder."

"The what?"

"It's what the Tillers call that sound you're hearing, the sound of the wind through the trees." Sophie nodded her head toward the outside.

"What's it a reminder of?" Claire asked, hoping for a good story to distract her.

"To wish," Sophie said, then she repeated herself, drawing out the word until it had a whistling quality to it: "wishhh, wisssh, wissssssh." She beamed at Claire. "I really like it. Nett told me about it."

A ping of surprise darted through Claire. She'd forgotten, as she often did, that Sophie had actually known Nett and Sena longer than Claire had, and shared a history with them that Claire did not. On the first day of their journey to Stonehaven, Claire had asked Sophie about a bunch of scratches she had on her legs—the same scratches that had started a bad fight with Mom back in Windemere's gallery. Sophie had launched into a rollicking and raucous story about accidentally watering a Hugging Bramble, and the amount of Tillering Francis and Nett had needed to do to get her out of its embrace while Sena laughed until she cried.

Turning over in her sleeping roll, Claire didn't think she'd ever be able to sleep—not with worries of Royalists and wraiths and war. Of Aquila and Anvil. Of Nett and Sena. But the journey so far had been exhausting, and her feet throbbed.

Knowing Sophie was watching, and comforted by the quiet crinkle of the maps, Claire finally nodded off.

When her eyes opened again, something had changed. Her breath caught—was it Sophie?

She lurched upright, and saw that her sister was curled next to her, her chest rising and falling as she slept. Here and there, a loud snore tripped out. Claire's heart resumed its normal rhythm. Sophie was still here. She hadn't gone anywhere. But then . . . what had woken her?

A flash of light played against the outside of the tent.

She almost called for Sophie, but if it was a Royalist's lantern . . . She sat there, frozen, torn about what to do. She *hated* not knowing.

With a quick tap to the pencil behind her ear, Claire shimmied out of her sleeping bag and crawled to the entrance, careful to avoid Fireblood. As silently as she could, she unsnapped one of the metal clasps, and peeked through.

No one was there.

From far, far off, there was a rumble of thunder.

The campsite was as it had been.

But just as she was about to snap the tent shut, there was another flash of light. A far-off bolt of lightning, too far for even the storm's rain to reach them.

But that wasn't what made Claire hold her breath. Because in that flash of light, something else had momentarily glittered.

There was the slightest flicker of movement. A slight pulse

of lightness against the dark. For one second, it seemed that maybe—that perhaps—a creature, swift as the frothy waters of the Rhona, stood at the lip of the river, drinking.

A deliciousness coursed through Claire, as sweet as warm honey. And for a second, she half thought that the movement was more than a trick of starlight. That maybe . . . just maybe . . .

Could it be the unicorn?

Her heart in her throat, Claire gingerly stepped out of the tent. She blinked.

The river was just the river.

She let out a breath. It had only been her imagination.

Except . . . There! On a log not too far from the tent were long, shimmering strands of silver.

They had not been there before.

A wonder as intricate and fragile as a snowflake crystallized inside Claire. The unicorn *was* here—or it had been.

"Soph—" Claire stopped herself before she could finish her sister's name.

Here was a chance to prove to Sophie she wasn't a coward. And if she found the unicorn first, she could ask him to give Sophie her magic. Maybe even, by the time Sophie woke up, she, too, would be a Gemmer.

As carefully as she could, Claire went back into the tent and reached for Sophie's rucksack, quietly pulling out the slender flute. It was as cool as a raindrop in her hand. The first time she'd played it, she had probably been too far away from the unicorn for it to hear.

Slipping back outside, Claire moved several yards away and stood in the clearing where she'd seen the strands of mane. The storm had passed right by them, it seemed, but the air still felt heavy and full. Holding the flute to her lips, she thought, *I wish*.

Then letting all her most secret wishes and hopes gather up in her, she released her breath . . .

There was no sound. No movement anywhere that she could see.

Pulling the flute away, she let it dangle from her fingers. She should be used to disappointment by now, but it felt as fresh and new as ever. She crouched down to collect the new hairs of unicorn mane. They perfectly matched the knot in her pocket.

Are you really going to give up that easily?

The thought came to her in Sophie's voice. It sounded so clear that she looked back at the tent to make sure Sophie wasn't awake and talking to her.

The unicorn was right there, Sophie's voice in her head admonished.

Looking down at the log, Claire noticed some leaves seemed to have been squished into the ground. Maybe that's the direction the unicorn took. She could explore a little more before waking Sophie.

Claire yanked a sapphire from her dress. With the ragged end of the silk cloak, she began to polish. It wasn't too bright, but it would be enough to weave through the trees.

But as she left her sleeping sister and the safety of the tent, she realized the trouble with light: it made everything beyond its sphere seem darker, made the place where she *was* seem small compared to where she was *not*. Dad always said knowledge was like that, too: that everything you learned in life helped you see how much more there was to know.

Claire looked down at the dim light in her hand, taking a few steps to the right. Was it her imagination or did the light seem stronger now? Moving left, she saw the sapphire dim. Heart pounding, she turned to the right again and began to walk quickly, trusting in her magic—trusting in all she did not yet know.

Every so often, she paused, seeing if there was a difference in the intensity of the light depending on which way she turned. She could hardly believe it, but it almost seemed like the light, the sapphire, was guiding her someplace.

When at last Claire reached another small slip of a waterfall that fed a tiny brook, she stopped and pulled the flute out again. Maybe *this* time . . .

Slipping the sapphire into her pocket, she again held the flute with both hands.

The wind rattled the nearby branches, sending a scattering of leaves to the earth, and she let her gaze travel up through the bare branches of the trees. At least she could now easily see the stars, and they blazed against the backdrop of night, looking not unlike the moontears. The moontears that needed the last unicorn to be woken. That needed her to call it, just as Arden's heir had called the unicorn princess to him before. *Stories repeat.*

Keeping her gaze on the bright points of light, she raised the flute to her lips. And as she did, she almost missed the slight ripple of darkness in the spaces between.

Almost.

Her heart leaped as a piece of midnight seemed to detach itself from the sky. It hurtled toward her, a bone-freezing coldness stalking behind it.

Wraith.

CHAPTER
18

Claire's breath turned to ice in her throat. She choked.

The creature landed on the ground, silent as shadows, long limbs folding as it absorbed the impact. Unable to yell a warning, unable to breathe, Claire watched as the monster slowly stood. Though slightly human in shape, all its limbs were too long to be human, and the misty blackness that rolled off it obscured its features. She had the sense that if she were to sink her fists into its cloak, her hands would push through, as though it were made of ink, until she hit the hard skeletal bone of the *thing* beneath.

Nearby, someone screamed. It sounded a little bit like Sophie, but in that moment, a thick darkness flooded all of Claire's senses—her ears, eyes, nose, mouth. The cold wasn't just the cold of a winter's night or the cold of a northern ocean.

It was the cold that belonged only to those alien, barren stretches of space.

It was a cold that wrapped. That suffocated. That dragged her under.

It was the cold of absolute fear . . .

And then, just as suddenly, the cold lifted.

"Claire! *Claire!*" Sophie was calling her name, as if she'd said it many times before, and Claire was only now responding. She realized she was no longer standing, but was lying flat on her back, the leaves gently cushioning her.

I'm fine, Claire tried to say, but her tongue felt heavy, as if it had indeed turned to ice.

"What's wrong with you?" Sophie asked, her voice sliding a scale up. Claire felt a slight pressure on her wrist as her sister took her pulse. Her sister's fingers were deliciously warm after the extreme cold of the wraith. She tried to speak again. "Sophie?"

"Claire!"

Sophie's thumb fell away as she threw herself around Claire, wrapping her into a feverish hug.

"What happened to the wraiths?" Claire managed to mumble.

Sophie pulled back, and Claire saw that her hair was wild, her eyes bloodshot. And abandoned next to her was a sword.

"Fireblood," Sophie said, her voice strained. "Aquila must have done something to it, because as soon as I took it out of the tent and into the moonlight, it began to glow the same way the ReflecTent does. I followed your sapphire to the clearing. I saw you about to play the flute, and a wraith just came from the sky—out of nowhere! It was like it was in slow motion. It landed on you, knocking you to the ground. And then without thinking, I ran at it with Fireblood."

"You were in a swordfight with a wraith?" Claire asked, impressed.

Sophie looked a little embarrassed. "I think I surprised it. I kind of just poked it and it ran, like shadows before light. I don't know why, exactly, but at least it's gone and you're . . . you're . . ." She dragged the back of her hand across her nose.

"Sophie—are you crying?"

"No," she said, sniffing. "Okay, fine. A little. Don't do something like that again! What were you thinking, sneaking away like that?!"

"It was the unicorn," Claire said, her words now sounding more shaded and whole, rather than two-dimensional as they had before. "He—or she!—was right near our tent. I found more of its mane, and thought I'd try to find it." She sighed, remembering her hope.

Sophie was quiet, then said in a low, serious voice, "That was really brave of you, Clairina. I need to tell you something, though." She stopped, seeming to gather her thoughts.

Claire was just about to prod, but a slight ripple in the darkness made the question die instantly on her tongue.

"Look," she croaked. Sophie turned around just in time to see another ripple in the shadowy trees beyond the meadow.

And then another.

And another.

The wraith hadn't left . . . it had returned. With more.

"RUN!"

Claire wasn't sure who said it—Sophie or herself—but her feet were already pounding the ground. They streaked across the field.

"Where's Fireblood?" Claire yelled.

"Behind," Sophie said, her voice catching. "But there are too many!"

Claire pumped her legs faster, her muscles screaming in protest after so recently being frozen. Her skirts grew heavy with the meadow's dew, slowing her down. But the forest wasn't any better. Thin branches whipped Claire as she ran by, the trees seeming to grab for her. Each time her jeweled gown snagged, she fell a step behind.

Hoisting the fabric in her hands, Claire tried to rip away from stubborn bramble—but this time, she couldn't free herself. She was stuck. Her breaths came as sharp and fast as her terrified thoughts. The thoughts that told her this time, there would be no escape.

"Claire!" Sophie had finally noticed Claire had fallen behind. Claire's heart stopped as her sister turned around, and began to run back toward her. Toward the wraiths.

Claire began to struggle again. She gripped one of the few remaining sapphires on her belt, and as her hand connected with the gem, she remembered. She might be a little sister. She might be a failed princess. But she was a Gemmer. And she could do something about this.

"STOP!" Claire shouted at her sister. "I have an idea!"

She brushed her skirt over the sapphire, and the glow came almost instantly. But it was a weak light, barely as bright as an old glow-in-the-dark sticker.

She needed more light!

She thought frantically of bright things—of crystals hung in sunny windows. Hubcaps in the school parking lot. Lights strung on an evergreen tree. Dad's glasses glinting in the sun during an afternoon spent by the poolside. Mom's special earrings from Venice. Her fingers tingled. Her heart hummed.

Just as the wraiths were about to reach her, their freezing breath beginning to numb her skin, the forest erupted in a clear turquoise light.

Claire laughed in relief as the light pulsed around her, spreading through the tree branches and up into the sky, illuminating everything.

Illuminating the wraiths . . . who were still charging forward, right into the blue light, as if it didn't bother them at all.

"IT'S NOT SUNLIGHT!" Sophie yelled from behind her. "*RUN!*"

Too late, Claire realized her mistake. Only sunlight stopped the wraiths—and the light she'd called from sapphires was not the same as the trapped sunlight in Nett's mossy marimo. Her light—the light of rocks melting under pressure far, far, far from the sun—was useless.

Claire squeezed her eyes tight. She didn't want the last thing she'd ever see to be the wraiths. *Mom, Dad, I love you!* she thought as the magic's hum trickled away from her.

Suddenly, the air filled with pounding hooves and shouts. Claire's eyes flew open.

Men and women on horseback galloped through the trees, each rider connected to the next by a glowing rope.

"Help!" Claire yelled as the thunderous hooves pounded the ground all around her. "I'm right here!"

But none of the riders seemed to look in her direction—or even acknowledge her shouts. Then she noticed why—they couldn't hear her! They all wore earmuffs, exactly the kind Mom liked to shove onto Claire's head on winter mornings.

And then, suddenly, she understood *why*. A sound like nothing Claire had ever heard before—something like a knife scraping a glass bottle, but a thousand times louder—split the air. It knocked the wind out of her, and she swayed.

Ropes of light crisscrossed against the night sky, then snagged on the monsters, pushing them back, pulling them down.

The riders wove expertly through the trees, their ropes only ever tangling around wraiths. Each time a rope hit one, it'd scream and rear back. If the wraith was lucky, it fled the second rope that bound it to the spot. Some, however, were shackled to the ground, writhing inside like billows of ink.

Letting go of her skirt, Claire threw her hands over her ears, only vaguely aware of the horses and chaos around her as she tried to beat back the inhuman screams.

Suddenly Claire's stomach swooped and her feet left the ground. A moment later, she was on the back of a horse, staring straight ahead at its ears.

"Stay still," a man's voice ordered loudly. "Tassel doesn't like wiggling."

Claire froze and the man kicked the horse into motion. Claire had never ridden a horse before, and she wished with all her heart that it had stayed that way. She didn't know what would be worse: falling off this surging avalanche, or staying in the woods, the wraiths' shrieks echoing and re-echoing in her ears.

Soon, though, the dark forest became a soothing blanket, erasing the already fading shrieks, and replacing them with the hums of crickets and other nightly creatures.

"Hey!" Claire said, finally able to hear herself. "Where are you taking me? Who are you?"

There was no answer. She struggled to turn around, but the man's arms kept her tightly in place. Panic swelled in her stomach, threatening to burst out. Where was Sophie? Her teeth clacked together with each stride of the horse, the forest bouncing before her.

After several more minutes with only hooves pounding as her answer, the rider finally pulled the horse to a halt.

The man waved his arms in front of him, as though trying to swat away flies. Then suddenly, his hand vanished completely—like it was cut right off.

Claire shrieked, lurching back, and the horse jittered slightly beneath them, unhappy with the unexpected shift in weight.

"Stop that," the man snapped too loudly. "I need to concentrate!" As he leaned forward even more, the rest of his arm disappeared.

A moment later, a slit seemed to appear in the air, and Claire was no longer standing before a vast swath of tangled trees, but was instead at the top of a hill, overlooking a valley. And below, a ring of glowing lanterns.

The man grunted a little and pulled back, and as he did, the trees that Claire thought had been there were swept away like a curtain. No, not *like*. The forest *was* a curtain! And now that the rider was holding it back, his arm had fully reappeared on the other side.

It was an illusion. Magic, and a powerful kind at that.

As the man nudged the horse forward and through the opening, Claire twisted around to watch the curtain fall seamlessly back into place, looking again like a vast wilderness.

She wasn't sure what kind of magic she'd just witnessed. A Tiller's vertical garden, maybe? Or an invisibility cloak? But she couldn't imagine that even the Spinners would have been able to weave a large enough cloak to hide an *entire* village.

Except, Claire saw, that was exactly what this was. Nestled in a valley below them, hidden by an illusion of wilderness:

A secret, magic village.

CHAPTER
19

With a click of his teeth, the rider urged the horse forward. As they bounced down the hillside, Claire's teeth rattled in her skull. Drawing nearer the encampment, she saw that what she had thought were glowing lanterns were actually tents lit from the inside.

Tiller-made? Or Spinner?

She needed to figure out—and quickly, before they asked her which guild she belonged to. She squinted harder at her surroundings, but even as she took in the tent's haloed edges, they seemed to blur slightly, as if they weren't quite there. She shivered.

"Who goes there?" a deep voice called out.

The horse stopped, and Claire saw that a man with a braided beard and a thick whip spiraled on his hip had appeared from a tent and had grabbed the reins. The rider behind Claire quickly dismounted, yanking his earmuffs off as he jumped down.

"It's me, Cotton!" the rider said, shaking out his shoulder-length hair. "What did you say, Ravel?" In the dim light, Claire could see that the rider had wrapped different colored threads around sections of his hair. Her hands grew clammy. This was a group of Spinners. Mira Fray was a Spinner . . . was she here, too?

Where oh *where* was Sophie? Chills racked Claire's body, and the world seemed to blur again. But the two Spinners seemed completely unaware of the storm of worry raging inside her.

"What did you find?" the bearded Ravel asked.

"Seven wraiths—can you believe it? They're about three miles from here. Bennu and Tulip are taking care of them."

Ravel nodded, sending his braided beard swinging. "And the blue light?"

"You were right," Cotton said. "It *was* a Gemglow. By her." He jerked his head toward Claire.

A second later, hands pulled Claire off the horse. As soon as her feet touched the ground, something invisible twisted around her wrists.

"Hey!" she protested, too scared to be polite. "Why—"

"Runaway Gemmer?" Ravel asked Cotton.

Cotton sucked in his cheeks and nodded. "I think so."

Claire frowned. The Spinner sounded as if he were speaking

around marbles. And she was cold. So, so cold. Maybe there was ice in her ears . . .

Ravel frowned down his beard at Claire. "Is she all right?"

"Wraith-burn," Cotton said, and he reached toward the saddlebag. "You're right, too, about the wraiths behaving oddly. They're starting to roam in groups." Pulling out a bottle, he poured something into a small wooden cup, then offered it to Claire. The liquid steamed slightly, though Claire hadn't seen him heat it.

"Go on, then," he told her. "It'll help with your shivers. If wraith-burn isn't treated, it'll slowly spread to the rest of your senses, and you'll feel nothing but cold ever again."

He undid whatever it was that had bound her wrists together, then pressed the cup into Claire's shaking fingers, and she sipped from it. A delicious warmth raced through her, warming her toes. She took another sip, and the ice in her ears seemed to crack.

"See?" Cotton said, smiling. And this time, his voice was as clear as a permanent marker on a white wall. He held out a small biscuit.

"Please," Claire said, ignoring the food. Now that she could feel again, her stomach was too full of knots to be tempted by anything. "Where is—"

But she was cut off as something whisked by her nose. A moment later, a tiny swan alighted on Ravel's hand. For a moment, it sat in his palm, looking exactly like the folded napkins at fancy restaurants. The swan flared its wings, and unfolded itself into a square piece of cloth with scribbles across it: a note.

Ravel glanced at it, then ran toward a second horse tied to a nearby tree branch. "We have to go!" he snapped. "Tulip's been hurt!"

"But what about the girl?"

"Put her in the infirmary!" Ravel said. "Hurry!"

There was a sharp tug on Claire's wrist as she was pulled into a dim tent. She blinked.

If she hadn't known it was a tent, she would have thought she was standing in the room of a cozy cottage, complete with wooden rafters on the ceiling. And from the rafters dangled multiple nets of knotted rope. They spun slightly in the air, like the mobiles hung over babies' cribs. Except Claire had the sinking feeling these nets weren't just for decoration . . .

Before she could finish her thought, Cotton had snapped his fingers and Claire was swept up into the air. The world swung back and forth as a thick net scooped her up into its valley. Its loose edges wove themselves together quickly, anchoring her to the ceiling above. She was trapped in a rope cage.

"Stay put," Cotton said, and as he ran out, the light went with him, plunging Claire into darkness as she dangled at least seven feet over the floor.

Where was she?

. . . And what had happened to Sophie?

Automatically, Claire's hand drifted to her ear, but instead of feeling the comforting wood of her new pencil, she felt only the texture of her hair.

A cry of dismay slipped out from Claire as she quickly patted the rest of her head, trying to see if the pencil had somehow gotten lost in her curls like it sometimes did. But no—it wasn't there. She'd lost the one thing that made her feel somewhat strong. And worst of all, it had been a gift from Terra.

Claire shifted her weight, and the net rocked. Closing her eyes, she tried to steady her thoughts despite the fact that everything around her was unstable, despite the fact that ever since the moment Anvil had left them at Stonehaven, everything had gone wrong. From her Gemmer classes to the test of the crystal flute . . . the crystal flute!

Slipping her hand into her gown's deep pocket, she pulled it out. Relief washed over her. It still shone, whole and beautiful, despite the earlier events of the night. She almost dropped it raising it to her lips, but she gave it one quick breath.

Nothing.

"Why won't you play?" Claire whispered.

"Psst!"

Sitting up, the world lurched again, but this time, she didn't close her eyes. Because there, scurrying in from the tent's entrance was . . . "*Sophie!*"

Sophie looked, as Dad would say, the worse for wear.

Her hair was a seaweed tangle and her hands and dress—if it could still be called that—were streaked with mud. Claire clung to the ropes and pulled herself into a kneeling position. "How did you get here?"

"Shhhh!" Sophie commanded. She tiptoed to the center of the tent and stood underneath Claire's net, looking up. Even though Sophie was tall, the net—and Claire—still dangled a couple of feet above her head.

"Over there," Claire whispered, pointing behind her to where she spied a stool. Sophie hurried over and dragged it to Claire's net. Finally eye-to-eye with her sister, Sophie grinned.

"Thank the diamonds above," Sophie breathed. Claire tried to smile at the Gemmer saying on her sister's lips, but it was hard. She scrambled as far away as she could from Sophie, who pulled out the Kompass. Sophie touched the eagle's beak that was carved into its cover. Then she pressed hard on the beak as if it were a button, and a small knife flicked out of the brass circle that Claire hadn't even realized was there. Typical Forgers. Always adding an edge to everything.

"How did you get here?" Claire murmured.

Never taking her eye from the rope as she began to saw, Sophie explained, "I was caught, too, and put in another rope thing, but they never checked my pockets. Don't wiggle! I need to get you out of here before the Tillers find us."

"Tillers?" Claire said, trying not to move more than just her lips. "This is a Spinner village."

"No it's not," Sophie said, her blade still sawing through the rope. "Didn't you see what the tent is made of?"

"Fabric—" Claire broke off, and stared harder at the orange walls. Now that the sun was starting to rise, she could see thin lines shooting through the walls like the veins on a leaf.

And that's exactly what the tent was, Claire realized in awe—orange leaves sewn together to wrap around the tent. She looked up at the ceiling and discovered it was actually a collection of wide autumn-ginger fronds, locking together to create a waterproof covering. It was the leaf roof that made the inside slightly orange, as any sunlight that floated through took on the color of the leaves' thin membranes.

"But," Claire said, her mind flashing back to Ravel with his whip and swan handkerchief and Cotton's thread-wrapped hair, "that doesn't make any sense—oof!"

The Kompass's knife had cut through the final knot, and Claire had tumbled to the ground.

"Sorry about that," Sophie said, extending her hand to help Claire stand up. "But we need to leave, now."

Cautiously, Sophie pulled back the tent's flap and peered from behind it. A second later, she scurried out, Claire following silently behind her.

She blinked as she took in their surroundings. Wherever they were wasn't like anyplace she'd ever seen before—either at home, or in Arden. Most of Arden's villages and towns she'd seen had a permanence to them, as if they'd been there a long time. This place felt like it might get up and walk to a new spot at any moment.

The community was cradled in a shallow valley and seemed more like a camping ground than an actual settlement. All the structures looked different. Some were tents of brightly colored silk, while other tents seemed to be woven of reeds and thin twigs like extravagant nests. But whether cloth or flora, the tops were all the same—covered with a fuzzy moss in an array of red, yellow, orange, and green. Claire could imagine what it might look like to people at the top of the valley—like an endless forest of autumn-tinged trees.

It was a place perfectly hidden.

As they darted between the tents, Claire thought she spotted Lieutenant Ravel—from last night. He still had a whip coiled at his hip.

Suddenly, a shout went out. A second later, men and women rushed from behind a silk tent, heading toward the orange one they'd just escaped from.

"They've noticed!" Sophie whispered. "Hurry, we need to hide."

"There," Claire said, pointing to a long wooden building that looked like a stable. "The horses!"

"Don't run," Sophie said, "it'll make us look even more suspicious."

It took all of Claire's will not to sprint, so she settled on a quick step, keeping her eyes on the ground. When they were only a few feet away they heard a voice shout, "They're gone! Fan out around the camp!"

She—and Sophie, too—sprinted toward the door.

"Check the tents!"

Claire pumped her legs harder as Sophie stretched out a hand and opened the door. Claire tumbled in after her and slammed the door shut.

Holding her breath, Claire waited for her eyes to adjust to the dimness. She heard a soft *skritch*, and something skittered by her ankles. Rats? She grabbed for Sophie's hand.

"What's up?" Sophie asked.

"I thought something moved."

She felt Sophie tense, but when nothing happened, Claire

began to feel silly. "Where are the horses?" she asked. "I don't see anything in the stalls, do you?"

Letting go of Sophie's hand, Claire pulled the last sapphire from her bedraggled belt. Her fingers tingled in anticipation. Using the corner of her sleeve, she polished light from the sapphire. A gemstone's light sparkles the same way a jewel does in the sun, and as Claire took it in, she felt momentarily soothed. It was the same color as other blue-tinged memories that sparkled: trips to the lake; the high summer skies of July; the turquoise of her favorite nail polish.

There was a sudden intake of breath from Sophie, and immediately, the skin on the back of Claire's neck prickled. Something was wrong.

Looking away from the blue light spilling over her hands, Claire saw her sister standing, mouth agape, as she peered over a stable door.

"Come, come look," Sophie whispered faintly. Claire crept forward to see a jumble of antlers, hooves, tails, and feathers that glinted copper in the dim blue light.

A chimera.

"There's one over here, too," Sophie said, pointing at the stall next to it. She hurried a few paces to look over the door of the next one. "Here, too! Why would they collect chimera?"

Claire couldn't begin to guess. The chimera hadn't moved in three hundred years.

She came up beside Sophie and this time, when she peered over the stall door, she didn't lurch away. A chimera lion lay curled inside, looking just like a house cat taking a nap on the radiator—if a house cat had a raccoon tail, antlers, and mouse ears, that is. In the wavering light, the copper of the chimera gleamed, creating an illusion of movement where there was none. Whatever Forger crafted this beast hundreds of years ago had taken time to etch in the look of luscious manes and a fuzzy tail. Its claws, though, were still sharp.

Claire frowned.

Had the claws been out a moment ago?

She took a step back and looked over her shoulder for Sophie. Her sister was by the door now, trying to figure out how to lock it. Suddenly, there was a loud screech.

"What are you doing?" Claire whisper-called. "We need to be quiet."

Sophie's head snapped up, and she stared back at her, eyes huge.

"It wasn't me," she whispered.

Apprehension itched between Claire's shoulder blades. Slowly, she turned back to the stall . . . just in time to see the lion chimera open its mouth, copper teeth shining—and roar.

CHAPTER
20

The chimera surged to its feet with the sound of a hundred clattering pots and pans. Its barrel chest pounded at the door and a jaw unhinged again, letting out its rusty roar.

Forgetting they were in hiding, forgetting they were the captives of a strange place, Claire screamed.

As the chimera rammed itself against the stall door again, she stumbled back into something warm and solid. Strong hands suddenly gripped Claire's arms and from somewhere above her head, she heard a new voice say, "Sit, Lixoon! Sit!"

There was the crack of a whip, and the chimera's jaws snapped shut. It tilted its massive head, considering the command.

Claire held her breath as—ever so slowly—it sank back down onto its haunches. The metal beast was still as could be, except for the racoonish tail that whipped back and forth, like an annoyed cat's.

The hands let go of Claire's shoulders, and without bothering to look back, Claire sprinted to Sophie, who had huddled against the far wall. Sophie's hand reached out for hers, tugging her closer. It was only then that Claire turned around to see who had commanded the chimera.

A woman wearing a simple green dress stood in front of them, an emerald scarf draped elegantly over her shoulders. Her short white hair fluffed above her head in a poof, giving her the resemblance of a dandelion gone to seed. She seemed unarmed, but the stern Lieutenant Ravel stood on her other side, recoiling his long whip.

"That's them," Ravel said grimly.

"I see," the woman responded. She stared at the children, her blue eyes pensive beneath the rather odd wreath that perched on her head like a strange bird. It seemed to be woven from flowers and twigs, though here and there Claire caught the gleam of gold and a few sparkly bits that glittered like diamonds. Perhaps they were.

"You're not supposed to be in here," she admonished them. "You were supposed to stay in the Quarantine Tents."

"Yes," Ravel agreed. "You've wasted everyone's time." He beckoned. "I'd advise that you move away from that stall— Serpio is only half as friendly as Lixoon."

Startled, Claire looked into the stall behind her. A fanged chimera with a scorpion's tail slowly tilted its head, looking up at her from where it was curled on the ground. Though chimera didn't have eyes, only shallow dents in their copper armor where the eyes would be on a normal creature, Claire had the distinct sense that it was watching her.

She sprang away from Serpio's stall, her mind scrambling for answers. For a little less than three hundred years, ever since the unicorns had been hunted to extinction, the chimera had been still, rusted by time and un-oiled by magic.

The unicorn.

Claire's heart galloped in her chest.

Though she hadn't found the unicorn last night, it still must be near—or had been near, in order to have woken the chimera. They were on the right path!

"Who are you?" Sophie demanded, still standing by the stall door. "Why should we trust you?"

"That's no way to talk to Mayor Nadia," Ravel said gruffly, but Mayor Nadia's expression remained politely puzzled.

"Why would you *not* trust us?" she asked, her hands spreading wide. "It's we who saved your lives from the wraiths. It's we who put you safely in a hammock while the effects of wraith-burn wore off."

"Who," Claire whispered, trying to speak up despite her mouth suddenly going dry, "exactly are you?"

Mayor Nadia reached out a hand to stroke Serpio's nose. "We're what all lost souls seek and young hearts yearn for. We're what you've been journeying for. We're . . ."—she paused dramatically—". . . *Woven Root.*"

Claire didn't really know what to say.

The old woman had said the words with utter certainty, as if Claire had asked what teachers did, and she'd responded with "teach." Not sure what to do, Claire did what she always did in times of confusion: she looked at Sophie. Sophie, however, was looking right back at her, equally baffled.

The old woman's eyebrows shot up. "My goodness," she murmured. "Is it possible . . . could it be . . . you *weren't* looking for us?"

"Mayor," Ravel said, clearly unnerved. "If we had known, we would have never—"

Nadia waved her hand, cutting him off. "What's done is done, Lieutenant," she said, the lines around her mouth deepening. "The girls are here, and that's a knot that can't be undone."

She turned to face them, and as she did so, Claire heard a high, faint tinkling. Looking at the scarves, she realized some of them had tiny bells sewn into their hems.

"And *here*," Nadia said, with an extravagant sweep of her arms, as if she were a ringmaster in a circus, "is the last place in Arden where jumbled magic is free to exist. We welcome you to the last community of alchemists."

Alchemists. Jumbled magic.

Not so long ago, these strange words would have been just that: strange words. But Claire had been in Arden long enough now (so, *so* long) that she knew exactly who the alchemists were—and how the rest of Arden treated them. Both of Sena's parents had been alchemists . . . before one had been executed and the other imprisoned.

Sophie must have been reminded of Sena, too. "Are you really?" she asked, eyes bright with curiosity. "I mean—you're *actually* alchemists? Do you know the Steeles?"

The question dangled in the air, and Claire suddenly had the distinct impression that Sophie had said something wrong, but she wasn't sure what or why. It was something to do with the stiffness Nadia suddenly held herself with, as if she were no longer human but a metal rod.

"We did," Nadia said at last, inclining her head. "Mathieu was a very kind man, and Sylvia burned with such brightness. The two greatest alchemists of our time. Such a tragedy what happened." She smiled sadly. "So you *did* intend to find us, if you know the Steeles."

Claire opened her mouth to say no, but Sophie spoke first. "Yes," she said emphatically. "They told us about Woven Root long ago, and we knew we had to come."

Nadia nodded. "That's how it is for many of us. Many seek Woven Root for different things: to explore their magic in freedom, or for protection from persecution. I myself came seeking treasure, though I found much more than that here. I discovered that freedom to live the way you want is its own kind of treasure, more valuable even than ancient masterpieces and works of great art. Now, please, your names?"

"I'm Andrea," Sophie said promptly, giving her middle name, then gestured to Claire. "And she's Elaina. We're so glad we've finally found Woven Root. I have *so* many questions!"

"All of which will be answered, eventually. After we get you both changed and fed. We can't have our guests looking . . ." Nadia scanned them up and down. ". . . like *that.*"

Nadia commanded the girls to follow her, leaving Lieutenant Ravel and the dimness of the chimera stables behind.

"Why did you lie? We don't have time for this," Claire murmured under her breath to Sophie as they trailed Nadia a couple of feet behind.

"Yes we do," Sophie insisted, but only after making sure Nadia was too busy talking to another member of the Wraith Watch to listen to them. "First of all, did you see those chimera? That's powerful magic. And did you see how the riders were able to quickly encircle the wraiths? They're clearly trained at tracking magical creatures. Maybe they can help us with our tracking skills. Third, this place is hidden. We can figure out our next steps here without worrying about the Gemmers or Royalists finding us."

Her death will be the key to our victory.

Mira Fray's voice resonated in Claire's thoughts. Maybe Sophie was right. Maybe they deserved a break, somewhere safe both from wraiths *and* Royalists like Jasper or Fray.

"This way!" Mayor Nadia called over her shoulder to them as the two members of Woven Root's Wraith Watch finished their business with her and walked away. Sophie and Claire followed her as they rounded a cluster of tall tents.

"*Oh!*" Claire gasped, while next to her, Sophie let out a whistle.

"Exhibition's Row," Mayor Nadia said, and Claire could tell

she was pleased with their reaction. "Best not to touch any-thing here without first asking permission."

In the bright light of morning, they could clearly see Woven Root's central square in all its jumbled splendor. Rows of brightly colored tents lined up across from one another like danc-ers preparing to take their final bow, as merchants called out gaily to one another, trying to entice their neighbor to leave their wares for just a moment and come see what they had to offer.

And the offerings!

Woven bookmarks that never lost their place or fell out, because they rooted themselves to the page. Pillows that promised to always stay cool on even the hottest summer nights. Seeds that were said to grow into willows that had ribbons instead of leaves. Everywhere Claire looked, she spotted something new, something wondrous, something impossible.

Claire wished she had her paint set. Or at least some felt markers. She'd even make do with a box of crayons, because the merchant tents of Woven Root demanded to be drawn.

Nadia smiled as they wove through the booths with opened mouths.

"You'll have time to explore before the welcome feast," she promised as she ushered them up a small incline and toward a blue and purple striped silk tent. "They'll be happy to see you—two Gemmers added to our ranks!"

Sophie said something so softly that Claire wasn't sure if she had imagined it until Nadia said, "Beg your pardon?"

"I said," Sophie said, "that I'm not . . . I don't have a craft."

"Really," Nadia murmured. "How unexpected. We know, of course, about those who lack magic, but none, if any, have ever been born here in Woven Root."

A blush crept into Sophie's cheeks, making her freckles look like stars against a pink sky. She shrugged defiantly. "It's not *so* unusual. I have a friend who is also . . . similarly inclined."

"No harm intended," Nadia said lightly. "I only meant I find it hard to believe that anyone can lack magic, really."

"What do you mean?" Claire asked, curious. She knew from Nett and her time in Arden that magic had seemed to fade since the Guild War, when the unicorns were believed to have been hunted to extinction. Everyone knew it was because the unicorns had gone away that the magic, too, had grown weaker, and lackies had been born—like their friend Thorn Barley in Greenwood Village.

"I only mean to say that magic is in the material," Nadia said, reminding Claire a bit of Scholar Terra. Nadia turned left and they began to walk up the steep incline, passing by a thundering waterfall that tossed rainbows playfully into the air before rushing through the valley.

"After all," Nadia continued, "the only magic we have isn't really magic at all. It's just the ability to see the potential in each block of stone, medallion of metal, loop of thread, or seed. If someone doesn't have magic, I think it's just because she hasn't learned enough about herself yet."

She stopped them in front of a small tent of blue and purple silks and swept the door flap back. "Now, let's get you out of those tatters—you look like you're unraveling."

Claire glanced down at her outfit—it was covered in bits of grass and clover left over from the wraith's attack, while Sophie's dress was frayed at the edges, and in some places, the beautiful silver embroidery that had spangled her gown was completely gone. Catching Claire's glance, Sophie crossed her eyes and stuck out her tongue before following Nadia through the entrance.

The tent was large inside, despite its small appearance on the outside. A carpet as lush as spring grass lay on the floor and the wooden furniture was painted in an array of patterns. It looked like the kind of cozy place one could hunker down in for long winter months.

Nadia opened a painted chest near a trundle bed and pulled out a soft sky blue tunic embroidered with swans and wide-legged trousers with golden roses growing from the hems. *Actually* growing, because even as Claire watched, a tiny rose-bud made of thread blossomed in tiny stitches. Sophie was given similar garments, but hers were a deep indigo lined with golden lilies and herons.

"It's beautiful," Sophie breathed.

"Yes, but it's also practical," Nadia said, and showed them an invisible seam that concealed a secret pocket. "For anything you can't bear to lose," she said. "Whatever you put in a Lock-it Pocket can only be found and taken out by you." She winked. "It's an old Spinner trick."

While Nadia left to retrieve some food, Claire and Sophie quickly changed and explored their surroundings.

"Claire," Sophie called, "it's our stuff!" She'd opened a painted chest next to one of the hammocks. Sure enough, their packs squatted there—torn and dusty—along with Fireblood . . . and Claire's pencil. Claire quickly snatched the pencil and nestled it securely into her hair. It wasn't hard—her curls weren't so much curls anymore as they were knots, but for once she didn't mind. There was no way her pencil would slip out again.

"My Wraith Watch recovered your items this morning," Nadia said as she bustled back in with bowls of steaming oatmeal. Setting them on a checkerboard table, she smiled at the girls. "I hope you'll be very comfortable here. I suggest you take a chance to explore your new home a bit. There will be a welcome feast tonight. It's tradition. We believe in full integration at Woven Root. Everyone knows everyone."

As Mayor Nadia spoke, dread crawled over Claire's shoulders. Should she say something? She didn't want to be rude, but what did Nadia mean by "new home"? They were safe here for *now*, sure, but they had to find the unicorn, and wake the moontears, and save Anvil and Aquila, and eventually find their way home.

"Wait," Sophie said, speaking up as Mayor Nadia moved to the exit. "We can't stay. We're looking for—um, some friends of ours. We've got to leave as soon as—"

"Leave?" Nadia paused near the flap, morning sunlight

outlining her so that she looked as if she'd been traced in gold. "Crossed-stars, no, my child. I'm sorry if I wasn't clear before. People are always welcomed in Woven Root, but they're never allowed to leave."

CHAPTER
21

What?!" Sophie yelled while Claire's gasp lodged hard and sharp in her chest.

During all their travels, Claire had known it was a possibility that she and Sophie might not ever make it home again.

She had only known it in such a way that it was a light sketch across a canvas: barely discernable and easily changed. Now, however, hearing a grown-up say it made the possibility burst forth in clear and terrifying detail.

Nadia adjusted a scarf, seeming perplexed by their reactions. "If we let people leave the safety of Woven Root, they could be tracked back here. We could bring down upon ourselves the fury of all four guilds if we were found out. People come here precisely to stay hidden. They put their trust in us. We can't risk their safety."

"Please—" Claire tried to say, but she was cut off before she could push the word out.

"Woven Root has very few rules," Nadia said firmly, "but this is the one rule we all abide by. There will be no exceptions. And if you ask again," she said as Sophie opened her mouth, "I'll have to assign some of the Wraith Watch to keep an eye on you. Or you'll again be confined to the infirmary until you come to the logical conclusion yourselves. With the wraiths so restless recently, I really can't afford to have even one of my watch off duty."

Claire held her breath, waiting for Sophie to talk back, but instead, Sophie nodded slowly. "Yes, we understand."

The mayor smiled at her. "Good, I'm glad we see eye-to-eye. And I do apologize—I myself was young once, and I used to travel and seek out my own adventures. But once I found Woven Root, I knew I had to stay. It'll grow on you. It always does."

Nadia smiled kindly, and for a moment, Claire forgot everything—forgot that Anvil had disappeared, forgot they'd left the moontears behind, forgot that the Royalists were after her. In that moment, she felt only the warmth and safety of Nadia's smile. It reminded her of something—reminded her, oddly, of home.

Maybe Nadia was right.

Maybe there *was* good reason to stay here, where it was safe, where they were hidden, where they'd be free to do what they wanted . . .

"Go on, then. Amuse yourselves. You may not pass the Camouflora, but you are free to explore within its confines as much as you please."

"Camouflora?" Claire asked.

"Haven't you seen it? Well, I guess that's the point," Nadia said, wrapping her scarf a little closer. "It's a jumbled Spinner and Tiller technique to train moss to mimic its surroundings. Our very talented Tillers and Spinners can grow Camouflora so strong that it can seem like an invisible curtain."

With that, she nodded to them, and walked off. And as she did, it seemed as if the hope and warmth Claire had felt for only a moment followed the mayor out of the tent. The cold truth set back in: they were trapped.

Claire whirled on Sophie. Fireblood again hung on her hip, even though it was technically Claire whom Sena had given it to originally. But that wasn't what was bothering Claire now, or at least, bothering her the *most*.

"Why did you give in?" she asked. "What about the Malchains? What about the moontears?"

"Relax," Sophie said, pulling her hair back into a ponytail. "We clearly weren't going to win that argument now, were we? Also, didn't you see that flute shop? Maybe someone there can make the crystal flute work. I think it's broken."

Claire felt her spirits lift. "You think so?"

She hadn't thought of it that way, that it could be the flute that was broken, and not her. But it made sense, now that she thought of it. According to Terra's story, the instrument had to be hundreds, if not thousands, of years old. In all that time, something probably had gone wrong with it. After all, Claire *had* to be Arden's heir. She had released the unicorn. She had proof.

Reaching into her pocket again, she pulled out the soft strands of unicorn mane. Without moonbeams touching them, they seemed slightly less wondrous than they had in the glade. But just by holding them, Claire felt a kind of peace enter her. The unicorn was still out there. There was still hope.

"Of course," Sophie said, turning her head so quickly that her ponytail snapped in her direction. "Every second here is time wasted, another second the moontears haven't been woken and the Malchains are all alone in that cottage. So stop lolly-gagging," she said, using a phrase Mom sometimes said when Claire stared a little too long out the kitchen window, day-dreaming of new art projects while the dishwater in the sink lost its suds and cooled. "We've got work to do."

CHAPTER
22

Entering the kaleidoscope of color and sound of Exhibition's Row once again, Claire half felt like she'd ended up in a carnival instead of a campsite. And just like at a carnival, it was almost impossible to keep track of Sophie.

Claire looked up from a display of flowering paints ("Watch your colors blossom across your scroll!") just in time to see Sophie talking animatedly from the opening of a quieter-looking tent.

"Fine eye," the merchant was saying with a nod to a small bottle set before Sophie, "that is my latest experiment: Unicorn Cream."

"You hear that, Claire?" Sophie asked, widening her eyes meaningfully at her sister. "*Unicorn* Cream." She spun around to address the merchant. "Does it, er, attract a unicorn with a certain scent or something?"

"Ha!" the merchant laughed. "Attract a unicorn—that's funny, girl. No, I call it that because it's meant to enhance guild magic, the same way a unicorn artifact would."

"Bramble, what are you telling our new arrivals?"

Claire turned to see the friendly-faced Cotton walking by, his arms full of firewood. The rider shook his head, the colorful threads in his hair swaying like a bouquet of sea anemones. "Mayor Nadia wouldn't be happy if she knew you were still trying to push your Unicorn Cream. These girls don't know any better."

"You always were a stick-in-the-mud," Bramble said, waving a dismissive hand. "You never know. Perhaps *this* could be the batch."

"I doubt it!" Cotton said as he continued past them with his heavy load. He looked down at the girls. "I'd stay away from experiments, if I were you. You never know what might happen. We recently lost our two strongest alchemists—the ones who taught us how to wake the chimera in the first place—to an experiment gone wrong at the seams of the world."

"Cotton!" a woman in an apron called as she stomped by, her hands full with a large cauldron. "Are you waiting for the firewood to take root? Let's get moving!"

As Cotton and the woman hurried away, the sisters turned their attention back to Bramble's wares.

"So," Sophie said, her disappointment as tangible as a pebble in Claire's shoe. "So . . . I guess the Unicorn Cream won't work."

"Cotton doesn't know what he's saying," Bramble said dismissively. "The Unicorn Cream might not be my greatest creation, but you won't find better Hollow Packs anywhere else." He lifted two rucksacks down from a shelf, one a soft powder blue and the other lavender. "Spinner-sewn to contain just short of everything, with root support so that they never feel heavier than your hair."

"What do you mean, 'just short of everything'?" Sophie asked, running her fingers across the fabric.

"I mean you can put everything in the world in it, except if you put the last thing in, it might tear." Bramble chuckled. "That's the theory, anyway—it's never been proven one way or the other."

"Perfect!" Sophie exclaimed, lighting up. She reached over to take the satchels.

"Hang on, miss." Bramble held up his hand. "That'll be fifty guilders—twenty-five apiece."

Sophie's face fell and she looked at Claire anxiously. "I, you see . . ."

Claire stepped forward and handed the man the last sapphire she'd pulled from her almost-a-princess dress before the mayor had thrown it away. The man's eyebrows shot up. "Gemmer-touched?" he asked, nodding. "That is indeed a fair trade. We don't get many—any, really—Gemmer items. Two Hollow Packs and . . . sixty guilders."

He counted out some coins and handed them to Sophie, who pocketed them silently before turning away.

Trying to cover up her sister's rudeness, Claire thanked the seller profusely before hurrying to catch up with Sophie.

"Which way to the flute stand?" Claire asked.

"I don't know," Sophie admitted. "It's just so big." Her eyes swept across the market. "We're not being practical about this. Let's split up. I'll search for the flute stand, while you be on the lookout for something that can help us track the unicorn. We can meet up at our tent before the welcome feast, and head over then."

It made sense. Claire knew slightly more about magical objects after her lessons at Stonehaven, but as she pulled the flute from her Lock-it Pocket and handed it to Sophie, she hesitated. "Are you sure we need to split up?" Claire asked.

Sophie wrinkled her nose, puzzled. "You don't mind try-ing to face down the wraiths by yourself, but you don't want to be alone at a market?"

"This is completely different," Claire protested. "That wasn't a choice."

"You'll be fine," Sophie said, and she shoved half the guil-ders from the sapphire into Claire's hands, before spinning around and walking away.

Claire would have protested harder, pushed back against her sister's bossiness, but she'd seen something funny in Sophie's eyes—something that told her that her sister wanted to be left alone. Turning in the opposite direction, she began to wander through the displays. Something had definitely upset Sophie, and if she had to guess, Claire would have said it had to do with being a lackie.

Lackie. Claire hated that word. Her sister didn't *lack* anything. But maybe Woven Root would be a good place for her to experiment . . .

Maybe the alchemists knew something . . .

Maybe . . .

Claire realized she was having those tempting thoughts again. The thoughts that said *stay where it's safe* and *leave well enough alone* and *Royalists!* But she shook her head, trying to make those thoughts go away, because she knew that, after all they needed to accomplish—saving the Malchains, finding the unicorn, and waking the moontears—they were eventually going to go home. Real home. And that was not here.

Claire wandered for a while, allowing herself to be dazzled by all the thriving activity of the Woven Root marketplace. It was so different from the echoing halls of Stonehaven, where people hammered and sweated all day to make even a little bit of magic stick. She stopped a moment to watch a teenage Spinner and Tiller work together to dip shirts into a cauldron of vegetable dye.

"Excuse me," Claire asked the wide-faced girl stirring the cauldron, "but what color is in there?"

"The color of invisibility," the Tiller girl said, and grinned as Claire's mouth fell open. The Spinner boy next to her nodded, and waved his hand at the empty clothesline above his head. "This batch is special ordered by the mayor."

Claire hesitated, then raised her hand. Her fingers brushed against something soft and light and slightly damp. A breeze brushed by, and the air was suddenly filled with the sound of rustling fabric, like ghosts' whispers.

"Are you interested in anything?" the Spinner boy asked. Claire was about to say no when she saw a little sign that read, "No tears, no tears! We fix everything."

"You fix everything?" Claire asked. "Could you fix a flute?"

"Everything cloth, that is," the boy amended. "I'm good with a needle and thread, but I'd have to be a Spyden to be able to patch a flute with just that."

"What's a Spyden?" Claire asked, desperate for anything that could help and aware of time slipping. "Where can I find one?"

From Claire's left, the Tiller girl chuckled. "You don't go seeking a Spyden, not if you know what's good for you." The girl began to stir the contents of the cauldron. "They're fascinating creatures, though, I give you that. They can patch any problem with their silk and are so good at the spinning wheel, they can spin answers out of thin air. Topher, I need you to keep stirring! Or else this batch will go bad."

As the boy hurried to help, Claire pondered the girl's words. Answers out of thin air . . . answers like where the last unicorn had gone? Claire wanted to press more, but the girl and boy were hunched over their dye frantically throwing in more petals and ground roots. Invisibility, it seemed, was no easy task, and Claire trudged away.

As the sun rose overhead and the day grew hot, Claire stumbled into a shop that appeared to be empty. It was made of woven branches and twigs that heaved and sighed slightly with the breeze that passed through the archways.

All along the walls, shelves were filled with wonderful objects, like never-popping soap bubbles, intricately carved boxes, candles that filled the air with taste instead of scent, and even a pair of gloves that promised to sense things just like skin. But what caught Claire's eyes was the fluttery wave of white roses. The petals swayed in the breeze, making a soft crinkly sound that reminded her of something.

They weren't roses—well, they were, but they hadn't been *grown*. They'd been folded. Folded out of . . .

Claire's breath caught as she scanned the nearby shelves.

Paper!

It had been so long since she'd held a fresh piece of paper. In Stonehaven, apprentices used slate and chalk to mark down their homework since paper—a Tiller specialty—was too difficult to attain on their lonely mountaintop. She knew she should be shopping for something more useful, like a Looking Glass or a Kompass, but this paper . . . it looked as smooth as cream and as soft as a unicorn.

"Can I help you?" a voice asked.

Claire's head sprang up, and she saw a man with brown skin, about Dad's age, standing at a bench near the back of the shop. He wore a tunic made of leaves sewn together and his trousers seemed to be made of woven bark, making him blend right in with the walls around him. She wouldn't have noticed him at all if he hadn't spoken.

Now the man dipped his head in greeting. "Would you like to buy some paper?"

She would, but . . . Claire shook her head. "I'm actually looking for something that will help us *look* for something."

A thoughtful expression crossed the merchant's face. "I think I have just the thing. But you'll have to wait a moment, is that all right?"

When Claire nodded, the man rustled off. First one minute passed, then two. She eyed the paper. Her fingers were tingling, eager to draw. Surely a single page wouldn't cost that much . . .

With one last glance toward the back, Claire pulled out a fresh piece of paper and tugged her pencil out from behind her ear. Then, she got to work.

She sketched in a picture of their house. Not Aunt Diana's mansion, but the small house where she and Sophie had shared a bedroom until Sophie moved into the small study. She could picture everything, down to the chipmunk holes in the stone walls and the spot on the driveway that was still a bit yellow after an incident where a much younger Sophie had decided they should paint it "gold" with permanent outdoor stain.

But when she was done drawing her home, it still didn't feel complete. In the corner, there was a little space left. Her art teacher had always said to take up the entire space. Suddenly, she knew just what to add.

Mom and her curly topknot and Dad with his clear-rim glasses. And as she shaded in their smiles, Claire felt something course out of her accompanied by the contented hum in her fingers. She was almost done, but she needed one more person to put in front of their house. She sketched in Sophie's dark ponytail, then laid the pencil down. The drawing was complete.

But as Claire stared at it, Pencil Mom opened her mouth, and though Claire could not hear her, she could make out the words on her lips: *We miss you.* Claire's breath caught. Was Mom really saying that—or was it only what Claire wanted to tell Mom?

Then, Pencil Dad seemed to speak: *We love you.*

A tear splattered onto the paper, and Claire rubbed her eyes. Something beautiful and delicately fragile spun itself inside Claire like a glass spider's web. It was a sweet sadness, to know that you were loved and missed.

The paper moved out from beneath Claire's fingertips.

"Oh!" She looked up to see that the seller had returned and was now inspecting her drawing under a glowing plant bud. "I can pay for that," she added hastily, feeling shame spread across her cheeks in a warm flush.

"That won't be necessary," the seller said, "paper is common enough, but thank you for offering." He slid the picture back to her, then held out a little pouch. Undoing the drawstring, he pulled out a thin golden spyglass, the kind that Claire imagined pirates must have used.

"This," he said, setting it on a cushion of black velvet, "is a rare beauty, both of Gemmer and Forger craft. It allows the viewer to see for almost unimaginable distances. With this, you can see the pearl spires of the Sunrise Isles' grand temples across the sea, or to the very top of Starscrape Mountain. Or . . . ," he raised an eyebrow at her, ". . . see your old home."

Claire hadn't realized her homesickness had been so obvious. And she didn't think that even a super special spyglass could see *her* home.

"Here," the seller said, offering the spyglass to her as another customer entered. "Take a look."

Slowly, she pressed the spyglass's cool rim to her eye. She blinked as an eddy of colors came into focus, and then the world snapped into place to show members of Woven Root tending the cooking fires and a man in an apron stringing lanterns between tents, decorating for the welcome feast. Suddenly, he jumped back as Mayor Nadia walked by, smiling and waving to the party preppers as she guided Lixoon, the lion-raccoon chimera, back to the stables. It was a peaceful and happy place, despite Claire's fears.

"No," she heard the seller say over her shoulder. "You need to look up to get outside of Woven Root." She felt him adjust her elbow slightly. There was another headache-inducing swirl of colors, and then she was looking farther, beyond all that, past the Camouflora illusion, all the way to a dark smudge against the horizon.

Spinning the lenses, Claire suddenly brought the image into sharp focus to see a hundred bells on top of a hundred towers. Fyrton! It was a Forger city that Claire knew.

Scanning the streets, she saw the sparkling bits of silver scraps that made up Silver Way, and the wall that she had scaled with the help of Nett's wisteria bush.

Then she was looking at a cobbled square, where an entirely different crowd from the one in Woven Root had gathered. At the center of the square was a massive statue of a bear snarling into the wind. And around it, lined up in neat rows, were twenty or so people in armor. As she watched with wonder, a man in chain mail demonstrated a sword maneuver. A second later, the lines of people mimicked him with their own swords. They were training.

Her stomach dropped. Not so long ago in Stonehaven, she'd stood with Zuli and Lapis and Geode as they mimicked Jasper's drills with the spear. And even less time had passed since she'd heard the Royalists' plans.

It seemed that Mira Fray would soon get her war.

CHAPTER
23

Claire lowered the spyglass. Arden was dangerous enough with a secret society after them and friends' blood being turned to stone; she couldn't imagine how much more terrifying this land would be in the middle of a war. There was so much they needed to accomplish, and all she wanted to do was run home, before things got worse.

But she—and not Sophie for once—had a plan.

The golden spyglass lay in her palm, a slender key to the solution. This spyglass would let her and Sophie search all Arden for the unicorn—without having to leave the protection of Woven Root. It was genius!

"Is that enough?" she asked as she plunked down all her guilders. But even Claire could tell it would not be enough.

The seller shook his head. "I'm afraid not," he said. He

picked up the drawstring bag and his fingers reached for the spyglass.

"Wait," Claire said, remembering what Nadia had told them. "I'm a Gemmer! Is there something I could make for you in exchange? I'm not really much good at anything—I explode things sometimes—but if you have a jewel, I can make it glow for you!"

"Ah." The seller's expression brightened. "That *is* interesting, but I'm afraid I have no gems and no need for explosions. But," he tilted his head, "if you include your rather charming drawing, I'll accept it as payment in full. I'll even give you a few extra sheets of paper."

"Thank you!" Claire said. At last, something was going right! Just then, a small hourglass chimed. Glancing at it, the seller nodded. "There's an hour to sunset and to your welcome feast."

"Already?" Claire exclaimed. She was going to be late to meet up with Sophie. "I gotta go!"

"Don't forget this," he said, waving the spyglass at her as she made for the door. She doubled back to take it with a smile, then darted through the door as the man called out with a chuckle: "It was good doing business with you."

Claire wove her way frantically through the tents, trying to find her way back to Mayor Nadia's. Thinking about home had only reminded her of everything that was at stake. They needed to get out of here.

But she found herself getting more and more lost in the

tangle of market stalls and magical wares. What had seemed delightful to her earlier in the day now seemed alarming and distracting—everything was too bright and too musical and too oblivious. Did no one know that the Royalists were planning a war? Didn't they care? Consumed by her questions, she didn't notice a wayward tree root until she tripped on it.

She just managed to catch herself before sprawling on the ground. Looking up, she saw a hunched figure hurrying toward her.

"Sophie!" Claire called, waving. "I'm over here—*Sophie*?!"

The girl who stood in front of Claire certainly looked like her sister. She was wearing the same outfit Claire had last seen her in. And there was still a constellation of freckles across her nose. But her hair, which had previously sprung from its ponytail in an inky fountain was no longer dark . . . but white.

Claire stared aghast. "What . . . what happened?!"

"I look awful!" Sophie wailed and buried her face in her hands. "I . . . I bought Bramble's unicorn potion. I thought it would wake my Gemmer magic but instead, it did *this*!"

Poor Sophie. It wasn't funny, but . . . Claire smothered a giggle.

"It's the inside that counts," Claire said, trying to sound soothing. And she must have succeeded at least a little bit, because Sophie peered through her fingers. Trying to think of a way to coax her sister out more, Claire asked, "Did you manage to bring the flute to a shop?"

"No," Sophie moaned. She dropped her hands. "I spent all

the guilders. I thought it would be worth it if the potion made me a Gemmer. Then I could try the flute, and that could work."

Hurt flared within Claire, but before it could entirely engulf her, something blew it out: understanding. Claire didn't feel *princess* enough, but then again . . . Sophie didn't feel *magic* enough.

"Sophie, it doesn't matter that you're not a Gemmer," Claire said softly. "You're still the bravest person I know."

Sophie sniffed.

"And," Claire cast about, trying to think of what would make her feel better, "it could have been worse. We're in an alchemist village, after all. Your hair could have turned into leaves or something."

Sophie stared at her a moment, then burst into laughter. "Ugh, you're right," she said, dragging an arm across her face, and sniffling slightly. "Bramble said the color change should only be temporary, anyway. And we should get going. We're late!"

Before Claire could say anything, Sophie had begun to join the crowd of people trickling to the campfires.

Claire quickened her pace to keep up. "Wait for—ow!" Her toe throbbed as she sprawled onto the ground, catching herself with her palms just before she planted face-first into the grass.

Sophie glanced over her shoulder. "Are you okay?"

"Fine," Claire muttered, the back of her neck warming. She stood and wiped her hands on her new clothes with a grimace. "Let's go—ow!"

"What's wrong with you?" Sophie asked. She walked over

to where Claire had tripped *again*. And fallen . . . *again*. "I know you're clumsy, but this is getting ridiculous!"

Scowling, Claire looked up at her sister. "I'm not doing it on purpose!"

Sophie opened her mouth to say something, but suddenly her lips snapped shut and her head whipped to the side. There was a rustle in the undergrowth, and then Claire thought she saw a movement, long and whiplike, shudder toward her through the fallen leaves.

A crawling sensation tickled Claire's shoulder blades and her skin tightened into goose bumps.

Please don't be a snake, Claire prayed. *Oh please!*

A spray of dirt exploded near Claire's feet, covering her in dark soil and leaf mulch. Yelping, she leaped away from—

—the tree root that had just burst through the dirt.

"What is going on?" Sophie cried, watching as the root spread fibrous hairs and pulled itself along the ground . . . toward Claire.

The rest of Woven Root had noticed now, and shouts filled the air.

Frozen in shock, Claire could only stare while the root, as wide as an elephant's trunk, reached for her ankle and wrapped around it.

With a scream, she tried to kick the root off her, but it was as tight as a too-small hair band on a wrist.

Crack!

Nadia suddenly appeared, cracking her whip expertly on the root.

The root slackened, then froze, all the tiny hairs lying as flat and still as the shadows on the moon.

Scooching out from its grasp, Claire lurched to her feet. "What's happening?"

Nadia's fluffy hair sprang out in all directions, but now she no longer looked like a dandelion: she looked like a lion. Her body seemed coiled, as if she were about to jump, and her eyes relentlessly scanned the scene of displays and tents that had been overturned as the alchemists of Woven Root had run for cover.

"There's an intruder," Nadia all but growled.

Claire couldn't breathe. Had the Royalists found them? Nadia had said the entire point of Woven Root was to keep people safe, but what would happen if it turned out they had led the Royalists straight here?

From the edge of the Camouflora, Claire could see Cotton sprinting over to them. "We got him!" he yelled. "Lieutenant Ravel has him!"

Him. She looked at Sophie, and could see her own horror reflected in Sophie's face. Could it be . . . *Jasper?*

But as the band of Wraith Watch marched toward them, Claire didn't see the thin, tall frame of Stonehaven's commander. In fact, she didn't see anyone not in uniform until the band stopped, and two of the watch stepped aside to reveal their small captive's shaggy black hair.

"Thank green and greenest!" Nettle Green cried as his bright brown eyes landed on Claire. "I've found you!"

CHAPTER
24

*N*ett!" Claire shrieked joyfully.

She only had a moment to note that his black hair tufted as usual and his brown skin had healthy undertones of pink—a far cry from the boy Claire had seen being dragged out of the swamp after a nasty encounter with razor mud—before the Woven Root command closed in around him again.

Mayor Nadia whirled on Claire. "You know this boy?"

Claire nodded. "Yes! And you might know him, too. He's Nettle Green, and an apprentice of Greenwood."

"Green?" a man from the forming crowd said. "Not Francis Green's grandson?"

"Yes!" Nett's voice piped up from behind the wall of tall commanders. A grin spread across Claire's face. Even under these circumstances, Nett couldn't resist answering a question he knew. She looked around to share the joke with Sophie, but Sophie seemed to have melted into the crowd.

"Elaina, is this true?"

It took Claire a moment to realize that Nadia was talking to her. "Yes," she said hastily as all eyes turned on her. Nett frowned slightly, but to her relief he didn't ask why Claire was suddenly being called Elaina. Claire held her breath as she could practically see another question forming in Nadia's eyes, one much more difficult to answer: How did a Gemmer and a lackie from Stonehaven know a Tiller?

"Sena Steele is his foster sister," Claire said, hoping this would explain away the question. She wished Sophie hadn't disappeared on her. She was *much* better at these kinds of things. "We were actually all traveling together and got separated . . ." Claire trailed off as Nett's face fell, and Claire had the feeling she was teetering on the edge of a cliff. "Nett, where's Sena?"

"That's why I needed to find you," he said slowly. "When she took me to Dampwood to cure me from the razor mud, the Tillers recognized her as one of the girls accused of stealing the Unicorn Harp."

"A Unicorn Harp was stolen?" Mayor Nadia interrupted.

"Yes," Nett mumbled, looking as miserable as a wet wool sweater. "And now Sena's going to pay for it."

"What do you mean?" Claire asked.

Nett's eyes shone overbright, and he let out a deep, shuddery breath. "As we speak, she's waiting for her trial in front of the Grand Council of Arden—in front of *all* the guilds. And if she's found guilty . . . she'll be exiled *from* Arden, not just the Forger Guild—or worse!"

Claire's heart plummeted.

"That's why I needed to find you. You can give testimony to the Grand Council of Arden and help me prove she's innocent! If enough of us say it, they just *have* to believe us!"

"I've heard enough," Mayor Nadia said. Her expression didn't brighten, exactly, but she did seem less likely to pounce. "If you, Nettle Green, seek the safety and protection of Woven Root, you are welcomed here. As for your foster sister . . . I am terribly sorry for your loss."

Nett looked alarmed. "Loss? She's not lost yet. Her trial isn't for another few days. There's still time."

"It is the rule of Woven Root to not meddle in the guilds' affairs. We welcome any who seek us, but we do not seek others."

Claire gaped at Nadia. "But Sena's just a girl!"

"Yes," Nadia said with a nod. "Exactly."

As Nadia and the rest of Woven Root made their way to the feast, Ravel released Nett. Running up to him, Claire hugged him. "Don't worry," she whispered. "We'll help you."

"It's *good* to see you," Nett said, squeezing her back. "You have no idea how long I've been looking for you!"

"And what about me?" Sophie asked, stepping forward.

His eyes widened. "Sophie! I found you! And your hair— it's white!" He considered it, then nodded. "I like it."

Sophie grinned. "Actually, Claire found me a little while ago. And it's Andrea for now—Claire is Elaina. The hair is fine, I guess." She walked over and hugged him tightly.

For a second, Claire felt left out. She'd had her sister all to herself and now she'd be sharing her again. From what she could gather from Nett and Sena's conversations, the three of them had become good friends. It was only later that Sophie had learned that she'd been framed for stealing the Unicorn Harp, when really it had been Sena who had done it. Claire was sure that Sophie would understand when Sena explained why she'd done it: to trade the harp for information on where her mother was.

"What happened? Where did you go?" Nett demanded, breaking through Claire's rush of thoughts. His head swiveled between the sisters so quickly that she thought it might just twist off.

"It's a long story," Claire said just as Sophie replied, "Stonehaven."

Nett's eyebrows shot straight up. "You went to the Gemmer village? And you came back alive?"

"Not all Gemmers are bad," Claire protested.

"But they did imprison us," Sophie pointed out.

Nett frowned thoughtfully. "No wonder the Root Tracker didn't work, then."

Claire had forgotten how Nett had a habit of throwing around words she didn't know. Some might have found it annoying, but she didn't mind. It meant that he didn't think of her as an outsider. The lonely days of Stonehaven faded just a little more.

"What's a Root Tracker?"

"All the trees in Arden are connected," Nett said. He bent down and patted the now still root as if it were a good dog. "You tap into one, you can tap into all of them. But I bet there weren't any trees in that Citadel of theirs, were there?"

Claire hadn't really thought of it, but now as she remembered the cool arches and echoing corridors, she realized that Nett was right. She shook her head.

"Interesting," Nett said with a nod. "So since there were no trees, the roots couldn't find you. I only got a sense of you yesterday morning. More of a *thud* than a sense, really."

"But how?" Sophie cut in, and Claire was surprised to hear an edge in her sister's voice. "If all Tillers can track people using tree roots, then why haven't we been found yet?"

Nett beamed with pride. "Not all Tillers can. It's highly advanced, and you have to have a good sense of the person you're tracking. I've only now gotten the hang of it, actually. I was worried I'd get here and you'd be two complete strangers. But this . . ." He looked at the tents of cloth and leaves that speckled the valley. "This is an alchemists' village, right? Why won't they *help*?"

He turned his face to the line of tents. Any other time, Claire knew he would've dived into the magical wares, asking questions, exclaiming over things he didn't think possible. But now he seemed like an autumn leaf, barely clinging on. She wished she had the magic to make people feel better—*be* better. It seemed more useful than knowing how to craft a Grail that didn't explode or produce a Gemglow brighter than Geode's. How long ago it seemed that had been her only worry!

But she did have something that might make Nett feel better.

"Here," she said, pulling out the spyglass and handing it to him. Nett looked at the object quizzically first, then gasped.

"Is this what I think it is?" he asked, light coming back to his eyes as he examined the jumbled object. "Does it actually work?"

Claire nodded. "I tried it out myself."

"Spectacular," Nett said, and Claire smiled. "Spectacular" was Sophie's favorite word, right after "Experience." "Forgers haven't been able to make a spyglass like this in years—at least, not without an entire museum's worth of unicorn artifacts."

"It's not just Forger magic; Gemmers helped, too," Claire said, remembering the day she'd first learned that glass was a Gemmer specialty as Nett fiddled with the lenses. Grandmaster Carnelian had shown them how molten glass could be blown into useful bowls or cups, and he'd finished off the lesson by using his breath to craft a glass swan that had been able to fly for a few moments before the magic left its wings.

Stonehaven held so many wonders—all of Arden did. It was a shame that the guilds didn't have a chance to see how beautiful the other crafts could be without worrying about inspectors and guild Grand Councils.

Maybe once they had found the unicorn and woken the moontears, things would change. Her heart twinged; she hoped the moontears were still safe. When Nett was done with the spyglass, she would try to peer through to Stonehaven and see what had happened to them. Most likely, Terra still had them safely locked in her desk, but Claire trusted Jasper just as much as she trusted a Stonehaven goat not to nibble on her dress.

A short yelp broke the air . . . and Nett sat hard on the ground.

The sisters looked at each other, eyes wide, before hurrying over to him.

"What's wrong?" Claire asked. "Did you hurt yourself?"

Nett seemed dazed. He shook his head.

"Did you see something?" Sophie asked sharply.

Taking a shaky breath, he nodded. "It's—it's Sena," he said, so slowly that it seemed like each letter must be a knife against his throat. "She . . . they—" He broke off, letting out a strangled cry. Claire waited, chest tight, for the words that came next.

"I saw," he said with a gulp, "they took Sena to the Drowning Fortress. And her trial is *over*. They found her guilty! They've locked her up and sentenced her to . . ." He swallowed. He looked like he was going to throw up. "To death."

For a moment, the only sound Claire could hear was the pounding of her heart in her ears, and her knees slightly swayed. She could barely breathe, let alone offer words of comfort as Nett wailed, "I'm too late!"

"We are *not*."

Claire glanced over at Sophie, who'd spoken. Her brown eyes were determined. Even though Sena had betrayed Sophie's trust, even though Sophie had no magic, she always did the brave thing. She always knew exactly what to say. "We leave tonight."

"But even if we escape," Claire protested, "how would we ever make it to the Drowning Fortress in time?"

"Isn't it obvious?" Sophie asked with a flick of her ponytail. "We steal a chimera."

Silent as the clouds drifting over the moon, Claire, Sophie, and Nett darted from one shadowed space to the next as they hurried again to the chimeras' stables.

Though Claire had done more sneaking in the past month than she had in her entire life, she found it hard to be quiet. For one, in between telling Nett all that had happened, she'd eaten a little too much of the potato pies and candied pears at the welcome feast. It had been since before the crystal flute's test that she'd devoured a full warm meal. And even that breakfast she hadn't enjoyed much because she'd been so angry with Sophie for getting them in trouble.

How long ago that worry now seemed.

How small.

How slight.

"Wait here," Sophie whispered as they crouched behind a hedge just next to the stable. She sidled off into the final few feet of darkness alone, Claire unable to watch.

She tried to focus on breathing as softly as possible, but for some reason, that only made her breath sound louder. Dropping her eyes to the ground, she stared at the little crush of blossoms at the toe of her boot, the white petals a stark contrast to the maroon and umber of autumn leaves. It was a combination she'd like to re-create with her pastels. They were like pearls resting on velvet or snowflakes set in a dark winter sky.

Or.

Like flowers of snow that trailed a unicorn's steps.

Her eyes flew to the hedge as if they already knew what she would see: four luminous strands spun of starlight. And perhaps it was the angle of moonlight, but these seemed even brighter and more beautiful than the ones she'd found before. The unicorn wasn't far.

"Sophie's waving at us," Nett whispered. "Let's go."

Pinching the strands off, Claire hastily wound them around her pencil and tucked them carefully behind her ear before hurrying after Nett.

Sophie waited until they reached her before she opened the door with ease. "Come on," she said, whispering over her shoulder. "Follow me." Then she shimmied into the darkness.

Claire tried, she really did. But her feet wouldn't move. Frowning, she again tried to take a step.

"Sophie—I'm stuck!"

"I am too!" Nett said. Claire looked behind to Nett's feet that had sunk into the ground. But it hadn't rained. There was no mud. Glancing down at her own feet, Claire almost forgot to stay quiet.

Her feet, too, were in the ground, but the earth around them was perfectly solid. It was just as though she'd stepped into an open chain and it had clasped around her, except this time, the earth itself was the manacle.

"Nett, what's happening?"

"I . . . think . . ." Nett huffed and puffed as he strained against the crushing weight of the earth on his feet. "That Sophie . . . set off some sort of . . . trap."

"Close."

If Claire hadn't already been stuck to the earth, she would have frozen. Instead, she could only just keep a yelp from coming out.

Mayor Nadia was behind them, holding a lantern in one hand, Ravel and his whip on one side and Cotton with a lasso at the ready.

"I warned you," Mayor Nadia said, sounding disappointed. "I cannot allow you to risk Woven Root and all we've worked for."

"But don't you see?" Claire said, finding her voice and surprising even herself. "It's not fair—you can't just keep your eyes shut when the world around you is falling apart! You have to *do* something! What kind of a safe place is this if you're ignoring the real problems Arden is facing? This land is falling apart—magic is *dying*, and you're all just celebrating in hiding as if it doesn't matter!"

Ravel took a step toward them, and something broke loose in Claire.

"Sophie!" she screamed. "Sophie—run!"

A split second later, Sophie came bursting out of the stable. And not through the door—through the *roof*.

Sophie soared over them, clinging to her tattered silk cloak. But her cloak was no longer hanging limply down her back. Instead, it billowed above her like a sail.

She looked like an avenging angel.

For a second, Claire half expected to see a chimera beneath her—some sort of flying creature, a metallic eagle perhaps. But all she saw was Sophie and the majestically billowing cloak, as if the cloak itself was what held her aloft . . .

"Don't leave me!" Claire said as the inhabitants of Woven Root watched below in awe.

"Throw your cloaks over your heads and blow!" Sophie yelled back.

Before Nadia or Ravel could stop them, Claire and Nett followed her instructions. A second later, Claire felt a massive tug on her arms as her cloak strained to join Sophie in the night air.

Sophie swooped down lower, and Claire reached up. Their fingers brushed by once, but it was enough. Their hands clasped together. There was a giant sucking sound as Sophie pulled Claire and Nett up from the ground, clumps of dirt clinging to Claire's boots as though they were the roots of an uprooted tree.

"Hang on!" Sophie cried, and she blew more air into the domed cloak above her. "Pull your feet up!"

Claire did as she was told, and from the corner of her eye, she saw Nett do the same—just in time for them to clear the Camouflora wall and float into the starry void of night.

CHAPTER
25

So you're a Spinner?!" Claire yelled across the rush of damp night air. The thought had come to her as the cloak billowed around Sophie in the sky, and now it seemed so obvious. She remembered how even back in Windemere, Sophie had always been the one interested in clothes, and how she'd seemed particularly fascinated with the beautiful, ancient tapestries hanging on Great-Aunt Diana's walls. And how, most of all, she was capable of weaving the most elaborate stories, even if they were part truth and part imagination. "When were you going to tell me?"

The sound of laughter—gleeful, wicked, wild, joyous—came back to her on the wind.

"I *am* a Spinner, aren't I?" Sophie called as she maneuvered a dizzying twist and floated toward Claire. "Here, let's tie the cloak to your rucksack so your arms don't get too tired."

"How is this happening?" Nett called as Sophie's fingers—Spinner fingers—quickly knotted the cloak securely to Claire's rucksack. The fabric billowed above her head like a parachute or—since she wasn't falling—like a mini hot air balloon.

"I'm not really sure!" Sophie said as she did one final tug on Claire's cloak. Nodding, she drifted toward Nett to help him adjust the cloak into a more comfortable position.

"One second, I was in the stable, *terrified* that this was it. That they were going to take you away from me. And then . . ."

"Then what?" Claire asked, adjusting her grip slightly around the shoulder of her rucksack as a new gust of wind buffeted her. It was cold up high, though she wasn't exactly sure how high they were. In a world without electric lights, the land beneath was an endless shadow. She only knew that they were higher than the trees, but lower than the moon.

"Then I heard your voice," Sophie said. "What you said about magic dying out. It was like something in me rose up, angry, like a fire. I didn't want magic to die. And I was just sick of it . . ."

"Sick of what?" Claire asked.

"Sick of being afraid."

Afraid? Claire had never thought of Sophie as afraid of anything.

"But I'm not scared anymore, Clairina!" she said. "I'm not afraid of—of anything! I'm not even afraid to die." Her voice showered over them, sounding magnificent and magical and free. But what did she mean, she wasn't afraid to die? It scared Claire a little. She wasn't going to die. None of them were. They were going to escape and go home, just as soon as they made sure Sena was safe.

Sophie was still talking, clearly ecstatic over her transformation. "You guys, it was like my whole body had become a song!"

"What kind of song?" Nett asked, curious as ever.

"Like . . . like a violin string," Sophie said. "Like a chord that was plucked. And the sound grew louder and louder, drowning out everything, until suddenly, I *knew* what I had to do to make the silk fly. Exactly which thread I needed to pluck so that the fabric would snag on air."

Nett had drifted a little too close; she gave him a slight push and he bounced forward, his legs swinging. Grinning, she turned to face Claire, and Claire could hear the wonder in her sister's voice. "Did you know silk comes from cocoons? The silk—I don't know—*told* me that it comes from moths. It knew that it could have wings."

"Told you?" Claire asked. "Told you how?" But she thought maybe she already knew.

"I've been hearing a soft chord in the background of everything for a while now, but it was never this loud. Never really meant anything to me. All of a sudden, it *did*."

There was another gust of wind, and Claire looked straight down. It was a mistake. Her stomach tilted as she saw her legs dangling freely in the air. Sophie might not be scared of anything anymore, but she was. Quickly, she looked up, out toward the horizon, just in time to see Sophie fling her arms out.

Sophie began to laugh again, a sound as exuberant and free as a rushing river, and just as fierce. "*Look* at us!"

And for a moment, Claire imagined what they must seem like to anyone on the ground glancing up—like three wisps of storm clouds or maybe even bits of dandelion seed buffeted by the wind. She glanced over to see Nett's hair being blown straight back, as if he had a hair dryer beneath his chin. A giggle slipped out and her stomach leveled.

Pumping her legs as though she were on a swing in the park, Claire propelled herself faster along the air currents, putting all her trust in Sophie, as she always had, to carry her.

⌒⌒

The fun of flying quickly faded.

Mostly because it wasn't really flying, it was floating. They had to catch updrafts, and were helpless to the whims of the wind, though Nett did figure out how to shimmy slightly so they could head the right way, toward Lake Drowning. Using Nett's knowledge of navigation (impressive for his age, but not necessarily in-depth) and the spyglass, they were able to coast in the lake's general direction.

As the night wore on, Claire's arms began to ache and she could barely remember a time when she didn't have them clinging above her head. At one point, when they'd all drifted together, they'd taken turns knotting the cloaks to the handles of one another's rucksacks. It was more comfortable, but Claire still hung onto the straps, just in case. Bobbing in and out of clouds wasn't as glamorous as it sounded or even looked—the low clouds they brushed against were cold and damp, soaking their cloaks so that they became heavier.

"There it is!" Nett said through chattering teeth. "Look!"

Claire did.

Silhouetted against a brightening sky were four towers jutting from the center of a large gray lake.

"Why four separate towers?" Claire asked above the rushing wind. "Why not just one fortress?"

"It *is* a single fortress," Nett called. "You'll see when we get closer. During the Guild War, the Forgers ran out of metal and began to take ore from the tiny island in the middle of Lake Drowning. Eventually, they destabilized the island, and the fortress began to sink. Now, three hundred years later, the first floor is completely underwater, but the second and third floors and the towers are accessible by boat. It makes it hard to—to attack . . ." His voice trailed off, and Claire guessed he was thinking about Sena.

It would be difficult enough to find her in the fortress, among the Grand Council of Arden, but then once they got her . . . how would they sneak her away? There were only three silk cloaks, and already the wind had ripped holes into them. Claire didn't think they would fly a second time.

The three children swung their legs harder, propelling and floating themselves as close to Lake Drowning and its fortress as possible, but eventually, even the strongest bursts of wind weren't able to keep them and their waterlogged cloaks aloft.

They dipped lower and lower, until Claire's toes skimmed the tops of evergreens.

"We're going to crash!" Nett yelled, and a second later, Claire felt a throbbing pain as her foot nailed a trunk. She dipped wildly.

"Keep swinging!" Sophie cried. "We're almost to the lake."

Anxiously, Claire blew air into the cloak above her. But it no longer billowed; instead, it looked more like a crumpled sock. There was a hard thump to her back—a helpful shove from Sophie. Claire spurted forward, just clearing the tree line as her tired cloak gave up. Gently she sank to the soft grass edging the lake, Nett and Sophie just a moment behind.

Gasping for breath, Claire took in their surroundings. They were safely hidden from view of the fortress. The rising sun had not yet burned off the hazy mist of Lake Drowning, and through it they could just make out a fleet of rowboats and the shining silver of armored guards. Forgers, Claire guessed. Most likely, the inspectors whose job it was to make sure all was in order along the trading routes of the Rhona River.

"What an Experience," Sophie breathed as she shrugged off her tattered cape. Her eyes were bright, and the wind had snapped pink into her cheeks. She looked like the very definition of healthy, and Claire was once again grateful to the unicorn that had cured her sister. And at the thought of a unicorn, her spirits rose.

Maybe they would rescue Sena, and tell her and Nett to go find Anvil so that she and this happy, healthy Sophie could just go home. But looking at her sister's flushed face—her sister who had just discovered that she, too, had magic—Claire knew there was no way she'd be able to get Sophie home anytime soon.

"How do we get in?" Sophie asked. "Ugh, I wished I hadn't left Fireblood in the stable. Everything happened so quickly!"

Nett shook his head. "Fireblood wouldn't be helpful here," he said. "And only grandmasters are allowed on Arden's Grand Council."

"But they probably don't come just by themselves, right?" Claire asked. She tried to remember Grandmaster Iris of Greenwood Village. There had been a boy who'd fetched her belongings and taken notes. "Wouldn't they have—what do you call them? Scribblers . . . ?"

"Scribes!" Nett said, "that's genius!" Claire flushed as he excitedly continued, "We just need to convince the inspectors that we're scribes for one of the grandmasters and they'll let us in."

"And how do we convince them?" Sophie asked, eyebrow cocked.

"We'll get . . ." Nett trailed off. "Oh," he said, seemingly stumped.

But Claire was already pulling her pencil out from behind her ear and opening her rucksack, looking for the extra pages she'd traded her picture of Mom and Dad for. "I can draw up papers," she said. "I saw a Spinner journeyman's papers once. I can make something similar for us."

Nett tilted his head. "Do you remember exactly what it looked like?"

"Yes," Claire said, but as soon as she said it, she began to doubt herself. "Well, I know it had her name on it and listed her rank . . ."

Sophie stood up and shook pieces of tree bark and sap from her trousers. "Maybe they won't look that closely if we *look* the part." She pointed toward Nett's soft shirt and Claire's tunic. "Our clothes are obviously Spinner-spun," she said. "We just need to style our hair to match what the inspectors will expect from Spinner scribes."

"That should work," Nett said, nodding so eagerly that Claire got the sense he would have said yes to anything—so long as it was a step toward saving Sena. "We need to hurry. We don't know how long she has!"

Sophie had lost her hair ribbon somewhere along the way, and her hair hung in front of her eyes like one of the ponies at the petting zoo. Her hair was slowly turning dark again, except for one stubborn streak of cream. It made her seem younger somehow, more vulnerable. But then Sophie tossed her head, and she was back to being the big sister. "Then what are we just standing around for?"

After that, they moved quickly. Sophie used the remains of the cloak to weave ribbons into Claire's hair and even somehow managed to work a few into one of Nett's tufts. When Nett had seen himself in the lake's reflection, he'd studied himself quietly, then given a sharp nod of approval. "I like it. It looks kind of like I sprouted my own blossom."

As they prepared, they occasionally peered behind the rock to keep an eye on the fleet of rowboats. Some of them had started to cross, and Claire hoped that meant that it was usual for grandmasters and their scribes to arrive late.

Finally, Nett declared that they looked enough like proper Spinners. "I *am* a proper Spinner," Sophie said, a delighted smile spreading across her face. But before they stepped behind the rock, a sudden fear snagged Claire. She reached out for Sophie.

"Is it safe?" Immediately, Claire felt foolish, but to her surprise, Sophie didn't laugh.

Instead, she leaned over and adjusted a bow in Claire's hair. "What *is* safe, anymore?" Sophie said quietly. "Starscrape Mountain, this place, home . . . Anything can happen at any time, Clairina."

And with that, she stepped out from behind the rock. Nett looked impressed and quickly followed.

Sophie glanced back, catching Claire's eye. *Ready?*

Claire gulped and nodded.

Ready.

CHAPTER
26

They approached the dock just as one of the rowboats broke away from the fleet and slipped into the mist. After a second, it disappeared the same way that sparks break away from a bonfire and disintegrate into the air. But the moment before the boat disappeared, Claire caught a glimpse of its passengers. They seemed familiar. One was oddly tall and spindly while the other appeared to be an older woman with white-blond hair . . . just like Mira Fray.

And beside her was . . .

Claire's heart stopped.

Commander Jasper.

Were they both part of the Grand Council?

Her heart jumped into action again, beating harder and faster. They may have avoided the Royalists on Starscrape, but by coming here, to Drowning Fortress, they had more or less walked directly into their arms.

"We need to go back," Claire hissed. "We need to plan!"

"Shh," Sophie whispered. "The inspectors!"

Two men stood in front of them, clearly Forgers by the long broadswords dangling at their hips and battle hammers across their backs. They seemed even more armed than the ones she'd glimpsed on the Rhona River, and she couldn't help but think a gathering of guilds in one place was like lighting a match around dried wood and expecting it not to burn.

"Papers?" the tallest inspector asked.

"Good afternoon!" Sophie said brightly. "We were wondering if we could borrow a rowboat—"

"Papers," the inspector said again, and held out an armored hand.

"Of—of course," Sophie said, her smile slipping slightly. "I'd love to, but we lost our papers recently. I can assure you, though, that we have permission to be here."

The inspector's eyes narrowed. "No papers, no entry."

His partner, a large woman with bulging biceps, looked them up and down coldly. "And without papers of any sort," she said, "we'll need to take you into custody. Hold out your hands."

Claire shuffled back, instinctively clutching her hands behind her back. Nett managed to keep his hands by his sides, though his fists clutched the extra fabric of his tunic.

"Stay back," Sophie said, so forcefully that Claire blinked.

She seemed to have surprised the inspectors, too. While they didn't step back, the woman hesitated.

"Clearly, we're Spinners," Sophie said, and Claire noticed that she kept her eyes wide. Claire thought that she was trying to look innocent, but the widened eyes only made her look more suspicious, as if she were looking for an escape.

"Maybe," the inspector said. "You're certainly dressed as such, but those other two are awfully quiet. I've never met such silent Spinners before."

"We're scribes," Nett squeaked out, "for . . . for Historian Mira Fray!"

The man snorted. "You're late. Historian Fray just took a rowboat, and she didn't mention anything about waiting on lost apprentices."

So. Claire had been right. Those had been the figures of Fray and Jasper slipping away into the fortress.

"What's in your packs?" the inspector asked. "Open them!"

Claire had the sudden sense of when you're on a sled, just starting to slide, and you realize the hill is steeper than you thought. But the only way out of the situation is to get to the bottom. And the only way to get away from the inspectors now was to complete the investigation. Slowly, Claire began to shrug off her rucksack.

"Stop," Sophie said sharply, and Claire froze as Sophie swung to face the inspectors. "This is highly unusual. How dare you not believe us?!"

The first inspector crossed his large arms. "I've had enough," he growled. "Hands together." There was a jangle as the inspector pulled a pair of handcuffs from his belt.

"No," Claire said. "Really! We're with . . . we're with Water Bobbin Fleet!" she said, frantically trying to remember anything about Spinners she could say to convince this Forger inspector otherwise. "You have to—"

"Let her go," a new voice said behind them. A familiar voice.

Sophie whipped around, and Claire heard her gasp of delight, "*Thorn!*"

Blood welled on Claire's lip as she bit down hard to stop from crying out. Hardly believing her ears, she turned to see a tall boy with blond hair and ears slightly too big for his head stride toward them. Thorn Barley, a member of Greenwood Village, Claire's friend, and judging by the deep red flush that unfurled across Sophie's cheeks, her older sister's crush.

Thorn looked different from the time Claire had last seen him—travel-worn and wearing a Fyrton cloak as he led her, Nett, and Sena to the entrance of the old Forger mines. *This* Thorn seemed older. Taller. With a start, Claire realized that he was standing with his shoulders thrown back. She hadn't realized that he used to slump.

"They're with me," he said now, confidence ringing in his voice.

"And who are you?" The inspector squinted.

Thorn set down a leather pack, and from the front pocket, he pulled out a small bundle of documents.

As the inspectors thumbed through them, Claire held her breath to stop herself from exploding with questions.

How had Thorn found them?

How did he come by these papers?

What had happened in the last month that gave him the courage to talk to the inspectors like that? Claire couldn't imagine the boy she'd met in Greenwood Village speaking so fearlessly.

You're not being fair, a tiny voice inside told her. *The Thorn who snuck to Fyrton and led you to the mines was definitely brave.*

Pushing the thought away, Claire looked at Sophie. But Sophie wasn't looking at her. Instead, she was beaming at Thorn, her eyes sparkling. He beamed back at her.

Oh brother.

Her sister was seriously embarrassing. Claire caught Nett's eye and he pulled a face. Despite the serious situation they were in, she couldn't stop a tiny grin.

"These seem to be in good order," the inspector said, sounding slightly disappointed as he handed them back. "You can take that one," he said, gesturing to the nearest rowboat.

"Thank you," Thorn said, and threw his pack in. The others hurried forward.

"Don't say anything yet," Thorn murmured, nodding his head toward the inspectors who still lingered nearby. "I'll explain later, I promise. Just get in the boat."

Quickly, Nett, Sophie, and Claire clambered in. Nett sat next to Claire, while Sophie sat next to Thorn, who picked up the oars. With a push from the inspectors, they floated out onto the lake.

Sophie managed to keep quiet until they were just out of hearing range from the shore.

"Thorn!" she practically squealed, and Claire stared at her older sister curiously, never having heard her talk in quite that tone before. "That was incredible! How did you get those fake papers?"

"Fake papers?" Thorn said, puzzled. "They're not fake."

Nett frowned. "But how did you get them, then? Grandmaster Iris is on trial, too, and I can't imagine she'd invite you to be her scribe even if she wasn't. No offense," he added quickly as Sophie glared at him. "It's just, you know . . . you're not *really* a Tiller." Everyone knew Thorn was a lackie and pitied him because of it. That's why he was so shy. Or used to be, anyway.

"I'll tell you," Thorn said as he pulled them through the silver water toward the looming towers. "But we just need to get somewhere private first." He nodded over Claire's shoulder, and she turned to see a boat with what looked like a Tiller grandmaster suddenly appear from the mist and slide silently by them.

"And there's the rest of the Drowning Fortress," Nett whispered. "By all that's green, it's beautiful!"

That's not exactly the word Claire would have chosen.

The sinking fortress was made of a dark gray rock she didn't recognize. There were no doors, as they had disappeared under the lake, but there were many massive round windows on the lowest level. Their glass, however, seemed to have been broken long ago, and now all the rowers aimed themselves toward one particular round window, gently guiding their rowboats inside.

"Here we go," Thorn cautioned as they quickly glided through.

Claire gasped in awe. She knew of cities where canals replaced roads, but Drowning Fortress was a castle with water-ways instead of halls. The roof had long since crumbled, leaving only arched rafters above them. It made Claire think of a giant rib cage—as if they'd been swallowed by a whale. Looking away, she peered over the side of the boat.

The lake's water was crystal clear, and she could see down below to what once must have been an open courtyard filled with gardens. She could make out the wavy shape of statues as well as a birdbath or two. The statues reminded her a bit of the sad mermaid stories, the ones that came in the grownup-looking fairy book that Sophie had insisted Dad read to them from.

"Claire," Nett said softly. "Look."

Leaning toward the surface, Claire caught the glimmer of scales, and peered closer, expecting to see a fish but—a gasp caught in her throat. The glimmer had been scales, but they weren't fish scales. They were wyvern scales.

The two-legged, dragon-like creatures lay at the bottom of the lake. Made by Gemmers who had gifted them with stone hearts, they were too heavy to swim.

But it wasn't only wyverns she could see through the

crystal-clear water. There was also the soft green of copper exposed to the elements—chimera, too, had drowned here.

"I think it's the remains of the Battle of Lake Drowning," Nett said quietly.

"Why haven't they cleaned it up?" Claire asked.

"To remind everyone of why the treaty was signed," Nett said. "The Drowning Fortress is the only place the Grand Council will meet—even though it continues to sink. Because it's in the water, it doesn't really belong to any of the guilds, and it's the most neutral spot in Arden for all four guilds to meet."

He stretched out a finger to the rafters, where Claire saw a massive chandelier made with four materials: stone, metal, plant, and thread. "Each guild has stories about Lake Drowning, stories that could make the case that this should belong to one guild or the other. And so here, when Queen Estelle disappeared, was where it was decided the treaty to end the war would be signed."

Just then a shout rang out, as a Tiller rowboat filled with thorn bushes accidently bumped into a rowboat outfitted with a sail—Spinners most likely. The Spinners in the boat glared at the trespasser and one angrily cracked a whip. No matter how neutral Nett claimed this fortress to be, it felt as neutral as a cat in a dog kennel.

"Where are they all going?" Claire asked.

"The council room," Thorn murmured. "There've been rumors of a rogue Gemmer who has been turning the minerals in blood into stone."

A slippery worry oozed over Claire, made her feel cold and clammy. "Who?"

Thorn shrugged. "As far as I know, two Spinners and a Tiller so far."

Claire exchanged a look with Sophie. It didn't seem anyone else knew about Anvil and Aquila's rubification. And the only Gemmer that she knew had left Stonehaven recently was Jasper . . . was this part of Fray and the Royalists' plan to seed confusion across the land? Glancing anxiously up at the sky, she wished that she knew how to read time by the shadows. She had no idea how many hours had trickled by.

But Thorn turned them away from the staircase, and down a narrow hallway, empty of boats.

"Where are *we* going?" Claire asked. "We need to—"

"Shh," Thorn said. "Don't say anything yet! There are ears all around."

Nodding mutely, Claire sat back. But she was . . . uncomfortable. Something inside her wouldn't settle at his words and instead, kept nudging her. It was weird how the inspectors had done exactly as Thorn said. And shouldn't he be worried about Sena?

There was a slight bump as Thorn drew them up to the bottom of a small staircase.

"Follow me," he said. He held out a hand to Sophie, and Claire watched as her sister placed her hand in his, and allowed him to help her onto the steps. Thorn held on to her sister's hand a little longer than Claire thought was necessary.

Quickly, she scrambled out and was surprised by how slick

the stone steps were. She gripped the guardrail as Thorn led them up the spiraling staircase.

"Are we headed up one of the towers?" Nett asked suddenly.

Thorn nodded. "Yes, to . . . here we go!" They'd arrived in front of a small door and Thorn pushed it open and beckoned them in.

Claire couldn't tell, exactly, how big the room was because it was crowded with fabrics. It could have either been a large room filled with too much cloth . . . or a little room filled with too much cloth.

Nett froze as Thorn locked the door. "You can tell us now what's going on," he said, and Claire was surprised to hear his voice so sharp. Nett liked everybody, always. "This is a Spinner room. How did you get access to it? Why aren't we in the dungeons rescuing Sena *right* now?"

"It's all right," Thorn said, smiling widely. "I promise you, Mira has a plan."

Claire's heart stopped. It didn't just stop—it ceased to exist. Her whole body felt as if it had been hollowed out, scraped empty like a jack-o'-lantern.

"What—what did you say?" she stammered out. "*Who* has a plan?"

"Mira Fray," Thorn said, seeming oblivious to the swirling terror that was starting to spin inside Claire, filling the empty space where her organs had once been. "She was a good friend of my Grand. You've heard of her, Nett. She's a famous historian—the historian's boat we snuck you onto, actually. Sophie and I used to visit her together and she'd tell us stories about unicorns. Isn't that right, Sophie?"

He looked at Sophie, smiling, but when he saw her expression, his smile dropped off. Claire couldn't blame him. The look on Sophie's face could only be described as a snarl.

"What did you do, Thorn?" Sophie said, and her tone was one of such anguish that Claire was momentarily reminded of wraith-burn. Of sorrow that suffocated and dragged.

"Nothing!" Thorn said defensively. "I mean, I did something, but it's a good thing!"

He reached out for the hem of Sophie's tattered cloak, and pulled at a frayed edge. Quickly, he knotted the loose threads to another one. Claire blinked. The hole that had been in the cloak was suddenly gone, completely repaired as if the tear had never been there at all.

"Did you just—Thorn, did you just . . . was that magic?" Nett asked, his voice shrill.

Thorn smiled triumphantly. "Yes it is. She gave it back to me."

"*Who* gave magic back to you?" Claire asked.

"That's what I've been trying to tell you." He looked at Sophie, whose mouth gaped open. "I did it, Sophie! I woke the queen."

CHAPTER
27

$\mathcal{S}$ilence crept into the room like a chill.

Sophie and Nett stared at Thorn, wearing twin expressions of befuddlement. Claire understood their looks of confusion because she felt exactly the same way. Queen Rock could only be woken with d'Astora Gemmer blood. The same kind of blood that had sealed Queen Estelle into the rock in the first place.

Claire's blood.

She would never wake the queen. And besides . . .

"Stonehaven says the Forgers destroyed Queen Rock," Claire pointed out.

"Is that what people are saying?" A strange expression skulked onto Thorn's face. "You should know better than to believe whatever you hear."

"But it makes more sense than what we're hearing from *you*," Sophie said, sounding more exasperated than perplexed. "Claire is the only one who could wake her, and she didn't!"

Thorn lifted his chin. "I said *I* woke the queen. It took me a little while to figure it out, but once Nett said that you," he nodded at Sophie, "climbed out of a well, I pieced it together. 'A place where fire meets water' and all that. The old wishing well that you said was actually a chimney where you came from. I figured out you two must be the lost Prince Martin's descendants, and I knew then that I needed your blood to wake the queen."

"But how did you get my blood?" Claire asked in shock.

He shrugged. "I wasn't sure, but when you tripped and split open your knee, it became a lot easier than I had thought."

"The handkerchief...," she said slowly, remembering how he had helped to dab her wounded knee for her.

Tugging on a silk cord, Thorn lit a chandelier above him. "And now the unicorns will return, the wraiths will be defeated, and magic will flourish again. It already has!"

"You don't understand," Claire croaked. Thorn's words seemed to wrap tight around her chest, suffocating her.

Thorn frowned. "What's there to understand?"

"Queen Estelle wasn't a hero," Sophie said, arms crossed. "She's not going to bring back the unicorns—she killed them all in the first place!"

But instead of looking aghast, Thorn laughed.

"Are you laughing at me?" Sophie shot back, looking so fierce that Thorn immediately stopped.

"No, no, I'm not," he rushed to assure her. "But it's funny, because I've met her. She's on her way now."

"Impossible," Nett said, while at the same time Sophie made a rude noise. "You probably only met someone pretending to be her."

"Then how would you explain this?" Thorn asked. He pulled something tiny and silver from the hem of his tunic and plunged it into his cloak. A needle, Claire realized as he began to stitch. The many shawls and scarves rustled around them as they watched. Then they began to flap, as though in a great wind.

Claire looked around. The door was still closed, and the only window was partially opened and high up. So where was the draft coming from?

"It's like I said," Thorn said as he continued to stitch. "With the queen back, wraiths will be under control . . ." He tied up his cloak and it billowed and swelled like a balloon. Or like the cloak was calling the wind to it and *trapping* it. Like a sail.

". . . the unicorns shall return . . ."

Claire stumbled forward. For a moment, she thought someone had accidentally nudged her, but then she realized a sudden gust had knocked against her. Her beribboned hair was now in her face, and Sophie's white-streaked ponytail whipped around.

"Thorn, stop it!" Sophie yelled over the howling wind. And suddenly, all was still. Claire's hair fell to her shoulders and Nett patted down his tunic. The only thing that moved was Thorn's cloak-bag, which lurched and bulged as if it contained a thousand balloons.

"And," Thorn finished, "true magic, *great* magic shall return."

With that, he opened the bag—and a punch of wind burst out.

The wind whirled in an upward spiral, twisting scarves and hair as the wind rushed toward the lone window like a living creature. There was a giant *BOOM* and the wind released itself out the window in a shower of broken glass.

Claire's mouth dropped open, and Sophie stared at Thorn. There could be no doubt.

Thorn had magic. He was a Spinner.

Queen Estelle d'Astora had returned.

Thorn looked at the girls—well, Sophie mostly, and gave a cocky little bow. It was so unlike Thorn—Thorn, the humble boy who'd shyly asked Claire to give a gift to her sister for him—that Claire wondered for a moment if she'd simply forgotten what Thorn looked like and this was a stranger in his place instead.

"Oh, Thorn," Sophie sighed, shaking her head sadly. "I don't think anyone gave you magic. I think you always had it."

Thorn's eyes narrowed. "What do you mean?"

Sophie looked around the room—at Nett, who was quickly slipping his hand into his rucksack, at Claire who was carefully pulling her pencil out from behind her ear. Sophie appeared calm, but Claire could tell by the way she bit her bottom lip, she was all attention. All anticipation.

"I think that you were always a Spinner," Sophie said. "You never needed the queen to give your magic back to you because you always had it."

A baffled snort filled the space. "I've never been able to do magic," Thorn said. "I couldn't even light a fire without needing a flint." He looked at Nett. "*You* know. You've known me practically my entire life. Have I ever had magic before?"

Nett shook his head, but Sophie let out a frustrated breath of air. "Let me show you."

She reached into her pocket and pulled out a figurine of a bird. It looked so real that Claire half expected it to take off. But she knew it wouldn't—it was just a statuette Thorn had made from straw.

Claire looked at Sophie, trying to figure out what she'd say next.

Sophie pushed the bird into Thorn's hand. "What do you see?" she asked.

"My bird," Thorn said, smiling faintly. "You carry it with you?"

"Not the point," Sophie huffed, the tips of her ears turning pink. "How did you make it?"

"I wove pieces of straw together."

Sophie's idea popped into Claire's head as clear as a bell.

Woven from river reeds. Maybe Thorn's bird didn't look so lifelike because he was a bad Tiller. Maybe it looked lifelike because he was good at *weaving* . . . because he was a Spinner.

"I think," Sophie said quietly as Thorn stared at the little bird in his hand, face expressionless. "I think that maybe guild magic hasn't weakened because the unicorns are gone. Is it possible that maybe—just maybe—it only seems that some people are born without magic because they don't have a chance to try a different craft? Because the guilds are kept so separate?"

Sophie glanced at Nett, who looked as if lightning had struck him. "I—I don't think I've read that theory anywhere," Nett stammered out. "I never thought—but maybe?" He fell silent, but Claire could practically see his thoughts darting around, slipping one over another to be heard.

"I'm not so sure about your theory," Thorn finally said. "But either way, you need to meet with Fray." He looked at Claire and added, "She's been wanting to talk with you."

"No!" Claire cried. Pressure built behind her eyes. "Fray doesn't want to talk to me. She wants to *kill* me! So they can win their needless war!"

"Wait." Thorn's eyes darted between Claire and Sophie. "War?"

"Yes, war!" Sophie exclaimed. "I bet it was the Royalists who started the rumor that Forgers destroyed Queen Rock. They're trying to divide the guilds even more than they are now so that they can . . . can . . ." She trailed off, looking angry—not at Thorn, but at herself for not having an answer. "So they can do something," she finished.

"So they can make it easier for the queen to rise," Nett said softly. His lower lip trembled. "It's a tactic written in *The Craft of War* by Admiral Belli Cose." He looked Thorn in the eye.

"That's what the Royalists want, right? To see the queen back on the throne?"

"Of course," Thorn said, spreading his hands out. "But why is that bad? Queen Estelle is a hero. Everyone says so—the legends wanted it! Even Francis believes it!"

Nett frowned. "Grandfather isn't a Royalist."

"You don't know everything, Nettle Green," Thorn snorted.

But something Thorn had said gnawed at Claire.

There was something missing to his story. "If you woke the queen the way you say you did," she addressed Thorn, "you would have needed a unicorn artifact. The harp wasn't the only thing that went missing around that time."

"The Unicorn Tooth," Nett gasped.

Claire nodded. "Right. The tooth was stolen from the Forger academy *before* Thorn joined us."

"So?" Thorn said, but his eyes widened. Claire knew she had him.

"So," she said, "that means you knew I could wake Queen Rock . . . but then you sent us into the abandoned mines. It wasn't a shortcut at all, was it?" She shook her head as the pattern snapped into place. "You sent us away so that you could get to the Sorrowful Plains first. But you didn't, because you weren't expecting a wyvern to help us."

"Thorn!" Sophie gasped, and Nett shook his head in disbelief at the boy who they had all thought was their friend.

Two notes of a trumpet sounded from somewhere deep in the castle.

Nett swayed slightly. "What if that's the call for execution? What if we're already too late—" He broke off and hurried to the door, his rucksack thumping loudly against his back. But before he could reach the door, there was a loud *crack*.

Nett sprawled onto the floor.

"Are you all right?" Claire asked, surprised. Nett usually wasn't clumsy, but a second later she saw why he'd fallen: wrapped around his ankle was the thin end of a whip, its handle clutched in Thorn's fist. Thorn gave a slight tug to the whip, and the first foot or so of cord broke off on its own, binding Nett's ankles together.

"Hey!" Nett said. "That hurts!"

"I'm sorry," Thorn said, looking slightly horrified by what he'd done, but still, he didn't drop the handle. "I can't let you leave without telling Mira."

He cracked the whip in Claire's direction. She yelped as she felt the cord rush by her, coiling into a mini-tornado above her head before dropping down.

But before the cord could settle around her, there was another deafening crack, and suddenly, the whip was wrapping itself around Thorn—its handle clutched tightly in Sophie's hand.

"I tried to tell you," Sophie said as the cord coiled around Thorn, binding him tight to the spot. "Queen Estelle doesn't give out magic. You've always had it. *I've* always had it. We just needed to be given a chance to try our options."

Claire watched as her sister bent down and quickly undid

the knot tying Nett's ankles together. A second later, the Tiller boy was on his feet, staring down in horror at Thorn.

The whip had wrapped carefully around Thorn, binding him mummy-like from his feet and ending right below his nose—allowing him to breathe, but not giving him a chance to yell for help. His blue eyes stayed fixed on Sophie.

Sophie met his gaze. "I'm sorry," she whispered. "But I can't let you put Claire in danger."

The trumpet sounded again.

"Hurry," Nett hissed, his hand already on the doorknob. Sophie nodded and walked to the door. Claire glanced once more at Thorn, then rushed to meet them. As she shut the door, she thought she heard a muffled sound that could have either been "Sophie" or "Sorry."

Or maybe, she hadn't heard it at all and only imagined it. Either way, they couldn't risk a known liar giving them away to Fray or Jasper—not when their enemies were so close. Not when she'd heard for herself what they wanted:

Her death will be the key to our victory.

CHAPTER
28

They ran down the winding stairs of the tower, back to where they'd tied up the rowboat, and jumped in. Sophie picked up an oar, but when Claire gently nudged her, Sophie scooted to the middle, letting Claire take her place instead. As she took the oar, Claire's heart ached for her sister. She didn't know what to say. Claire had never had a boyfriend—well, except for the neighbor boy when she was three but that didn't count—but she could guess that whatever Sophie was going through was not fun.

"The spyglass," Claire said, searching for a distraction. She nudged Sophie's Hollow Pack with her toe. "Use it to locate Sena."

Giving a short nod, Sophie dug into her pack and pulled out the little spyglass. Holding it to her eye, she began to sweep the walls.

"I don't see her," Sophie whispered. "I can't find cells, anywhere. I only see the—" She stopped short and looked at Nett. "I'll try again," she mumbled.

Nett stared straight ahead, pretending not to understand, but Nett was smart, and Claire knew that he had put it together, just as she had: Sophie must have spotted the execution platform.

"Dungeons don't usually have windows," Claire said. "Try looking into the shadows."

"I don't—" Sophie began, then gasped. "I found her!" She pulled the spyglass away from her eye and pointed. "That way."

Slowly, Claire and Nett dragged them through the water-filled passageways, as Sophie pulled her knees to her chest, watching to make sure they didn't bump into the walls or another boat. Claire's arms began to ache but she didn't mind. All that mattered was that they get to Sena and smuggle her out of here.

There was a loud *skritch* as the bottom of her oar hit something, and she realized it was the sunken floor—they were in shallower water now. The passageway they'd been floating down continued to get narrower and narrower, but from here, they could not see where it ended. The walls had changed, too. They were no longer the color of slate like the rest of the Drowning Fortress, but a velvety black.

"She's this way," Sophie said, and Claire heard the confidence in her voice.

"All right, then," Nett said. "We'll . . . have to get out and wade the rest of the way. Wait!" he said as Sophie threw one leg over. "If you have any food in your pack, I'd leave it on the boat—just in case."

Claire suddenly had a very bad feeling. "In case of what?"

"Ah," Nett said, looking sorry he'd said anything at all. "There are stories—rumors, really—of a lake monster that some Tillers may have accidentally crafted."

Sophie blinked. "Come again?"

Nett shrugged. "I don't think it *really* exists. But there were rumors a few years ago that a young Tiller journeyman accidentally grew a water plant that drifts around the lake like an animal. It's called a Gelatinous Fish."

"So, a jellyfish?" Claire asked.

"No, *Gelly* fish . . . but it's really not a fish at all, just a cross between white snakeroot and a jungle trapper. You know, the plant that eats small bugs."

"Oh good," Sophie said, sounding relieved. "So it only eats insects."

"I didn't say that."

Sophie stared hard at him. "Right, then. I'm sure it can't be here where the water is so shallow."

Still, it was with an uncomfortable splash that they clambered out of the boat and into the water-clogged passageway. Claire pulled her beribboned hair up into a bun, carefully removing the pencil to slip it into her tunic's Lock-it Pocket— just in case. They waded slowly. The roof had been fixed here, and there was no sunlight to illuminate the lake's waters. It was all murk and gloom, except for a few sleepy sparkles in the black rock walls.

You can know a stone's intentions by how it feels, *how it* shines, *and what it* says, Scholar Pumus's squeaky voice sounded in Claire's mind as her first lesson in Identification came back to her. Reaching out a hand, she brushed one sparkle with her fingertips.

It was hard, but softer compared to most stone, and in its reflective depths, she could make out layers of color, like bits of broken rainbows. She wanted to sink into the colors, allow them to swirl around her as she sank into the rock—wait, what?

Claire yanked her hand away, as quickly as if she had been burned. No, she was not falling for *that* again. Opals—and not just any opals. Mesmerizing Opals, expertly Gemmer-crafted. Even now, she could feel their glow calling to her thoughts.

In fact, *all* the glittery spots were opals, trapping light . . . and she knew how easily they could trap the mind, too.

"How much farther?" Claire whispered.

Sophie held the spyglass to her eye. "A few more steps."

"Does she look all right?" Nett asked anxiously.

"As well as can be expected," Sophie said, squinting into the spyglass.

The passageway began to go up now, the water slowly shrinking back until finally Claire could see the slippery flagstones beneath her feet. Her wet shoes sloshed and squished loudly.

Pain flared in Claire's ankle. She screamed.

"Claire, what—Sophie!" Nett yelled as blood began to billow around Claire's ankle. The Gelly! It's got her!"

Claire yelped again as a second nip got her ankle. She kicked out, trying to shake whatever was on her foot, but it was too heavy. And with her own blood darkening the waters she couldn't see where the Gelly was, or even what it looked like.

Suddenly, she felt what seemed to be rubbery tentacles, or lake weed, wrapping around her ankle, pulling her back into the deeper waters.

"Grab her!" Nett shouted, and both he and Sophie grabbed Claire by the arms trying to pull her out of the plant's grasp. "Harder!"

"Hang on, Claire!" Sophie yelled. "Don't let go."

At least, that's what Claire thought her sister was saying. It was too hard to know exactly. The pain intensified. Black dots swarmed the edges of her vision. The passageway darkened. She needed . . .

"Light!" Claire wheezed out. "The marimo!"

It stayed dark—could they hear her above the splashing? Had she even spoken, or had the pain silenced her?

A burst of white light shot through the entire passage, Nett's marimo glowing as brightly as a miniature sun. And as its light spilled over the glittering passageway, the opals exploded into color.

"Close your eyes!" Claire gasped out. "Don't let the light die!"

She knew that if any of them looked at the Mesmerizing Opals while the light shone off them, they would become entranced by the stone and would be no better than puppets, their minds numb and unable to think for themselves.

Squinting through her lashes, she saw a bit of gleam in the murky, bloody water. The pain was becoming unbearable now—she had to act quickly. Letting go of one of Sophie's hands, she plunged her fist into the roiling water. Nothing . . . nothing . . . there! Her fingers closed around a loose opal.

"The marimo isn't going to last!" Nett shouted, his eyes squeezed shut. "If you have a plan, do it now!"

Claire yanked the opal out. If she could get the angle of the stone right, she'd be able to sway the fish, catching its eyes and its thoughts.

The Gelly squeezed.

Claire screamed. Searing pain shot up her leg. She was going to pass out! Her hand dropped. She had been foolish to think that—

Suddenly, the tentacle's grip on her ankle slackened slightly. Looking down, Claire realized that she'd finally gotten the opal in position: she'd made contact with whatever constituted the Gelly fish's eyes.

And now it was weakening, its mind becoming too distracted to focus on the big meal in front of it.

Taking advantage, Claire kicked out at the creature. A second later, she fell forward onto Nett and Sophie as the Gelly suddenly released her ankle. Splashing, she twisted to look back at the passageway.

Squinting, she saw that the water had stilled, only a few ripples spreading across the surface. Claire still held the opal. She moved her hand to the right, and the ripples seemed to follow it. It was as though even the water was willing to do whatever the opal wanted.

Careful not to stare at the opals' hidden rainbows, which she knew would hypnotize her just as much as it had hypnotized the Gelly fish, she pulled her arm back, and threw. The stone arced over the watery passageway, still trailing rainbows in the marimo's light, before sinking into the water. There was a flurry of ripples, and then the water was still.

The Gelly was gone. And as the marimo's light winked out, the opals' whispering rainbows did, too.

"Away from the water," Nett croaked out, and Claire ran the last few steps to dry land before collapsing onto the ground, not caring that it was damp, not caring that her wound still bled freely—she was just grateful to even be alive.

"That's what you call a rescue?" A familiar voice called out a little farther down the hall. "I think I would have been better off on my own. At least it would have been quieter."

Though her feet still throbbed and her heart pounded twice as fast as normal, Claire felt a delighted grin stretch across her face.

"Hi," Sena Steele called as she poked her head out of a cell where she'd clearly watched the whole scene. "What took you so long?"

"SENA!" Nett yelped and ran down the rest of the passageway to his foster sister. Claire made to follow.

"Ouch!" She had to stop. Her feet still hurt.

"Wait a second," Sophie said. "Let's see what the Gelly did." Claire sat on the slimy floor while Sophie took a look at her foot. There were two little punctures at the back of her ankle where something—teeth, Claire supposed—had sunk into her skin. Though the wounds were deep, they weren't bleeding as much as it had appeared when she was in the water. Even so, Claire could barely look at the injury without the black spots blurring her vision.

"We need to clean these up," Sophie said. Her fingers lightly prodded the sensitive skin around one of the wounds. "Hang on." She rummaged through her Hollow Pack.

"You're not going to stitch me up," Claire protested. "I don't care if you are a Spinner."

"I gathered some first aid things in Woven Root," Sophie said, and pulled out a white square of cloth. "The seller who sold it to me said it'd get rid of any infection."

"No stitches," Claire repeated through gritted teeth. Ignoring her, Sophie quickly placed the cloth on the wound, then counted to three before whipping it away. She gasped.

"What's wrong?" Claire asked, still not wanting to look.

"The cuts—they're gone!"

"Really?" Claire looked down and saw that Sophie was right. The bite marks were totally gone, replaced by smooth, pale skin that was only slightly pinker than the rest.

"That's some magic," Sophie said, holding up the cloth. "I'm impressed." She offered Claire a hand, and Claire scrambled to her feet. Not only did her ankle no longer hurt, but the exhaustion from their travels seemed to have lifted somewhat.

They hurried down the passageway just in time to hear Nett quickly wrapping up a summary of what had happened since they'd been separated from Sena—Claire had never heard him talk quite so fast.

". . . the-queen-is-actually-evil-and-Thorn-is-a-Spinner-and-by-the-way-he-says-that-he's-woken-the-queen-from-the-stone-and-Sophie-and-Claire-are-kind-of-princesses."

"Huh," Sena said, looking at Claire and Sophie with a critical eye. "Not exactly what I'd imagined."

"It's good to see you, too," Claire said, grinning.

The redhead flashed her sharp smile, but then the smile hesitated, Sena's confidence flagging slightly as she saw who was behind Claire.

"Hi Sophie . . ." Sena trailed off, and Claire knew she must not have known what to say to the girl whom she'd set up to be the thief of the Unicorn Harp.

"Say, 'I'm sorry,'" Nett instructed in a stage whisper.

Sena's yellow gaze dropped to the ground, and she mumbled, "Sorry."

Sophie stood a moment, and Claire wondered if this was going to be one of those times Sophie would refuse an apology and hold a grudge.

"I think," Sophie said, her eyes sweeping the dank cell, "that you've had a fair enough punishment. But I have something else to say."

Sena cringed. "What?"

"Thank you," Sophie said. "From what Claire's told me, without you, she probably would have ended up as wraith bait."

"Maybe not wraith bait," Sena said, nodding seriously, "but definitely Forger rust."

"All right, all right," Claire interrupted, ready for this conversation to be over. "We need to get you out of here."

"Yes," Nett agreed. "The Grand Council might come down at any moment."

"You're wrong," a voice called out from down the passageway. Claire froze as she saw the flicking orange of a torch make its way toward them. "We're already here."

The torch lifted closer to the bearer's face to reveal the thin features of Mira Fray.

CHAPTER
29

$\int$ophie launched herself in front of Claire. "You can't have her!" she shouted. "Claire's death isn't the key to anyone's victory!"

"No," Fray sighed as she came to a stop in front of them. "She most certainly is not." The Spinner wore a navy gown, trimmed with hundreds of swinging blue tassels. But the threads didn't swing with her motion. Some swung forward while others swung back or to the side, as if each thread had a mind of its own. And maybe they did.

"But," Claire said, taking a step back, "why do you want me, then?"

"We don't," Fray said, a shake of her head sending her many long, white braids dancing. "You're much more useful to us alive."

"But we heard you say it!" Sophie exclaimed. "We heard you telling Jasper that her death would be the key to your victory." But even as the words left Sophie's mouth, Claire realized that wasn't quite right. What Fray had said was that *the girl's* death would be key. They'd never heard a name.

Claire felt a push as Sophie nudged her away from the bars.

"Stay away from Claire," Sophie said shakily. "She's no use to anyone. She's not even a real princess—she's just a sister!"

Mira's eyebrows shot up. "Somehow, I don't believe that. And neither do you, I think. But no, Claire's death is not key, either. Though if you keep squawking, it will come much sooner than you think."

"But then—" Sophie pressed, but Nett let out a yelp.

"NO," Nett cried, flinging his arms wide as if he could stop one of Arden's most famous and powerful Spinners from marching on. "YOU LEAVE SENA ALONE!"

This time, Fray didn't say anything.

A creeping horror began to twine through Claire, and slowly—so slowly!—she pieced together Nett's shout . . . and Fray's silence. The girl whose death was key to victory was not Claire, the supposed Gemmer princess of Arden. Nor was it Sophie, who was also Prince Martin's descendant.

It was *Sena*.

But . . .

"Why?" Claire's voice rang out as she tried to scan for an escape. If she could keep Fray distracted, maybe Nett or Sophie could think of a plan. "Why do you want Sena to die? What did she do wrong?"

"Besides steal the Unicorn Harp?" Fray shrugged. "Nothing, really. Nothing worse than Grandmaster Iris of Greenwood's lie about possessing said object. Nothing worse than anything my Royalists have done to collect unicorn artifacts. But all this was done for the greater good of Arden, as will be Sena's death."

"You're not going to hurt her," Nett said, stretching to his full height, which was only a little bit taller than Claire. "I won't let you!"

"Ah," Fray said softly, taking Nett in, who looked as puffed up as a hedgehog. "You're Francis's grandson, aren't you? Yes, he wasn't too happy about this plan, but he's not in a position to help her."

"Please," Sena said, and Claire whipped around to see the Forger girl standing with both hands wrapped around her bars. "If I have to die—can't you at least tell me why?"

Picking up her gown, Fray stepped over to come nearer to Sena. "Because of your parents, my dear."

"It's not Sena's fault her parents fell in love!" Nett yelled. "Why do you keep punishing her?"

"I'm not punishing her," Fray said, never taking her eyes from Sena's. "I'm using her as a lure."

"Lure for what?" Claire asked, sneaking a glance at Sophie. But she didn't have her thinking face on. Instead, she looked sick.

Fray sighed. "I expected more cunning from a Gemmer princess of Arden. I just said, *for her parents.*"

"My parents are dead," Sena spat. "Or as good as. Papa was

executed years ago and Mama is held somewhere in the laby-rinth of the old capital—according to my sources."

"Your sources are wrong," Fray said. "I am the greatest historian of our time. Nothing occurs in Arden without me knowing. That includes a faked execution. That includes a rescue to save a wife. That includes rumors of a pair of alche-mists in hiding as they experiment with a great and danger-ous magic. One that could tear at the very seams of our world as we know it."

Sena looked as though she'd been hit with a hammer. She visibly swayed on her feet. "Papa—he's alive? And with Mama?"

"For now," Fray acknowledged. "But they won't be for long."

The Steeles—they were alive! And that strange phrase again . . . the seams of the world. Where had she heard it before? With sudden understanding, Claire remembered. Cot-ton. Cotton had said the strongest alchemists—the very ones who had taught everyone how to wake the chimera—went missing when their experiment had gone wrong *at the seams of the world*. Sena's parents had been to Woven Root!

"You've set a trap!" Sophie's eyes flashed. "You're using Sena as bait so then—what? Wait, I know."

Sophie's expression was terrible to behold. "You'll make the execution public and coax them out to rescue their daugh-ter. And when they do, you'll parent-nap them. And you'll find a way to use this to drive the guilds even further apart, just like how *you* started the rumor that the Forgers destroyed

Queen Rock and Unicorn Rock. So that finally when you're ready to take over, there will be no one to stand against you."

"That is a very good guess, yes." Fray nodded approvingly. "I always thought you were clever, even if you were obsessed with unicorns."

Claire's stomach lurched. Sophie knew Fray before Claire had ever laid eyes on her. Her sister had spent much of her first days in Arden talking with the famed historian, seeking out the legends of unicorns.

"So you'll kill me just so you can have power!" Sena yelled through the bars, looking more mad than scared. "You're despicable!"

Shaking her head, Fray peered into the cell. "I'll have power, yes, I'll admit to it. But I'm not doing it for myself. I'm doing it for Arden. I'm making the path clear for Queen Estelle's return, because only *she* can bring magic back to its full strength. Only she can rid the land of wraiths. And she needs your parents."

She smiled sadly, and snapped her fingers. Two men melted from the shadows, and though they did not wear the Royalist blue cloaks, Claire recognized them from that horrible night on the Sorrowful Plains.

"And if that means one little girl must be killed," Fray said, tone as slippery as oil, and words as vile as lake slime, "then so be it."

The *drip, drip, drip* of the dank cell was as loud as a drum in the dark belly of the Drowning Fortress.

Claire hunched miserably in a corner, trying to avoid Sena's boots as the Forger girl paced up and down the cell, her red braid whipping behind her with each quick turn. Sena always had a spark of a temper, but with the turn of events, Claire wasn't sure when it would burst into a full-fledged forest fire. It was better to just stay out of her way.

Besides, Claire was still wrestling with the idea that the conversation she and Sophie overheard at Stonehaven was never about her, but Sena.

Shifting uncomfortably, Claire tried to think of an escape plan, but it was hard to concentrate on anything but Fray's echoing words—so horrible that they seemed to have their own kind of glue.

"Hey," she said gently, trying to make her voice soothing like Mom's when they were feverish. Her hand went to her ribboned bun, where she'd returned the nubby pencil from her Lock-it Pocket once Fray had inspected her. "Maybe I can draw us out of here again."

Sophie's lips twisted. "You could barely do it last time. And that was just a doorknob to a door that already existed."

Again, her voice was flat, like a picture without highlights or shadows. If only Sophie were a drawing, Claire would know how to fix it. But sisters were more complicated than sketches.

There just had to be a way out of here, a way to save themselves and go back to their search for the unicorn.

Wait a minute . . . *the unicorn!*

"Sophie," Claire said, dragging herself to her knees. "The flute!"

"What about it?"

"Get it out!"

The silver strand of unicorn mane she'd found outside the chimeras' stable streaked through her memory, bright and guiding like a flare. It was still wrapped safely around her pencil. "Maybe it'll work this time. Maybe, like the princess in the story, we needed to be in, what's the word? *Mortal Danger* for it to work. The unicorn will appear and its magic can destroy the locks—they can open anything, you know—and we can ride away on it and—"

"Claire—"

But Claire ignored her sister, her mind galloping ahead, just barely keeping up with the words that were spilling out of her. "I don't think we've been tracking the unicorn at all—I think he has been following us! He wants to save us, I just know it, and—"

"THERE IS NO UNICORN!"

Claire flinched as Sophie's shout filled the cell. Sena and Nett had gone silent, backed away to the far side of the cell, as if to give Claire space to hear the words right.

Sophie surged to her feet, still shouting, "THERE NEVER HAS BEEN."

"What are you *saying?*" Claire demanded, anger rising. "I released the unicorn from Unicorn Rock! It saved you!"

Sophie shook her head. "If that unicorn is somehow still alive, it is probably unfathomably far away by now, if a hunter hasn't caught up to it. He's *never* followed us."

"But," Claire protested, "we've found the unicorn mane everywhere—"

She stopped as Sophie made a sound. Claire guessed it was a laugh, but it was about as similar to laughter as a grimace was to a grin.

"What you found—that wasn't unicorn mane," Sophie said.

"Of course it was," Claire said, her own voice tight. "*You* said it was. In the moonlight, it was all shiny and silvery like—" She stopped. She had been about to say like spider's silk. But that wasn't entirely right. It had been silvery, yes, but more like silk thread.

Like the silver embroidery thread used to decorate lavender dresses one might wear to her sister's Grand Test.

The same thread that would catch on the underbrush as the sister ran away from deadly enemies. The same thread that had unraveled from her sister's dress.

An eerie calm spread through Claire, a numbness that froze her anger, damming it in place. Her ears popped, and her mouth went dry.

"You lied to me," Claire whispered.

"You didn't want to stay! You wanted to go home!" Sophie yelled. "*You said that.* It was the only way to keep you in Arden—"

The dam broke.

"SO YOU TRICKED ME?" Claire's fury flowed fast and fluid.

"You don't understand," Sophie protested. "I *told* you. I needed magic—"

"*YOU* NEEDED?!" Claire shouted. "WHAT ABOUT WHAT *I* NEED?"

Sophie was never the easiest to get along with. She always got to choose the movie for family nights. She always picked the color scheme for their annual family picture. She always decided their Experiences.

But this . . . this *lie.* This was beyond anything Sophie had ever done before. To pretend they were on the trail of a unicorn when they were not? To lie *repeatedly* to her own sister?

The fact of it hit Claire hard. She couldn't believe it.

And yet . . .

And yet the most terrible thing of all was that she *could.*

It might have been the worst lie Sophie had ever told her, but it was not the first.

Claire squeezed her eyes shut. She couldn't bear even to *look* at Sophie.

Sophie had lied to Claire to make Claire stay with her, but before Arden, Sophie had pushed her away. She had chosen to hang out with her older friends rather than stay home with Claire. Sophie was always leaving her behind . . . except when she needed something from her.

A raw cry tumbled from Claire, as her thoughts hit and bruised, her anger pummeling her insides.

"You didn't even give me a chance! You just assume because

I'm your little sister—because I'm not actually the Gemmer princess—that I'm not brave enough to help!"

"Claire—"

"No," Claire said, standing up on shaky legs. "You don't get to say anything, not now." Tears, hot and salty, landed on her tongue. She hadn't even realized she'd been crying.

"You say you wanted to help Arden, but all we've done is cause more problems. Anvil and Aquila will probably never move again. The queen is back. And the last unicorn is probably already gone for good. You just keep wanting to go on adventure after adventure without thinking about how your actions affect others! You don't care about *me* at all. I—I *hate* you."

The silence, punctuated only by the dripping ceiling, gaped wide as a crocodile's jaws between them. It felt as though it would devour them both whole.

Nett and Sena were standing there watching the whole thing in shock. Claire didn't look up at them but could feel their stares, the questions they weren't asking.

And then, a sound escaped Sophie's corner of the cell. A sniffle.

Suddenly, Claire realized her sister was crying. She was so surprised by it that for a minute she sat there, unsure what to do, her anger transforming instantaneously, as if by magic, into something else. Into curiosity. And worry.

"Sophie?" Forgetting to feel sorry for herself, Claire shuffled over to her sister. It was hard to tell in the dim light of the cell, but Claire thought her sister's skin looked waxy, and there were tight lines in her face that hadn't been there before.

"Hey," Claire said softly. "Are you okay?"

Sophie only moaned in response.

"Nett?" Claire cried, voice wobbly. "Can you come over here?" Something in her voice must have told Nett this was an emergency. A second later, he was there, crouching next to Sophie. He placed the back of his hand against Sophie's forehead, and she let out a low moan.

"She has a fever," Nett said. "She's burning up."

"But she's shivering!"

"My head . . . ," Sophie mumbled. "It hurts."

"Lay her down," Nett instructed. "Sena, is there any way you can make a fire?"

Biting her lip, Sena nodded. A few minutes later, using the heat from a buckle on Claire's boot and strips of cloth from their tunics, Sena had managed to kindle a small blaze.

As the flame's warmth flickered out, Claire brushed her sister's hair off her sweaty forehead. How had this happened? She thought of the night before, when they'd flown through the clouds. They'd been cool and wet, and the wind had rushed by them, shooting goose bumps up their arms.

A hint of a bad memory crept into the back of her mind—fluorescent lights, beeping monitors, hushed voices, nurses' shoes squeaking quietly along linoleum hospital floors. But Claire pushed that memory away. This was different. Sophie had gotten a chill, was all. Probably from all that flying.

Sophie wasn't *sick*-sick, not anymore. The unicorn from the rock had cured her.

Hadn't it?

Slowly, though, Sophie's shivers grew less violent, and the rise and fall of her chest grew steady.

"Claire?" Sophie's voice was but a thread of itself, thin and on the edge of breaking. "There's something else I've been keeping from you."

Claire's body went numb.

"Before we left," Sophie said. "Do you remember how I was late to the Grand Test?"

Claire nodded. "You were mad at me," she whispered.

Sophie shook her head, and her fingers brushed the spot above her collarbone, where Claire knew there was a pink scar shaped like a single star.

"It was because Terra pulled me aside. She wanted to see my scar. I think she wanted proof of your story. And then she told me that she thought—that maybe—the unicorn hadn't cured me. That he had only stopped me from dying of the arrow wound . . . and not anything else."

Anything else. The rare illness that even the doctors at home did not understand.

"She said," Sophie continued, "that unicorn magic is extremely powerful, but it works in mysterious ways. Their magic can sometimes save lives, she said, but more often than not it changes lives. I didn't know what she meant, but now . . . I thought I was fine. And if I'm not—" Her words cut off, as abrupt as a cliff. And Claire was tumbling over it.

Sophie wasn't healed. She was still sick.

"You didn't tell me . . . ," Claire said, too stunned to think.

"I tried to," Sophie said. She took a deep shuddery breath. "I wanted to. I just wanted to protect you from feeling sad. I thought maybe if we stayed in Arden a little longer, I'd discover my magic, and it would, I don't know, save me. But if the unicorn couldn't . . . there's no magic that can."

A coldness hundreds of times worse than the cold of the wraiths filled Claire's chest. What did you do when even magic couldn't help?

There was no way out of this cell—and even if there had been, there was no unicorn following them. Or maybe, there was no unicorn at all.

There was, for the first time in Claire's life, no hope.

CHAPTER
30

Time passed funny when your heart had broken. For Claire, it was as if her heart had been torn into a *before*—when Sophie might be annoying, stubborn, and bossy, but she had still always been a big sister, looking out for her—and *after*, when Sophie had entirely ceased to be who Claire had thought she was. With her heart in two pieces, it was like she'd lost the ability to count heartbeats, let alone seconds, minutes, or hours.

Sophie fell asleep, but Claire had no such luck. She wasn't sure how long she'd cried, her knees tucked into her chest. Then she wasn't sure how long she'd sat there, staring into the void of her kneecaps. Maybe she had even fallen asleep for a time, she wasn't really sure.

It was Nett's and Sena's quiet whispers that hauled Claire away from the expanding hole in her chest. Lifting her head, she squinted through the darkness. She had no idea how long or little she'd been lost in her misery, and Sophie was still asleep.

Standing up, she went to go sit next to Nett and Sena, and their conversation immediately dropped off.

"Please," Claire said, leaning her back against the damp wall. "Keep talking. I need . . . I need a distraction."

Nett ducked his head. "I was telling Sena about the crystal flute you told me about."

"Forgers craft magic flutes all the time," Sena added, "but I've never heard of one being crystal before."

The crystal flute's story prodded a question in Claire that she'd forgotten she'd wondered about.

"Nett," Claire said slowly. "There are so many legends about unicorns—*The Unicorn Princess and Her Crystal Flute*, the story about the moon's tears turning into unicorns, the fact that there are new unicorns in the moontear necklace waiting to be released—but which story is *right*?"

Nett paused, considering. "I don't think there *is* one right story, and that all the rest are wrong. Maybe they're all wrong, even, but when they're listened to together, you get the full truth."

"What?" Claire asked, frustrated.

"I think I get it," Sena said. "Think of a coloring page. You can give two people the exact same page with an outline of a unicorn. Each person can color in the unicorn any way they want, but at the end of the day, the picture is still a unicorn—no matter how you got there."

For one split second, Claire thought she understood. Not in the same way she knew one plus one equals two, but from the side, as if she'd finally seen the 3-D image in a bunch of fuzzy dots and knew that if she looked at it square on, it'd disappear.

Nett bobbed his head. "There are some historians," he added, "like Eliza the Ebullient, who try to link them all together. She thought that maybe unicorns didn't come from the moon at all, but were shooting stars that had been wished upon and had fallen to earth."

Sena tilted her head, looking thoughtfully at the small, contained fire. "That kind of makes sense. Wishing stars and wishing hearts can't be all that different, can they? And," she turned to look at Claire and said solemnly, "sometimes, they do come true."

It was such an unexpected thing to hear from Sena that Claire almost believed her.

Almost.

"Maybe Sophie's right, then," Claire said. "She thought that the unicorn ran too far away. Or was hunted down. Or after three hundred years just, you know . . ." She couldn't bring herself to finish the sentence.

Sena tilted her head as she considered. "There's a good chance the unicorn's still alive, especially if Thorn's telling the truth about Queen Rock."

Nett trailed his finger in some of the lake slime that had been allowed to grow in the cell. "There's something I don't get," he said, looking up. "Even if Sophie was lying to you about the unicorn mane all along."

"What?" Claire asked.

"The flute should have worked," Nett said. "You're a Gemmer, you're related to Prince Martin, and there are no other direct relatives here, other than Sophie. By all accounts, you should be the heir of Arden—" He broke off, and Claire knew why.

An orange light bobbed toward them, and then there was the sound of a soft splash as someone anchored a boat. Two figures waded toward them.

"This way, Your Majesty," Mira Fray said to another woman, who looked very familiar as the orange light glinted off her spectacles.

"Hello, children," Scholar Terra said as she came to a halt. "It's good to see you again."

CHAPTER
31

It was a joke.

It *had* to be a joke. Scholar Terra . . . was Queen Estelle? It made no sense.

"What—what are you doing here?" Claire stared at Terra, dumbstruck. Everyone else—Nett, Sena, even Sophie—faded into the background as she took in her teacher.

"I do so wish you hadn't run away," Terra sighed. "Your princess training was coming along so well. Slowly, I admit, but well."

Terra took another step closer, and for the first time, Claire noticed that the scholar now leaned on a cane. And not just any cane, a beautifully bejeweled one with a ram's head for the handle. Grandmaster Carnelian's cane.

"I don't understand," Claire said, desperation welling deep

within. "How can you be Queen Estelle?" She remembered Terra's study, full of unicorn paintings, rugs, and other decorations. "You love unicorns!"

Terra smiled, and pushed back her spectacles. It was the first time Claire had seen the woman without her many lenses of glass. If she had, maybe she would have realized sooner who Terra was. Because her uncovered eyes were not jet black. They were gray, and not just any gray. The same gray as Dad's eyes. The same color as Claire's.

"I am fascinated by them, true," Terra said, her fingers playing with the ram's horns. "They are powerful beyond imagining. They are pure magic. But love?" She shook her head. "How could anyone love such heartless creatures?"

"Scholar Terra," Claire said, her chest tight, "*please*. I don't understand! Why didn't you tell us who you are?"

She was vaguely aware of Sena and Nett circling around Sophie, trying to shrink into the shadows.

Terra's fingers lightly brushed the spectacles pushed up on her forehead. "I saw the Petrified Forest lingering on you. I had a sense of what you believed about me, and so I thought it best to remain concealed, and train you to a point where maybe, possibly, you could wake the moontears. But it wasn't until you told me the unicorn, too, had returned that I began to think we could really get anywhere."

"But . . . " Claire could hardly speak. "You're from *Stonehaven*. You've lived there your entire life, and the queen has been stone for at least three hundred years!"

Terra shook her head, and her jewelry that Claire once had thought was so pretty now seemed to glitter like predatory eyes. "Claire, you know better than that. You know Gemmers have ways of ensnaring the mind."

Claire's mouth went dry as she remembered the Identification Class when she'd stumbled upon a Mesmerizing Opal, and how surprised Scholar Pumus had been that one still existed within the Citadel. And she had just seen a tunnel full of carefully carved opals. With the Royalists aiding Terra, it would not have been hard for Terra to get her hands on one.

But then . . . had *she* been Mesmerized?

"Don't worry," Terra said, seeming to see the question in Claire's thoughts. "I had no need to Mesmerize you. You needed no convincing, and I needed to keep your mind clear while we studied the moontears. And I admit, though I am the most powerful Gemmer to have ever lived, Mesmerizing an entire village was not easy. Jasper in particular was stubborn, so I had to lure him the old-fashioned way, with promises of power. But I really had no choice. Secrets weaken the more people who know. And in the last three hundred years, I have learned patience."

Terra sighed, and Claire was surprised to hear it tinged with real emotion: with sadness. "There really are so few Gemmers left, but no matter. With your help, Princess Claire, we will return our guild to its former glory."

But Claire would never forget how, before she found Sophie in Arden, she'd been trapped in the Petrified Forest, and had heard the screams and whinnies of hundreds of unicorns being hunted—and all of it led by the queen herself.

"No," Claire squeaked. "You had your chance three hundred years ago. You killed unicorns. You drove the guilds apart! You don't *deserve* to be queen!"

"Watch yourself," Fray called from the shadows. An eerie rustle filled the cell as Fray's fringe all shifted in Claire's direction.

"Mira . . . ," Terra said warningly, and slowly the fringe fell flat. Terra's eyes flashed as she turned her attention back to Claire. "I think you'll soon change your mind. You see, I have a theory."

And as Terra tilted her head, the movement was so achingly familiar Claire almost cried out. It was the same way Sophie moved when she was weighing new information.

"What . . . what kind of theory?" Claire asked.

Terra stepped toward the door, leaning on her bejeweled cane. "One that could explain your sister's predicament."

Sophie's illness.

Terra had been able to Mesmerize an entire village.

And now she was offering what Claire wanted most in the world. Fear formed a lump of ice in her throat. She did not want to follow Terra. She did not trust the queen.

But Sophie was sick.

And Claire would rather face a hundred wraiths than lose what might be the only chance she'd have to heal Sophie once and for all. So in the end, there wasn't really a choice.

"Claire," Sophie whispered. "Don't."

But for once, Claire did not listen—she followed the queen.

Terra ushered Claire farther into the tunnels underneath the Drowning Fortress. The farther they went, the drier it became, until Claire sensed that they must have long since passed the boundaries of the lake. The walls were no longer polished smooth, but were instead roughly hewn, as if they'd been done in a hurry. Here and there, Claire spotted deep gashes in the rock, as if someone had run a rake through wet cement . . . or sharp claws.

Where was Terra taking her? Only the dim, red halo of Terra's single ruby earring cast any light. Finally, Terra stopped outside the mouth of a wide, dark tunnel that made Claire feel as though she were standing before the mouth of a beast. A cool draft emanated from the darkness, and there was the low moan of air rushing by, similar to the sound of blowing into a glass bottle.

Terra stepped into the passageway, but Claire stopped short. She wasn't afraid of the dark, not anymore, but still . . . the passage gave her a bad feeling. It felt like the sky before a thunderstorm, gathering wind and electricity and sound.

"Coming?" Terra's voice arched back to her.

Trying to bide time, Claire asked, "What—what is this place?"

"Don't be afraid, Claire." Terra smiled at her, a comforting smile—but because of its comfort, it sent chills up her back. Still, Claire gritted her teeth and walked forward.

At first, there didn't seem to be anything different about this tunnel. The dark was dark, and only that.

And then—a shift.

The murk began to roll and turn. It seemed almost as though a great beast were moving through the dark, and yet the beast seemed to be a part of the darkness, a shadow of shadows.

And Claire knew what kinds of creatures were forged of shadows.

Wraiths.

They were walking into a tunnel of a hundred of them—or maybe a hundred thousand. Wraiths, everywhere, surging and clawing and shifting. She could feel their restlessness. The cold wrapped around Claire, encasing every limb. She wanted to scream—she wanted to *run*. But she was mobile as stone; as sharp as a petal. And as the creatures prowled toward her, seeming no more substantial than thought—but just as dangerous—Claire felt herself unravel.

It had all come to this. This darkness. This terror. This intense feeling of being completely alone, of falling backward and away from everything she'd ever known.

Fear filled her. Fear tore at her. Fear *was* Claire.

And as Fear took hold of her, it pushed out reason. Then her senses. Until all that was left was a crumb of herself in a vast swell of emptiness.

"Enough!"

A cry streaked across the darkness, like a firework in the night. It burned its way to her, a sparkling lifeline, and Claire grabbed it.

She opened her eyes to find herself collapsed on the hard floor of the tunnel, Terra standing between her and the wraiths.

Almost immediately, Claire wanted to shut her eyes again. But the wraiths stayed back—a shifting wall of black ice.

A smile twisted across Terra's lips.

"Let us pass," she said. And immediately, the darkness lightened. The wraiths parted like paper between scissors. In the light of Terra's earring, Claire could now make out the vague outlines of an arched door.

Claire did not understand.

"You can control the wraiths?" she breathed as she scrambled to her feet. "How?"

"They listen to me," Terra said simply. "They recognize that the strongest should lead. That the powerful deserve to rule. And in Arden, that person is *me*."

She looked at Claire. "Only *I* can control the wraiths. Only *I* can command them to stay in the shadowed places, in the chambers of the earth that are so deep humans would never find them."

Thoughts tumbled over one another in Claire's mind. The Royalists said the wraiths would be gone when the queen returned. But they weren't *gone*, exactly. Just subdued into submission. Still, the power—the *magic*—was incredible . . . Incredible enough to save Sophie?

Terra moved toward the door at the other end of the passageway, and though Claire was still afraid of her, she was more afraid of the wraiths, and hurried to stay by Terra's side. By the glow of Terra's ruby, Claire could see that unlike the other doors of this underground palace, which were built of worn wood, this one was entirely made of stone. It was carved in a pattern of leaves and flowers that her artist's eyes recognized. Before she could nab onto the memory, the queen was speaking again.

"The unicorns did not deserve their magic," Terra said, putting one hand on the center of the stone door. "They did not use it, or when they did, it was never quite what you expected. They are wild creatures. Untamable. They don't listen to the desires of humans. They don't care what we want or need. If you have the power to gift immortality to others . . . wouldn't you? If you could cure illnesses, if you could stop death, wouldn't you?"

Red light threw shadows onto the queen's face, and Claire could not tell if she was sneering or grimacing in some internal pain.

"You, Claire Martinson," Terra continued, "are a fool if you believe the unicorn would willingly help your sister. The only way a unicorn can help you is if it's a *dead* unicorn."

The queen pressed her hand and the stone door swung inward as if it had the weight of a few feathers. On the other side . . .

Claire gasped. She was staring at a chamber of treasures.

Jewels and gold and silk hangings lined the walls. Crowns glittered even in the dim light while a collection of golden scepters leaned against shelves. And in the center was a pedestal with four indentions in the middle.

And inside those indentions sparkled the moontears.

The stone door gritted shut with a loud boom, leaving

Claire locked in the treasure chamber with only Terra. But though the queen had not increased the light of her ruby, the windowless room was far from dark. There was a pale, iridescent glow coming from one of the shelves that seemed to wash the room in moonlight, even though Claire knew that many feet of dirt and rock lay between here and the sky.

At first glance, the glowing shelf did not seem to be organized in any particular manner. For next to a fine bone comb was a pearl necklace, a leather belt, and . . .

Claire breathed in deeply through her nose, trying to calm her roiling stomach. The next item a Royalist had added to the pile was a chalice—a chalice carved from the leg of a unicorn, its bone hollowed out to form the cup while its snow-white hoof formed the base. The leg still had hair on it, though it was yellowed with age.

She looked at the pile of treasure with new eyes.

Not a necklace of pearls, but a necklace of teeth—unicorn teeth. A comb of unicorn bone. A belt of unicorn hide.

Artifacts like these, Claire knew, strengthened guild magic, but Nett had said that the artifacts were only a fraction as powerful as a breathing unicorn. But then, you had to ask a unicorn to help you . . . you didn't have to ask permission from a chalice.

Claire buried her face in her hands, trying to calm her stomach. These gruesome artifacts were all that was left of the star-kissed creatures that once roamed Arden. Now they were just bits of hair and bone and skin. How had she ever mistaken the dull silver threads of Sophie's dress for precious unicorn mane?

"Now there, no need to despair," Terra said, misreading Claire entirely. "I am sure the two of us can find a way to help each other."

Peering between her fingers, Claire watched the queen walk over to the shelf and place the necklace of unicorn teeth around her neck and buckle the belt around her waist. Then the queen turned to Claire. "The flute, please."

"What?" Claire asked, stalling for time, even though she could feel the weight of the instrument in her Lock-it Pocket.

"Do you want to save your sister?"

The answer was simple and yet . . . Claire's heart hammered as she pulled the flute out from her pocket.

"What—what do you want me to do?" Claire asked.

"Call a unicorn, of course. Call one, and we shall use that unicorn to wake more unicorns. Your sister will be healed. Arden will be what it once was. That is what you want, is it not?"

Claire stared at her. It *was* what she wanted for Arden. But how could she believe that Terra—*Queen Estelle*—wouldn't just return to her selfish, murderous ways?

After all, Queen Estelle had killed unicorns. She'd ordered Royalists to kidnap Claire. No matter what the queen claimed, her intentions couldn't be cured.

But Terra . . .

Terra had been kind to them. Terra had taught Claire magic,

had brought her to a diamond-lit sing-along to tell her that she belonged to Stonehaven. And how badly Claire had wanted to believe that! How badly she'd wanted to be the Gemmer princess, heir of Arden.

"I can't," was all Claire said. Because that much, at least, she knew. "I already tried and failed. You *know* that."

The queen drummed her fingers along the cane. "I have a theory. And I need to test it."

Theory. There was that word again. The word that reminded her so much of her older sister. Terra was an older sister, too. Prince Martin, Claire's many-times great-grandfather, had been her little brother. And yet, he thought it was better to turn his sister to stone and steal away to another world where he could keep the moontears safe. She couldn't imagine anything awful enough that would justify her turning Sophie into stone.

Claire suddenly felt sickened.

Because if Prince Martin had done so, the queen truly must be evil. What person wanted to have an allegiance with the wraiths?

"I can't," Claire whispered again. "I'm not Arden's heir. And besides, the unicorn probably doesn't even exist." Sophie's deceit curled up from her memory like smoke.

"I suggest you give it another try," Queen Estelle said, her voice hardening, sounding less and less like Scholar Terra and more like that cold voice that echoed eternally through the Petrified Forest.

Claire's fingers were beginning to sweat. She looked at the

queen, dressed in the unicorn artifacts. What was she planning to do?

"You try my patience, Princess," Estelle warned.

Princess. That's what Claire had wanted to be so badly at Stonehaven. A princess who could wake the moontears and save Arden. A princess whom Sophie would see as brave and more than just her little sister who needed to be protected from the truth. As more than just the youngest Martinson.

Suddenly, Claire's heart began to pound.

She *was* the youngest Martinson, but that didn't necessarily mean that Sophie was the *oldest* Martinson in Arden, or that Claire was the only Gemmer princess in Arden.

Someone had to have put the ladder in Windemere's fireplace. And that someone had died . . . but what if she hadn't? What if she had simply found herself in another world?

Claire fought to keep her expression neutral as the queen slowly raised the ram-head cane.

"I'll do it," Claire squeaked, pretending to be afraid. She could follow the queen's command—stall long enough to figure out how to get out of this dangerous situation—and the unicorn would still be safe, no matter what the queen's new theory was.

Claire brought the flute to her lips. She closed her eyes, and thought of the unicorn that had sprung from the rock on the Sorrowful Plains. Thought of the sheer joy of that moment, the all-encompassing hope, the terrible beauty of its magic unleashed. And the way it charged at Sophie as though knowing where it was needed most—healing at least her arrow wound only to vanish before Claire could even blink.

How she wished it had not vanished. Where had it gone? *Please be okay*, she thought.

She pressed her lips to the flute, and let her breath come naturally, flowing into the instrument, the hope and pain and fear and confusion all mingling together into that one stream of breath, into that one thought.

No sound came forth.

No majestic beast stormed into the room.

Claire had failed—again. And this time it was for the best. She almost laughed—she never expected to be so glad that she wasn't a princess! At least the last unicorn, if it was still out there somewhere in Arden, would remain safe for now.

She moved the flute away from her lips.

And that's when she heard the scream.

CHAPTER
32

No, not a scream—a *screech*!

Metallic snakes scraped under the stone door. But that wasn't right, either. These snakes weren't sleek and scaly, but fuzzy and fibrous, like the Root Tracker that had tapped Claire. Quicker than a blink, the metal roots—for that's what they were—writhed up the stone door, crisscrossing over one another, tying knots that Claire knew would never be undone.

Then the roots began to tighten . . . tighten . . . tighten—

The door disintegrated in an explosion of dirt and grit. Pebbles rained over her and Claire threw her arms over her head.

"Claire?" Sophie's voice came from behind a cloud of dust. "Where are you?!"

"Here!" Claire said, coughing as the dust coated her tongue. She let go of the crystal flute, and it hurtled toward the floor.

There was a shattering sound, like glass but purer, and Claire had the fleeting thought that it was ironic that the only time she could make it sound was when she broke it. But she didn't have to be the chosen princess to know what was right.

Though the crystal flute had been meant to be a gift, it had been turned into a curse. No creature should be at the beck and call of another.

As long as the unicorn was out there, Estelle would hunt, and maybe next time, she would figure out who the real heir of Arden was, just as Claire had just done.

Sweeping her hands in front of her, she hit something hard: the pedestal! Quickly, she wrapped her fingers around the moontear necklace and pulled—but something pulled back.

As the cloud of dust settled, Claire saw that Terra, too, had reached for the moontears. And that her hands were clutched around them just as tightly as Claire's.

"Let go!" Claire shouted, pulling. But the queen stayed still—and how could she have expected otherwise? Queen Estelle had been rock for three hundred years. She knew how to stand her ground.

"In a way," Queen Estelle said quietly, "I am sorry. There are so few Gemmers left. Stonehaven's magic has crumbled beyond almost any recognition and my court shall be very empty—for a while, at any rate. But," she let out a sigh, "why is it that family must always disappoint?"

And with that, she raised Carnelian's ram cane high.

Claire braced—not knowing what kind of magic a unicorn huntress would unleash—but the blow or spell never came.

Instead, the queen's gray eyes widened. "I was right!"

Confused, Claire looked over her shoulder as Sophie catapulted herself out from the cloud of dust, Sena and Nett just behind.

"LEAVE HER ALONE!" Sophie screamed. Her white-streaked hair was a tangled mane flying loose behind her, and in her hands was a purple ribbon, the same shade as her usual ponytail ribbon, but longer . . . much, much longer.

Sophie flicked her wrist, and the ribbon streamed through the air, momentarily looking like a dragon's tail in flight. Suddenly, there was a gentle hug as the ribbon looped around Claire's middle, and yanked her from the path of the queen's cane. Claire lost her grip on the moontears and hit the ground, rolling across the treasure room floor until she reached the far corner.

By the time Claire had caught her breath, the ribbon was again crisscrossing through the air, back toward the queen, more specifically, the queen's eyes. Sophie was trying to blindfold the queen!

"How dare you!" Estelle shrieked, and the next second the hairband disintegrated into purple dust. While Sophie, Nett, and Sena coughed, Estelle slammed her cane on the floor. And as she did, she let out a bellowing cry. "Wraiths—to me!"

A hum of magic rippled out, like rings in a pond, rushing into Claire and her friends. But Claire couldn't tell what the queen had done until she looked at her sister. Sophie was running in slow motion, as if her blood were slowly turning to stone.

An image of the Malchains—frozen somewhere on Starscrape Mountain—flashed through her mind. Queen Estelle's spectacles could see many things . . . why shouldn't they be able to see all the way down to the rest of Stonehaven's ghost town? Estelle had probably seen Anvil talking to Claire and Sophie, and then, once she'd settled the Martinsons, she must have snuck out of the Citadel and trailed Anvil, tracking him to Aquila and the forest cottage.

No wonder Terra had been late to gather them that first morning at Stonehaven! But, though Sophie, Sena, and Nett were clearly under some great weight, her friends were not frozen completely into rock. Not yet, anyway.

Claire wiggled her fingers and took a step forward. She felt absolutely fine—even if she was terrified.

"Claire," Sophie whispered urgently, "you have to do something! We've all been cursed."

"How did you get here?" Claire asked, dazed.

"Thorn!" Nett said, as if that were an explanation. He moved even more slowly, as he was helping a limping Sena who bled freely from her arm.

Glancing at the queen, Claire saw Estelle was hunched over the cane, breathing deeply. So, even with all her power and unicorn artifacts, she was weak. But the wraiths would be here at any moment.

Mom always said Claire had a unique way of looking at the world, seeing its details and patterns. That's what made her such a good artist. There must have been some way to get out of here. *Some* plan that the queen would have overlooked. She scrambled to a treasure chest and flung it open. But instead of a collection of forgotten magical swords, all she found were silken slippers encrusted with garnets.

"Remember your lessons!" Sophie said, speaking slowly around her heavy tongue. "Courage!"

Claire shook her head, rattled, stressed—none of her lessons had ever really worked. She had never cracked open the moontears. That's why she and Sophie had gone looking for the unicorn in the first place.

"Lessons," Estelle scoffed. "She could barely make a Gemglow."

"Claire!" Sophie yelled, drowning out the queen's insidious words. "You're powerful! You made a Grail explode!"

But Claire didn't know how to explode things *on purpose*. All she *could* remember were the droning lectures about minerals in the earth's crust. Supposedly, they would get to magma later . . .

An idea sparked.

Estelle seemed to have gathered back her strength, and she raised her cane again to finish the magic that would turn the blood in her friends' veins to rubies. Claire was out of time. What she knew would have to be enough.

She would have to be enough.

"Get back!" Claire shouted. And as her friends scooted back, Claire lunged toward a rock shelf, polishing the rough worn rock, letting the heat of her anger, her frustration, her shame call to the heat that the rock must have once known—and invited it to join her.

It grew hot—but not hot enough.

Terra strode toward her, illuminated by the unicorn artifacts that decorated her figure. Unicorn artifacts made the magic, Claire knew. They made any craft stronger. They made it *more*. If only Sophie hadn't lied to her. If only the unicorn mane in her pocket was real, and not just silver threads from a torn dress. If only—

—Suddenly, Claire was *too* hot. She lurched back, just in time to see the stone shelves melt like a candle into a pool of lava, separating the children from the queen.

"Impressive," the queen sneered. "A d'Astora through and through. But I have unicorn artifacts, too." She stepped forward and tapped the molten puddle with her cane. It immediately began to cool back into rough stone.

But apparently by doing so, she also released Sophie, Sena, and Nett from whatever spell she'd put on them.

"Try again!" Sophie cried, diving toward Claire now that she was able to move freely. "You've been learning how to wake the moontears—how to *break them open!*"

And at her sister's words, Claire understood what she needed to do. She pressed harder, urging the hum in her hands to go into the rock. She didn't just need to melt rock. *She needed to break the earth open.*

But she was tired. If only Sena had a hammer or Nett could call oak roots to tear through the layers of dirt beneath them. She felt her strength draining.

"Come on, Claire." She suddenly felt Sophie's hand in hers. "You can do this."

Squeezing back tightly, Claire lunged for a diamond scepter that had fallen into the softening rock. Diamonds knew heat—pressure—intimately. And as Claire slammed the scepter diamond-first into the ground, image after image tumbled into her mind: The Royalists ordering Sophie's death on the Sorrowful Plains. The strange, blood-stone trees of the Petrified Forest as they shrieked the queen's secrets. Sophie thinking Claire needed lies in order to be brave. Sophie's crumpling face as Claire said *I hate you.*

Claire's heart broke all over again.

And the earth split open.

Magma billowed up from the hole, a geyser of lava and hot stone, creating a continuous, roaring wall of molten rock between them. Protecting the Martinson sisters and their friends—but also trapping them in, for the exit was on the other side of the curtain of fiery stone.

"Wraiths—to ME!" they heard Estelle cry.

"Get away!" Claire cried to Sophie, who already had her back up against the far wall.

"We can't," Sena snapped. "We're blocked."

"And it's hot!" Nett said, sweat coursing down his face. It could have been the heat—the same kind of heat that made the desert shimmer—but Claire thought she saw the threads of the embroidered dandelion fluff on Nett's shirt unhook themselves from his tunic and drip down his shirt, almost as if the very thread was melting.

Shaking her head, Claire tried to focus. She was tired. She was spent. But she still had to try.

"Give me a moment," she said, fighting both heat and exhaustion. She swayed on her feet. If it got any hotter she was going to faint. "I can . . . I can . . ." but she couldn't. She sat down hard, too weak to stand, let alone craft anything else. And looking around at her friends, they were weak and exhausted, too.

"Look," Sena cried. The protective geyser of lava was no longer red, but turning a mottled gray. It was cooling, and as it cooled—it built a wall of new rock. Rock without cracks. Rock without weakness.

"The wraiths," Nett murmured. "The temperature always drops around them—the queen is sealing us in!"

And so she was. Claire hadn't protected them at all. Instead, she'd crafted their own tomb.

CHAPTER
33

I can wait," Queen Estelle called through the rock. "Oh yes, I can outlast you, uni . . ." But the end of her sentence was garbled. The last of the soft rock had hardened, and silence now encased them.

"What do we do now?" Nett asked. He placed his hand on the walls around them. "There are no plants this deep."

"Sena, there's metal here," Sophie said. "Can you do anything?"

Sena bit her lip. "I can try, but I've never been properly trained. Even Claire has had more guild schooling than me. And," she winced, "my arm." Her blood was dripping to the floor, splattering the rock.

"I can help with that," Sophie said. She tore a scrap from the bottom of her tunic. Holding it up, she frowned. "I could have sworn there were embroidered herons on this."

"Maybe they flew away," Claire joked weakly, but inside she was far from laughing. The air was stale. She was suddenly very aware of the hundreds of tons of soil that must be above her. Of the squeezing, tightening embrace of the earth. Of the sweat coursing down her cheeks. Though the piece of the treasure chamber she'd cornered them into was large, it wouldn't have an infinite supply of air.

She staggered to her feet to check the original wall for anything. A hairline crack. A spider's hole. Ignoring her panic, Claire placed her hand on the wall. It was hard to keep her palm pressed against it. Not because it was too hot or too cold, but because it *buzzed*. It hummed with an intense vibration that shook her very bones.

But it didn't feel like magic.

It didn't come from her. It didn't even come from the rock. Instead, it felt like it was coming from something that was *inside* the rock. The next second, she could make out a great grinding sound, like rusty door hinges or massive gears. She splayed her fingertips out farther.

BOOM!

Claire and the others scrambled back as the walls of the chamber shook.

BOOM!

She had just enough warning to jump back as the original wall cracked.

A gleaming head shoved its way through, followed by a lion's body and gleaming raccoon's tail. The chimera shook himself free of rock dust as the woman on his back held on to his copper mane. Woven around the woman's wrists were multicolored threads, which seemed to exactly match the once beautiful embroidery of Nett's, Sophie's, and Claire's Woven Root tunics.

"There you are!" Mayor Nadia said triumphantly. She dropped her leather reins and leaned toward them, hand outstretched. "Get on!"

"Mayor Nadia? What—*how?*"

But Claire thought she knew exactly why Nadia was here. *Nadia.* Who was obsessed with the treasures of all the guilds. Nadia, who had come to Woven Root and decided never to leave. If there was one thing she'd learned in Arden it was this: A rock was never just a rock. A story was never just a tale. And people were always, always more than they first appeared. Terra had been a reminder of that. And so, Claire was about to test out *her* theory when she heard Sena's delighted, "Lixoon!"

She bounded toward the lion chimera and before Claire could warn her, threw herself at its copper face. "I missed you!"

The lion chimera opened its massive mouth, and a surprising sound—somewhere between a harmonica's sigh and a snuffle—came out.

Startled, Claire looked at Nett, whose eyes had widened in surprise. "I think," he said, "it's purring."

Just then, a second chimera's head poked through, this one not as beautiful as the lion-raccoon but clearly useful as

Claire could see a drill had been attached to the chimera snake-scorpion Serpio's tail. And astride Serpio, as sturdy as an anchor thread, sat Cotton.

"No time for lollygagging!" Nadia said. "Get on, now!"

Sophie launched herself toward Lixoon, while Claire took a running leap. The air whooshed out of her as her stomach hit the hard metal of the chimera's copper side. She felt a pull on her tunic as Nadia dropped the reins and pulled Claire up the last few inches.

Suddenly, Claire could hear shouts on the other side of the new wall, and the sound of pick-axes.

"We need to go!" Nett said, looking anxious on the scorpion chimera behind Sena and Cotton.

"Agreed," Nadia said, and tightened the reins. Lixoon swiveled on well-oiled haunches and loped back toward the tunnel.

"Where are we going?" Claire shouted as their ears popped.

"Under the lake!" Nadia shouted back. "Arden is crisscrossed with tunnels left over from the Guild War! Gemmer-made, of course. We'll be out of here in no time."

Nadia kicked the chimera, urging him into a higher gear. As they twisted and churned through a seemingly endless tunnel, Claire began to feel sick. Or maybe it was the low, churning hum of warning that rattled her bones.

There was no rock in this section of tunnel, only soil that shifted and clambered over itself. Claire tried to open her mouth to warn Nadia, but she felt too sick.

Nadia, though, seemed to know how Claire was feeling,

because she leaned forward and shouted something in Lixoon's ear—and in the next moment, the chimera's joints
clanked in protest as it hastened its speed.

But the soil was shifting faster.

"Hurry!" Claire screamed. There was a slow rumble, the
sense of everything falling in, and then—

"Keep your head down!" Nadia roared.

Finally: a twist of light!

Lixoon shot toward it and they exploded into a stream of
noontime sun. A moment later, a fountain of soil and copper shot
into the sky as Serpio rocketed out of the tunnel behind them.

They had all made it! Relief bubbled out of Claire in the
form of hysterical laughter. Never had sun been so welcomed
or felt so good. Lake Drowning was nowhere to be seen, but
Claire saw several riders on Woven Root horses coming toward
them through the trees.

"The guilds have spotted us!" Ravel shouted as he galloped
his horse toward them. "We can stay ahead of them, if we leave
now!"

Nodding, Nadia tightened the reins, and Lixoon shot
forward.

"Nadia!" Claire shouted over the rush of wind. "Thank you
for rescuing us!"

"I can't hear you," Nadia called back. "Tell me when we're
safe."

But Claire didn't think such a time would ever come
again. So she leaned in and said it anyway: "Thank you, Aunt
Diana."

CHAPTER 34

Before I was Mayor Nadia of Woven Root, leader of the alchemists, I was Diana Martinson, world-renowned collector and explorer." Nadia's—*Aunt Diana's*—fingers flew as she knotted the ties of her tent, sealing them off from the curious eyes of the other alchemists.

After fleeing Drowning Lake, they had galloped into the forest that they had flown over. In the dark shade of the trees, Nadia had called for them to halt, then had leaned forward and pinched the air. A moment later, the Camouflora curtain had been pulled aside to reveal the many tents of Woven Root.

"Of course the village travels—why else would we use tents?" Nadia had said when she noticed their astonished faces. "Camouflora works wonders, but the only way to truly stay hidden is to not get caught."

Diana. Nadia. The letters were all the same, Claire realized.

When they'd arrived, they'd been greeted by clamoring alchemists, desperately wanting to know what had happened. Nadia had instructed Ravel to gather Woven Root for an emergency council, but first, she had said, she wanted to talk to the children. Alone.

Claire now sat in Nadia's tent, her arm brushing Sophie's as they both stared at the framed drawing on the desk. Pencil Mom and Pencil Dad stood, waving, while Pencil Sophie seemed to have snuck off the page somewhere.

Sophie rested her head on Claire's shoulder. "It looks just like them," she murmured.

"Is that your family?" Sena asked from Claire's other side. Nett and Sena sat there, looking slightly windswept. Both seemed tired, but Sena seemed changed, like a jewel that had been polished by Gemmers and now glowed. And why shouldn't she? She'd just learned her family was alive, after all. And Fireblood gleamed proudly on her hip.

"Yes," Nadia answered for Claire as, satisfied with her ties, she came to join them. "That is my nephew and his wife. I recognized them at once." Nadia/Diana tapped Pencil Dad fondly, and said, "He always liked stories. I did too! I remember sitting in Windemere, in a window nook overlooking the pond, and listening to my father tell stories about Arden, a land filled with treasures. In fact, it was those stories of magical objects that made me interested in art collecting in the first place."

Sophie reached out and gripped Claire's hand, as Nadia—Great-Aunt Diana—told them her story.

"I spent my life looking for a way into the world that Grandpa Martin described. Arden. And when I discovered his journals, I finally did."

She paused for a moment, taking a big breath. "At first, I just took some treasures—small ones. A coin here, a scrap of tapestry there. And each time I said it would be the last . . . until I heard about the Tablecloth of Everlasting Feasts or an hourglass that *saved* you time instead of spending it."

Nadia flipped the hourglass on her desk. "Time slips through Arden differently than it does at home. I didn't realize it, but as I collected treasures, I missed important moments in your father's life. Graduation, the birth of two daughters." She shook her head. "Unforgiveable things to miss."

"And when did you figure out who we were?" Sophie asked.

The old woman leaned back in her chair, her eyes closed. "I saw the picture, and realized that you'd given me false names. False names that just so happened to be the middle names of my grandnieces."

Her eyes opened. "But I realized before I put it together that I was wrong, before I knew who you were. Because, you, Claire, were right. We can't just stay in hiding while Arden slips away from us. I love Arden. Arden is why I never came home. And now these Royalists destroying monuments and spreading rumors around about their fake queen," she said disdainfully.

Claire and Sophie looked at each other. "Actually, Mayor Nadia?"

"Just Nadia is fine. It's the name I chose for myself."

"Nadia," Claire corrected, "the queen *is* the queen."

And so Claire began to tell their story, from the time Dad got the call of Diana's disappearance, to the journey she'd undertaken to find Sophie, to Sophie's reason for why she wanted to come to Arden in the first place, and how they had discovered their family's legacy: the Great Unicorn Treasure of Arden was not simply a moontear necklace, but the key to a future of unicorns.

And then Claire shared how they'd lost them—given them to Terra, who was actually Estelle, the same way Nadia was actually Diana. And how Estelle would not save Arden from danger, but was the biggest threat of all.

How they'd left the moontears behind at Stonehaven, after Claire failed to be the Gemmer princess of Arden who could play the crystal flute.

"The heir of Arden . . . ," Nett piped up, looking at Nadia questioningly. "*You're* the oldest Martinson, beside Queen Estelle. *You're* the Gemmer heir."

It was the same realization that Claire had had before she blew the flute for the final time.

Her chest constricted, but she forced her confession out.

"I broke the flute," Claire said. "I'm so sorry. I thought the unicorn would be safer if it didn't exist." She could hardly bear to look at Nadia. "I didn't realize until you arrived with the chimera that *you* were Great-Aunt Diana—that we had already met the heir! If we still had the flute, the unicorn could be here now, helping Sophie!"

"Maybe," Nadia said, "but then again, maybe not. Think on it. Who, in the story Estelle read to you, in the end became ruler after the old king died?"

Sophie shrugged, her ponytail bouncing, a new ribbon securing her hair. "I don't know. I missed that part of Claire's test." A shot of white still lingered in her dark hair, looking as if she'd washed her hair in snow.

Claire scrunched her eyes up, remembering. "The king chose a Tiller gardener to become king after him."

"Exactly." Nadia nodded. "So maybe everyone is looking at it wrong. It's not the *heir* that calls the unicorn. Maybe it's the *unicorn* that chooses the heir."

Her aunt's theory wasn't really comforting, and the relief Claire had felt at being again under Woven Root's protection had completely evaporated.

"Fine, then," Claire said. "I get it, I'm not the princess . . . but I *am* a sister. We still need to find the unicorn. Sophie's still sick!"

"I actually feel okay," Sophie said, rubbing her forehead. "It's only now and then that everything starts to hurt." And yes, out here, in a brightly lit tent, she could see that Sophie practically seemed to glow with good health, though her eyes still seemed too bright and shiny.

"But that's not good enough," Claire insisted. "You have to be completely better."

Nadia opened her drawer and pulled out a quill and paper. "Sophie, your turn," she said. "Tell me everything."

As Sophie talked, Claire studied Nadia. Sophie and Nadia weren't so dissimilar. Both of them had come to Arden to run away from something. Both of them liked to collect things, though one collected art while the other preferred experiences.

Patterns form in rock and in us, Queen Estelle had said when Claire still thought she was only Scholar Terra. *Stories repeat.*

Just not when Claire needed them to. Why couldn't the tale of the king's daughter repeat? Why couldn't the unicorn come and rescue Sophie, like he had the dying princess?

Something tickled her thoughts, like a delayed sneeze. There was something she was missing, a detail she'd overlooked . . .

"Wait a second," Nett interrupted Sophie's account, "I thought you said earlier that you weren't at the Grand Test. That you missed the retelling of *The Unicorn Princess and Her Crystal Flute?*"

Sophie nodded. "I got there late. After Terra said there was something off within me, that I was still sick, I spent the rest of the night and all the morning in the Citadel's library, trying to find something, anything, that could help me. I fell asleep reading, and didn't wake up until after the Grand Test had started."

But Claire wasn't listening anymore. Because Queen Estelle had said more than just that to Sophie. She'd also said unicorn magic can sometimes save lives, but more often than not it *changes* lives. What else had they learned about unicorns?

They could open doors—any door, even hidden ones in Stonehaven's tallest tower.

They could also heal. Claire looked down at her ankle. Its skin was entirely smooth, not even a hint of pink where the Gelly had bitten her.

And around unicorns, they'd learned, magic was always at its strongest—powerful enough to split the earth.

"Claire, are you there?"

Claire blinked, and realized the others were staring at her, Sophie waving her hand at Claire's face.

"Hey," Sophie spoke again. "You okay?"

Claire didn't know. Her mind was racing, galloping ahead so fast she could barely keep up.

Lines connect to form pictures. Patterns form.

Before Claire had shattered the flute, she'd played it four times. Once, at the Grand Test. Once, in the woods, before the wraith attacked. Once, when she was tied up in Woven Root. And once again in Queen Estelle's treasure room. Each time, the flute had stayed silent. Each time, the unicorn had not come.

But someone else had.

Stories repeat.

"What's wrong?" Sophie looked alarmed now. "Why do you look like that?"

The tent, the desk, Nadia, Nett, and Sena all seemed to fade away, until all that Claire could see was Sophie.

The unicorn chooses the heir.

Claire took a deep breath. "I don't think you're sick anymore, Sophie. I think that when the unicorn saved your life on the Sorrowful Plains, he did more than just save your life . . . Do you get what I'm saying?"

The others suddenly became very still—except for Sophie.

"No," Sophie snapped. "Stop being so mysterious!"

In another time, in another place, in another world, Claire would have been pleased that for once, she got to be the sister with a secret. But now . . . she looked down again at her perfectly healed ankle, then up at the spangled tent.

Wishing stars and wishing hearts.

"Sophie," Claire said. "You're not sick. You're becoming a unicorn."

CHAPTER 35

The sun was warm on Claire's cheek, but the breeze was crisp and cool. Change was in the air, and autumn was slowly coloring Arden's trees. Passersby eyed Claire while she waited outside the alchemists' headquarters.

Nadia was in there now, along with Sena and Nett, laying out the story for the alchemists, hoping to forge an alliance with Woven Root. They'd decided it would be best if those known to Arden spoke first—especially the daughter of one of their own, acclaimed missing alchemists Sylvia and Mathieu Steele. Then Sophie and Claire would be called in for questioning. And Claire knew there would be many, many questions.

About the impending war between the Gemmers and the other guilds.

About the Forgers who had been turned to stone.

About the rumors of a legendary queen's return . . . and what that would truly mean.

So as she waited, Claire found a mossy rock and sat down to savor the silence. She had a feeling that soon, very soon, there wouldn't be time at all to just sit and watch the shadows of the leaves dance on the ground.

"Claire, you're avoiding me."

Claire looked up to see Sophie standing in front of her, hands on her hips.

"I'm not," Claire said automatically.

"But you're still doing it," Sophie said. "Scoot over." When Claire had, Sophie sat down next to her. "Whenever it's just you and me, you suddenly have to ask Nadia something. Or find Nett."

Claire looked at Sophie and was surprised to recognize the expression on her face. It wasn't one she'd ever seen on her big sister, but it was one that Claire knew she herself wore often. It was the look of being alone. Of being left behind.

Claire suddenly felt horrible. Sophie was right. She *had* been avoiding her. She didn't know what to say. She didn't know what to do. What did it mean, to have a unicorn as a sister? Or a sister as a unicorn? When would her sister stop being her human sister with a dark ponytail and freckles on her nose, and become that creature of blazing light? The creature with a spiraling horn that could wake the moontears?

Claire already hated the streak of white in Sophie's hair left over from Bramble's failed experiment.

She leaned into Sophie. "I'm sorry," she whispered. "I'm here for you."

A warm weight settled onto Claire's head as Sophie rested her head against hers. "Clairina," Sophie said, her voice so quiet it was barely even a whisper. "I'm . . . I'm *scared*. The queen knows who—what—I am. She'll be after me."

And Sophie—always brave, fearless Sophie—looked so sad that Claire wanted to cry. But it wasn't her turn to cry anymore. If Sophie was scared, then Claire would be brave for her, just as Sophie had been for Claire so many times.

"We'll find a way," Claire promised Sophie. "We'll find a way to wake the moontears. You don't have to change—the other unicorn is still out there."

After a moment, Sophie said softly, "You're right. We'll find a way."

"But there are so many things to find a way for," Claire said, feeling momentarily helpless. "The guilds are on the brink of war. Anvil and Aquila are frozen statues. And Estelle—she has terrible, terrible plans."

"One thing at a time," Sophie said, and she said it so calmly—so gracefully, so wisely—that Claire already felt her slipping away from her. "We can do it. After all, Arden is magic."

"Magic is in the material," Claire said, the words coming easily, as if she'd always lived in a land of enchantment.

"Well, you're pretty good material," Sophie said. "Magic is just the potential something has to grow and change. You have it, and now . . ." She gave a weak laugh. "I guess I have it, too."

She reached out and gripped Claire's hand. "We'll go home soon," she said, squeezing. "I can feel it."

And for a moment, with Sophie's hand in hers, Claire thought she felt it, too.

EPILOGUE

The unicorn dreamed.

He rushed through meadows of stars and tore through galaxies of green grass.

He dreamed of a sharp cold, the tingle of snowflakes, and the warm tickle of his mother's nose against his ear, calling him to wake. He dreamed of mornings racing the wind alongside his sisters and of nights with his brothers chasing the falling stars that scraped the mountaintops. He dreamed of muscles stretching, hearts beating, his song mingling with the wild shout of the world.

But the stars were quieter now, the earth sleepy. His family was all gone, except for the changeling. She knew now, the girl who had contained a wish so big it'd taken up her entire heart. The girl who had been so close to death that he'd had to do the one thing he could to save her. He could help her. Even now, he could feel her reaching out to him, as moonlight trickled into her soul. And in her dreams, she searched for him.

If only he could tell her where he was. If only he *knew* where he was.

The unicorn was a tornado locked in a box. The tide contained in a thimble. A sun under a bushel basket. He was—

"*Trapped!*"

The tent swung wildly around Sophie as she rolled out of her hammock and her feet slammed into the ground. Her heart raced, as if she, too, had just galloped across a meadow of stars. With her hand (and they were still hands, thank the diamonds above, and not hooves that could split the earth), she pushed dark hair out of her eyes.

Sophie knew the moment before she heard the slight hiss of metal that Sena had drawn Fireblood.

"What's happening?" Sena demanded, just as a tousled Nett sleepily asked, "What's wrong?"

"Nothing's wrong," Sophie said, feeling as though her blood had been replaced by sunlight. Though her heart raced and sweat dampened her cheeks, she felt like laughing. She felt like triumph. How weird it had been, to share a dream with the unicorn. How utterly and completely spectacular!

And for a moment, she'd even seen him: a creature of wind and radiance. Though long whiskers covered his muzzle and the once snowy flank appeared tinged with a rain-wash gray, there was still starfire in his eyes, and the tip of his glorious horn twisted to a sharp point. This was not a docile creature.

And at last, Sophie knew why the unicorn hadn't come, when Claire (Princess Claire!) had called with her flute.

Trapped.

And the images the unicorn shared: a lock, a thimble, a basket. Metal, thread, reed. Forger, Spinner, Tiller. One of the guilds had already found the unicorn.

"Claire!" Sophie said, fumbling in the dark toward her sister's hammock. "I know where the unicorn is! Or, at least, I have an idea. He's—Claire?!"

The hammock in front of her swayed slightly in the night's breeze . . . empty.

No, not completely empty.

There, on top of the blanket that Claire should be snuggling under, was a paper flower. Picking it up, Sophie saw faint pencil marks crawling up it like smudged ants.

S—

The queen knows what you are. Which means you need to stay safe, in Woven Root. But I'll fix this. I promise.

ACKNOWLEDGMENTS

Inspiration, dedication, and courage aren't just the rules for magic—they're also the rules of writing. And, over the course of crafting *Secret in the Stone*, I relied on many people to find the necessary inspiration, dedication, and courage to set my fingers to the keyboard and dive headfirst into the story.

A tremendous amount of thanks is owed to the incredible team at Glasstown Entertainment: Laura Parker, Lexa Hillyer, Emily Berge, and Lynley Bird. A special thanks to Emily, whose enthusiasm and knowledge of childhood classics makes me excited to write, and to Lexa, who knows how to spot the potential in a writer and bring forth all the possibilities. Thank you, too, to literary agent extraordinaire Stephen Barbara, who always knows which road leads to the most unicorns, and to the rest of Inkwell Management Literary Agency, especially Lyndsey Blessing and Claire Draper.

Many thanks to my Bloomsbury family, who have adopted me in more ways than one. There's no one else I'd rather go on a quest with than my editor Sarah Shumway, whose thoughtfulness, curiosity, and willingness for adventure gives me the courage to plunge back into the pages. Claire and Sophie are lucky to have you as their guide. Thank you as well to Cindy Loh, Erica Barmash, Anna Bernard, Bethany Buck, Alexis Castellanos, John Candell, Phoebe Dyer, Beth Eller, Alona Fryman, Emily Gerbner, Cristina Gilbert, Courtney Griffin, Melissa Kavonic, Erica Loberg, Donna Mark, Elizabeth Mason, Patricia McHugh, Linda Minton, Brittany Mitchell, Oona Patrick, Annette Pollert-Morgan, Emily Ritter, Claire Stetzer, and Nick Sweeney. And across the Atlantic, a heartful thanks to the members of the UK team who have provided such a warm welcome: Elise Burns, Naomi Burt, Nicholas Church, Laura Main Ellen, Maia Fjord, Cesca Hopwood, Lena Kraemer, Fabia Ma, Lucy Mackay-Sim, Emily Marples, Emily Moran, and Emily Monckton-Milnes. And of course, thank you to Vivienne To and Matt Saunders, the illustrators of my US and UK covers, respectively, and who would each earn an A+++ in magic art school. Your beautiful covers have been one of my biggest delights in this authoring journey.

And speaking of magical learning, I am incredibly grateful to the many teachers I've had, and not just those who were in the school classroom. Thank you to Pat Righter, Cindy Lamberjack, Buff Whaley, Kathleen Prater, Jennie Pitman, Carolyn F., Susan Maul—all of whom have pointed me in the direction of magic in the real world, either on horseback, on ice, in music, or in thread. I am also very grateful to my North Park Avenue neighbors and friends for allowing me to spend my childhood running through their backyards and playing the make-believe games that were all a rehearsal for writing this story. Special thanks to the Blythe, Howald, Mills, Molander, Rodriguez, Reiffers, Snyder, and Williams families. Finally, a huge, massive thank you to Master Librarian Jennifer Burns and St. Luke Catholic Elementary School for your boundless enthusiasm and support—go Rams!

The learning process never really ends. I've learned so much about storytelling—and continue to do so through Sarah Jane Abbott, Melissa Albert, Rhoda Belleza, Kati Gyulassy, Kristina Pérez, Tara Sonin, Annie Stone, and Angela Velez. Thank you in particular to Medea Asatiani, Catherine Bates, and Matthew Richman who truly gave me the courage to persevere and whose feedback was invaluable. Often, the best teachers of all are years younger. *Secret in the Stone* would not be the book it is today without the sharp eyes of Liz Silva, D. J. Silva, Molly Silva, Katie Blacquier, Charlotte Blacquier, and Eliza Blacquier. I also have so much gratitude for Amelia Possanza, Mariel Freyre, and Caroline Dunphy, who all told me go write—and look! I finally did.

A most heartfelt thank you to Marguerite, Zoltán, Gabriella, and Matthias Benko who are always ready to talk about magic, quests, and unicorns at any moment. A special thank you to Papa, who knew what I was trying to say, even before I knew myself. You all continue to be my greatest source of inspiration. And finally, thank you to my husband, Andrej Ficnar, who will complain that he is mentioned last, but that is only because I would never have gotten to these final sentences without his willingness to venture into new worlds with me. You are the perfect ending for this story, and a perfect beginning for the next one.